To Rachael

Hope you enjoy!

ma...

New writing from Warwick

Warwick MA in Writing

Ball Bearing Press

manifest: New writing from Warwick

ISBN 978-0-9934292-4-8
First published in Great Britain by Ball Bearing Press

A catalogue record of this book is available from the British Library

Set and designed by The Book Refinery Ltd

Cover Design by Gaia Lamperti

Contents

Foreword

Welcome to the 2018 writing collection from the Warwick Creative Writing Programme. A single foreword to tie such a diverse compilation wasn't an easy task. Words like 'snapshot', or 'glimpse into A' and 'hints of B' come up a lot in these. It's not that these introductory clichés aren't truthful in some ways. We do have a snapshot of time here (both topically and stylistically), and we do get a glimpse into a collective contemporary which hints at a much needed re-evaluation of myth and fable. But such expressions do little more than take a reductive approach through loaded abstracts to writing which, in terms of construction, is still in a state of process.

And it's not often we are fortunate enough to see writing in process. In a way it's not so much a snapshot of something in the past as it is the very real possibility to see into the future. And no, I don't mean this in relation to book trends, or the next big thing or anything like that. Though that may interest some, what these writers have accomplished here is a variety of voices which naturally answer to our current climate – it is filled not so much with tomorrow's answers but with a constant state of questioning regarding our present concerns. We have playful applications of genre and theme with historical fiction, fantasy, detective dramas, self-destructive protagonists and modern day failures and outcasts. We get explorations of authority in relation to gender discourses and racism, and expressions of hopelessness as linked to power dynamics. We get the overarching fear of death, of dying, and also the fear of unexpected lives. These narratives, whether fitting to recognisable patterns or experimental in nature, are also acknowledgements of the personal dramas in which these discourses take place. It fills me with hope when I see writing that doesn't lose sight of the apparently lesser everyday dramas. Though we may see a 15th century dynastic matriarch, or characters like Clytemnestra, or even an adaptation of The Odyssey, the importance of these pieces is in the personal presentation of their ideas – the personal landscapes in which ideological battles, injustices, and the anxieties of living are played out. And so, organically tied to their historical bearings, you'll also find coming of age narratives and young adult preoccupations, with characters finding it hard to merely accept their place in the world, actively challenging power structures as well as sinking further into the recognisable shapes of modern emptiness and fake friends and guilt and denial and acceptance.

But the writers here present us with affirmations of life too, showing an understanding of drama past the simple spotlighting of images of suffering. Though a character may migrate from a war-torn Philippines after World War II, or though they may be trapped in toxic relationships, what matters here is the clarity of vision with which the writers present us not so much with judgements about a character's pain, but with what they truly want. And so we also find happiness in these pages. We find nostalgic joy, like that of a boy discovering the pain and exhilaration of love for the first time. We find deep-seated yearning and the possibility of shared pleasure in incompatible couples. And we find also the quiet lives of characters who've lived through personal tragedies and are rebuilding themselves. The risks these authors take therefore go beyond form (that is not to say that they aren't experimenting with form). But in a context presently so focused with typifying success in relatable, easily consumable figures, it's refreshing to see a group so devoted to a practice whose complexity relies on desire and frustration, on attempting to find love, and navigating friendships and family.

It's a pretty hard time to be a writer. The whole thing may at first appear to be paved with illusions made up by a language which just doesn't fit the pleasure of storytelling and opening intellectual exchanges. Making it. Industry this and that. Trends. Know your audience. Social media. Be authentic but strong, always so strong. And, after all that: destroy your ego… The writers in this anthology present us with hope for future writing in a language based on compassion, and more importantly, they give us ways to understand said hope in the face of so much uncertainty: it is still how we communicate, how we share our stories, how we act in our given contexts which portrays the real drama of living.

I want to congratulate all the writers in this anthology, and wish them all the best in their present and future projects. May this publication not be a snapshot, but a breathing testament to the importance of creating.

Gonzalo Ceron Garcia

50 East

M. René Bradshaw

'Perhaps, one day, we will all come together, and stand firmly together like hens defending their chicks.'
– Nicanor Parra

'I have two daughters.
They are all I ever wanted from the earth.
Or almost all.
I also wanted one piece of ground:
One city trapped by hills. One urban river.
An island in its element.
So I could say mine. *My* own.
And mean it."
– Eavan Boland

Chapter One

A half an hour before first light, Florentina pulled her daughter's clunking Chevy minivan into the high school parking lot with her thoughts fixed on heating frozen hash brown patties and French toast sticks. As she shifted into neutral and yanked up the parking brake, the wooden rosary beads dangling from the rearview mirror rattled against the Virgin Mary figurine that pardoned speeding from her dashboard shrine.

In the driver's seat, Florentina's feet just skimmed the gas pedal if she didn't perch on the seat's edge. She crossed herself, sighed, and immediately crossed herself again. Herbal cough drops in waxed papers littered the Mother's tiny lacquered sandals, and she unwrapped one of these sticky brown lozenges, letting it slowly melt beneath her tongue as the menthol vapours curled with her breath inside the cooling car.

Florentina Choi, eighty, diabetic, survivor of the Second World War, starvation, her husband's death, and exile, shifted uncomfortably and ran her arthritic fingers over the soft folds of her belly. At fifteen, she escaped with her family to the mountains surrounding Manila when the Japanese invaded in 1942. In 1945, she boarded an ocean liner to Los Angeles – several months after American troops wandered into their jungle encampment and announced that the war was over, and had been, for nearly half a year. Her hands, which were deformed into rigid claws from decades of scouring pots and bathing children and ancient aunties, were punished with doubled return by the dry valley air when she first gripped the van's hard plastic steering wheel every morning. It was not that she begrudged the pain, but that she feared her own growing superstitions.

You can try to hide your deepest feelings so you forget where you placed them. But when all the years and the cold that you were not born into finally get trapped inside your bones, you should be careful to watch how your shadow falls behind you.

The bleating of sheep pricked Florentina's foot-dragging. She hopped out of the driver's side onto the gravel and shut the van's rusty door with a necessary slam. The bleating was louder than usual – but singular, more insistent – and she wondered whether a young ewe had gotten out again. For the last ten years, she had worked in the cafeteria at Olive Vale's high school. Its agricultural department, the only one of its kind on this side of the Sierra Nevada mountains, kept livestock on campus, and a sheep or a pig would escape the animal enclosures at least once every semester.

Walking across the parking lot and onto the fields soaked with dew, she called for the sheepdog Ennis, who slept in a shed behind the cow pens and was allowed to patrol the runs freely. But the old girl didn't come.

Distracted, Florentina noticed that the classroom lights were on in the neighbouring chemistry building, though she was usually the first to arrive. Glass crunched beneath her work sneakers as she approached. From behind the half-open door, a blast of light illuminated the inside against the school's engulfing darkness. The small window in the door was shattered, and the handle lock must have been jimmied from the inside. She shoved the door uncertainly but hard enough for it to swing all the way back and hit the concrete wall. The remaining shards in the window scattered across the classroom's entrance, and she stepped over them and into the hard florescent light.

Florentina had seen many things. She had seen unnatural fighting between men before she was given the word *genocide*. She had seen women give birth in the open air and then bury their stillborn babies with their own hands. She had seen her father's tall silhouette disappear behind the chain-linked fence of a death camp. But what she saw in the classroom that winter morning was the worst thing she had seen since settling in California.

A lamb was collapsed against the wall a few feet in front of the door, its front legs buckled beneath its chest. It raised its head and screamed, spitting out blood and bile. After falling several times, the lamb managed to stand and totter toward her with a bandy-legged trot. It was so slathered in blood and bits of innards that it looked like it had rolled in it all, like a dog. Florentina saw the root behind its damaged locomotion: a mutilated stump hung from its side in splinters of bone caked with dust and blood – the bottom half of its front right limb had been severed off. The lamb screamed once more, and then heaved a long pneumatic sigh before crumpling on its side again. She strode over to it and kneeled on the chilly linoleum floor. Blood frothed at its lips, but its eyes widened and blinked.

Florentina rose to leave, but on the demonstration table, in front of the rows of desks, a sheep lay with its legs pointing stiffly to the ceiling. The meat above its woolly neck was a slick of blood peaked with shredded flesh. A single eyeball dangled beside its muzzle, and both empty sockets brimmed with blood. Snaking purple intestines crawled from its abdomen, branched around neat piles of soggy textbooks, and knotted with bloody shards of glass that blossomed from its anus. Florentina turned and ran out of the classroom, her sneakers slipping and squealing on handfuls of flesh and shit.

Back at the van, she fumbled the buttons on her flip phone. Her hands kept seizing into twisted fists, causing frustration to curdle in her throat. But as the 911 operator patiently coaxed the details from her shaky pauses and clumsy English, she ached to crane her neck behind her. Rocking back and forth on her heels, she waited for the sirens to approach like an announcement of deliverance, and then she imagined a smoker's wheezing on her neck and she imagined the promise of a knife in a man's eyes, a crown of midges aflame in lamplight, the glint of a golden rotting tooth, the sound of piss falling on water, macaque monkeys howling in treetop canopies, all of it running in the wrong order.

Florentina remembered Ennis and turned back to the school. This time her call for the dog quickened into a whimper of the Lord's Prayer as her fear and the high-pitched twangs of her native Tagalog broke the metronome of a thousand Sunday mornings. *Your will be done, on earth as it is in heaven.*

She tilted her trembling lips toward the fingernail of moon floating above the fields, and her frozen prayer drifted several inches away from her face in white threadlike breaths, hovered for an instant, and then vanished just as shooting pinks and yellows began to wrinkle over the moon and the stars. *And do not bring us to the time of trial, but rescue us from the evil one.*

The evil one.

After a lifetime – several lifetimes, even – more wars in the islands, and several oceans between them, had the Jap finally found her?

Undercurrents

Ed Butterfield

Three years ago tomorrow, two police officers dragged the waterlogged corpse of Sean Spencer out of the sea. He was my oldest friend. A shy, sensitive type, cut from the cloth of honesty and quiet conviction, he grew up in possession of a furious intellect and manifest ambition. More known than liked by most, but that never really seemed to bother him. He had a girlfriend and a future to look forward to, one well beyond the confines of this worn-out town.

The night before, we'd been in high spirits: fifty-four barely adult teenagers cavorting our way down the high street after stepping out of the gates of the local sixth form college for the final time. We bounced from pub to pub and drank in every place we could squeeze into. Anywhere that would take our money and not kick us out for being too rowdy. We laughed and celebrated the end of an era by drinking ourselves silly until last orders were called.

The following morning, we all lined up on the beach behind a strip of police tape, hungover and sobering in the sea breeze, while the officers took our names and statements. We had more questions than we did answers. No one could remember how drunk he'd been, or whether he'd said anything alarming or unusual. No one remembered seeing him leave. Everyone just wanted to know how he'd ended up floating face down in the water. The sergeant couldn't say for sure – she said they might never know exactly what had happened, even after an autopsy – but she gave us all a likely version of events: Sean was drunk and wandered onto the beach on his way home; he thought that going into the water might clear his head; he lost his footing and didn't realise the power of the waves; he panicked and tried to swim against the current, but the sheer force of the water exhausted him, dragged him down beneath the surface and drowned him. His body had been found barefoot; his shoes were further up the beach, sat in the sand with the socks balled up inside.

By lunchtime, people had already started to drift away, back to their homes and their lives. Only two of us stayed: me and Lauren. His girlfriend. My best friend. I held her in my arms and comforted her while she soaked my sleeves with tears. When they took his body away, I took her home and told her that I would always be there for her, no matter what. That I wasn't going anywhere.

I know you're not supposed to speak ill of the dead. But whenever I picture him lying there on that beach beneath a sheet, bare toes sticking out at the bottom, I can't help but think of his death as anything other than an insolent waste.

You can usually rely on the trains to run late around here. It's a staple feature of this part of the country. Doesn't matter where you're going or when you travel, if it's to or from the coast. Just ignore the timetable. You're better off trying to read tea leaves. Yesterday, of course, had to be different; the trains were right on time. The cosmic forces of the universe were carrying me along, sweeping me out towards the east coast at a frankly astonishing speed given Northern Rail's usual standards. Back to the motherland. Home turf. The place where it all began.

Lauren was waiting on the platform when I got off the train, scanning the carriage doors for my face, eyes hidden behind a pair of strawberry sunglasses. She was trying to look cool, curling her lips up in that surly pout she always thought made her look intense and mysterious. If I didn't know the curve of her face so well I might have thought it was a look of spite that she carried with her wherever she went. But it's only ever temporary. When she caught sight of me she was all smiles and excitement.

'Hello stranger,' she said, bundling into my open arms.

'Hi.'

I hadn't seen her in almost a year, but she hadn't changed a bit. All the details were just as they always were. The mousy hair scrunched up in a loose bun. The paper-thin vintage tee with a picture of someone taking a picture on it, oversized and sliding down one shoulder. The just-a-bit-too-much-makeup undercutting the intended vibe of apathy to the outside world. She smelled the same as she always does too: cherry blossom perfume and hair products. There were wristbands running up her arms from festivals she went to years ago, and she still wore that ring with a letter L Scrabble tile on it. L for Lauren, she always told people. I know she only bought it to help her tell left from right.

'It's so good to see you,' she said into the creases of my shirt.

'Yeah. You too.'

'Come on, I'm parked outside.'

'I was worried you might be.'

She led me by the arm through the station concourse and out into the meagre heat of the day. Sitting in the middle of the car park, shining under the pale sunlight like a vision from a nightmare, was her bright green Nissan Micra. The only car in the world that looks and smells like a giant bowl of stewed cabbage.

'I can't believe you're still driving this thing,' I said, climbing into the passenger seat.

'Yeah, for now. I'm saving up for something better.'

'You only live around the corner. We could have walked, spared ourselves the shame.'

'Walk then, if that's how you feel.' She turned the key and the engine spat into life. 'Come on, out you get. You ungrateful shit.'

'Just get out of here before anyone sees us.'

We pulled out of the car park and onto the main road, accelerating past rows of boarded-up stores and charity shops. The scars of a town starved of public investment. No wonder my parents upped sticks as soon as I left for university. I leaned against my hand to hide my face from passers-by until Lauren caught on to what I was doing. She wound the windows down, cranked the volume up full blast on the crackling stereo and howled into the open air.

'Look at us!' she shouted, blaring the horn in time with the music. 'We're having so much fun!'

When we got back to her parents' house, Lauren showed me up to her brother's redecorated old bedroom, cold and impersonal now that he's off chasing success down south. I dumped my bag and wandered along to her bedroom, but she wasn't there. I hadn't been inside her room since the beginning of secondary school when we first got to know each other, back when the walls were covered in boyband posters and the duvet was decorated with pink and purple flowers. The flowers were long gone. In their place, bedding bearing the names of capital cities around the world, covered in pictures of vintage suitcases and stamps. The posters were gone too; now the walls were off-white and bare.

'There you are,' said Lauren, poking her head through the door behind me. 'I thought you'd wandered off.'

'Oh, sorry. I thought you'd be in here.'

'Hiding from you?'

'Something like that.'

'Come on, you must be starving. Let's get some dinner.'

We ate pizzas in the living room from plates balanced on our laps and washed them down with a bottle of red poached from Lauren's parents' wine rack. They were away in Madeira – their third trip of the year so far – and wouldn't notice they were one short when they got back. Her dad's a bank manager and her mum owns the beauty salon in the old town where Lauren works. They've always liked me, and I've always found them bearable in short bursts. But they've got a nice house, all mod cons in the kitchen and a fancy home cinema system, so they must be doing something right.

'Right, come on then,' she said when our plates were empty. 'Fill me in.'

'What?'

'Tell me everything.'

'There's nothing to tell you.'

'Oh, come *on!* Loosen up a bit.'

'I don't know what you want me to say.'

'Let's just talk like we always used to.'

'Okay,' I said, swilling my wine before polishing off the glass. 'Talk away.'

'How's life?'

'It's alright.'

'How was uni?'

‘Uni was pretty good. Enjoyed it.’

‘And where’s a degree in history going to take you?’

‘Oh, I don’t know. I’ll probably just spend my life getting lost inside museums.’

‘Ah. Impressive.’ She picked at bits of sediment floating in her glass. ‘And are there any girls to tell me about?’

‘Not really.’

‘Not *really?*’

‘I mean, none at all.’

‘Right. Well, what with your excellent postgraduate prospects I’m sure you’d have your pick of the girls round here.’

‘I think I’d rather chop my own cock off.’

‘Doesn’t sound like you’ve been putting it to much use anyway.’

‘Yeah, yeah. Like you’ve been getting any action.’

I froze and closed my eyes. A moment of silence began to curdle in the air.

‘Lauren, I’m so—’

‘Do you want some more wine?’

I couldn’t look at her as she rose to her feet.

‘Yeah,’ I said. ‘Yeah, sure.’

Later that evening, we sat together on the sofa beneath an old blanket and half-watched some mawkish chick flick about a guy who marries a girl out of sympathy for her terminal illness. Halfway through, she laid her head on my shoulder and began to tell me about the things that kept her awake night, the way she always would when we were our younger selves.

‘I just feel so alone all the time.’ The words were sticking in her throat. ‘I don’t know what to do.’

‘You’re trapping yourself in the same old habits. You need to make a change. When did you last try something new?’

‘I can’t remember.’

‘Do something exciting. Be impulsive. Try not to worry too much.’

By the time the film had finished, she was asleep, her body rising and falling with the breaths that whispered through her nose. My arm was numb and I couldn't feel a thing in my fingers. All I could feel was the weight of her, a profound ache that sat somewhere beneath the surface of my bones.

Earlier this afternoon, I stood at the bottom of the town's cemetery holding a bunch of flowers and wishing I'd worn a coat. The morning sunlight reaching in through the windows had promised a fragile warmth, but by the time we left the house it was to the indifference of grey skies. At Lauren's behest, I was wearing the brightest clothes that I own: a cobalt-coloured jacket, a pink shirt, blue jeans, green shoes. She'd chosen a flower-petal sundress, bright yellow in spite of the drab palette of the day, and her shoulders were covered by a white cardigan. Mourners tend to wear black, of course, but days like today were about celebrating Sean's life, not mourning his death. Which, I'm told, is a very different thing indeed.

They buried him next to the hedge that separates the cemetery from the primary school that he and I went to. As I approached the headstone to lay down my flowers, the thought occurred to me that he'd come full circle; that it was the very same scrap of a boy who used to cry at school when the girls made him play kiss chase that was now lying in a box six feet beneath me. I never quite worked out what Lauren saw in him. He was a good mate, but he was crap with girls. He always seemed suspicious of romantic attention, like it was something he couldn't quite figure out. Why him? And what did she ever do that made him feel so different about it all?

Graveyards are dishonest places. They fill me with disgust. It's not the rows of rotting corpses that I have a problem with. It's the idea of burial grounds as final resting places. Nice, neat little plots of land, well-maintained with the grass clipped at the edges. Life's not like that. Life's a mess. People live lives full of clutter and chaos. Some are short, some are long, and some are so long the end can't come soon enough. But each one sprawls out in its own unique way. The business of the graveyard is just the business of reduction. Reduction to a narrow space where people only ever existed in death; reduction to a few lines chiselled into a chunk of stone. Sean's parents had chosen the inscription that's now meant to stand in for him forever: *The brightest stars burn fast and strong.* I'm not sure if it's supposed to sound like such an affront to the living.

I felt Lauren's hand on my arm and remembered that this was her moment, that I was treading all over it. I took a step back and watched her shuffle forwards, cradling her gift-wrapped arrangement of pink and white carnations surrounding a single red rose. She ran her fingers against the flower petals and began to talk to the ground. It was a conversation I wasn't meant to overhear. All that was audible was the soft, sonorous sound of her voice, a mystery humming between the headstones.

As soon as we left the cemetery, we headed for the nearest pub. It was always going to end up like this. Day drinking in places that never got to know us, telling stories about the present to avoid reminiscing about the past. We sat in spaces that weren't ours and tried to get comfortable, but the buildings didn't seem to want us around. The chairs we chose were old and rickety. The tables stood unsteady on uneven floorboards. When I tried to play a song on the old jukebox at The Castle, the machine swallowed my money and wouldn't give it back. In the tiny front room of The Gatehouse, a talking parrot called Henry heckled me from his perch while I tried to tell the story of a friend from university who revised so hard he overslept for his final exam.

By the time we arrived at The Anchor, the locals had grown wise to the fact that one of us wasn't from around here anymore. I went to the bar for a round of drinks and noticed a lad in a tracksuit down the other end eyeing me with contempt over an empty pint glass.

'Two pints of cider, please,' I said to the barmaid. Her hands were the size of pit shovels.

'Four quid, love.'

She turned away to pour the drinks while I fumbled in my wallet for change. The twentysomething tracksuit addressed me from the far end of the bar.

'Jesus Christ.'

I caught his eye. 'Everything alright mate?'

'Yeah. Elton John just wants his jacket back.'

I counted out my money into neat piles and passed them to the barmaid in exchange for my drinks. As I turned away, he had another go.

'Bit early for tourist season, aren't you?'

'Sorry?'

'Tourist season.' He stressed each syllable as if I was the idiot. 'Your lot aren't normally round here this early.'

'I grew up here mate. I went to school up the road.'

'Don't sound like it.'

'What does it matter to you anyway?'

'It matters because I don't like tourists.'

'You do realise it's only the remnants of tourism that keep a town like this afloat, right?'

'What?'

'Don't bite the hand that feeds.'

'What the fuck are you talking about?'

'Oh, forget it,' I said, heading back to the table.

'Posh prick,' he shouted after me.

'What's all that about?' Lauren asked as I passed her drink across the table. I took a large gulp of my own fizzing liquid.

'Nothing,' I said. My face felt warm and flushed. I took another large mouthful before putting my glass down on the table. 'Just a minute.'

'Where are you going?'

I ignored her and marched back to the bar. 'Hey,' I said, tapping the lad on the shoulder. He swung around and straightened up. I hadn't realised how tall he was before.

'What?'

'Don't speak to people like that. It's rude.'

'And what?'

'And. Well.' I had run out of things to say. 'I want you to apologise.'

He picked his empty pint glass off the bar. 'You trying to start something, pal?'

'No. I just—'

'You wanna take this outside?'

A hand clamped around my arm and started to pull me away.

'Sorry,' said Lauren, dragging me with surprising force. 'He's had a bad day. He doesn't know what he's saying.'

I stumbled backwards, eyes locked with the lad at the bar as he showered me with obscenities.

'What the fuck are you playing at?' she hissed. 'You're gonna get your head kicked in.'

'Fucking chav bastard,' I said. My chest had tightened and my head was starting to swirl. 'Thinks he can speak to me like that.'

'He can say whatever he wants, and he can do a hell of a lot worse.' I turned to face her. Her eyes dug into me like knives, savaging my pride. 'Sit down. This is *not* the time for it.'

I slumped into my seat and stared into the remainder of my drink. When I looked up, I saw the barmaid striding towards our table with a face like a hurricane, shaking her head and clenching her monstrous fists.

We sat for a while on the edge of the promenade wall, picking at portions of fish and chips and watching the tide gather in the distance. The waves murmured and purled as they crept up the shore, lapping over the twisted runnels that ran across the sand like hands reaching up from the sea. To our right, the beached wreckage of a fishing boat lay sinking into the silt; behind it, the pier stretched out like an old finger pointing towards the horizon.

'Why are fish and chips always so disappointing?' Lauren asked, pushing the last of her portion around the polystyrene tray. 'They're never as good as you think they're going to be.'

I scooped up scraps of batter into my mouth. 'Isn't that just like everything at the seaside?'

'I suppose. It must be shit coming here on holiday. Driving all this way just to sit around getting greasy fingers and waiting for the sun to come out.'

'Yeah.' I put my tray down on the wall in the space between our legs. 'I'm sorry for embarrassing you in the pub.'

'The only person you embarrassed was yourself,' she said, suppressing a smirk. 'Do you want to finish my chips?'

'Thanks,' I said, clawing at her leftovers.

'You know, I wouldn't miss them if I left.'

'The chips or the chavs?'

'Oh, just the chips. The kids are alright as long as you don't start fights with them.'

'Do you ever think about leaving?'

'Sometimes.'

'Why don't you?'

'Because it doesn't work like that.' She pushed herself off from the edge of the wall and arced through the air onto the sand. 'Come on. Let's have a walk before the tide comes in.'

We walked up the beach in step, in silence, following the trail of weeds and driftwood lying along the high tide line. The daylight was starting to fade. I wanted to build a fire, but I didn't have anything to light it with, so we pushed on instead, continuing north to the place where the beach gets narrower and steeper, where the cliffs start to rise up to the left-hand side and the sand gives way to fine fragments of shingle and larger weathered rocks. We reached a low stone platform where the beach fell away on the far side into a small inlet and sat down against the cliff face to look out at the desolate seascape. Two block brushstrokes: grey on dark grey.

'I sometimes come and sit out here on weekends,' Lauren said. 'In the evening, when all the people have gone home. I sit and watch the tide roll in, and everything just looks so peaceful. It's strange when you know what it's capable of.'

'Yeah.' The waves built and broke before us, scraping back and scratching at the stones before coming again in soft, persistent ripples.

'Do you think he knew he was going to die?'

'Lauren—'

'Because sometimes people pass out from the shock of the cold before they even know what's happening.'

'You can't keep doing this to yourself.'

'Doing what?'

'Going over everything. Opening up old wounds.'

'Why am I not allowed to talk about him?'

'That's not what I'm saying.'

'Well what are you saying then? Because right now it seems like you're telling me I should forget he ever existed.'

My fingers fell on top of hers. 'This isn't remembering him. It's just remembering how he died.'

She shook her head and laughed. Her hand twisted beneath my grip. 'It's just like no one else is even bothered, you know?'

'You can't remember him for everyone who ever knew him. You have to start letting him go.'

'You make it sound so easy.'

'It is. It's easier than you're making it. All this sitting around fixating on the waves that took him isn't helping. It's just prolonging the pain.' I pressed my palm against hers, interlinking my fingers with her own. 'You should get away from here.'

'I can't leave him behind.'

'You're not leaving him behind. He's not here anymore.' I looked down at our interlaced fingers. Her hand felt so natural in mine. I raised my head. Her eyes were shining in the half-light. 'You have to try to move on. It's what he would have wanted.'

I hadn't kissed her before. I wasn't sure what to expect. She didn't flinch – she didn't move at all, in fact – until my free hand reached out to rest on her leg. She broke away, drawing in a sharp breath through her nose, and for a moment I was sure that the feeling had passed. Then she moved towards me again, kissing me with force, pushing hot breath out against my top lip. In my mind, I was pulling at her clothes and she was pulling at mine; we uncovered ourselves, exposing our bodies to the air, to the world, with cold hands running over hot skin. I felt her clawing at my back, nails digging down around my spine.

'Fuck me,' I heard her say. The words were coarse and strangled. 'Fuck me.'

It was over too soon. I rolled away onto my back and tried to chase a feeling that had already escaped me, but there was nothing to hold onto.

The memory of it was already a blur. I heard the scrabbling of loose stones beside me, and when I looked I couldn't see her body. The darkness had congealed around our distraction.

'You okay?'

'Yeah. Fine.'

'Maybe we should have done that back at your place.'

'Yeah. Maybe.'

She rose to her feet and stood over me, a featureless form against the night sky.

'I'm going home.'

'Okay,' I said, looking up at the absent sky. I heard the rocks shift beneath her feet as she walked away down the beach. 'I'll catch you up.'

I don't know how long I've been lying here listening to the strengthening rush of the waves. I haven't tried to get up yet. A heaviness has descended over my half-naked body; the weight of something awful that I can't seem to shake. I lay in the darkness and sink deeper into the depths of my regret. I wonder how close the water is to washing over my toes. I wonder how many minutes I am from being submerged.

The Queen of Mycenae

Costanza Casati

> ‘I brooded on this trial, this ancient blood feud / year by year. At last my hour came. / Here I stand and here I struck / and here my work is done.’
>
> – Aeschylus, *Agamemnon*, ll. 1396-1399

Chapter One

Prey

Clytemnestra looks down at the steep ravine but cannot see any trace of dead bodies. She remembers crouching in the forest when she was little, watching the elders drag criminals and weak babies up the trail and throw them down into the gorge Spartans call Ceadas. Down the cliff, the rocks are as sharp as freshly cast iron and as slippery as raw fish. Clytemnestra used to hide and pray for all of those men whose death would be long and painful; she could not pray for the babies, the thought made her restless. If she walked closer to the edge of the ravine, she could feel a soft breeze caressing her skin. Her mother had told her that the dead infants lying at the bottom of the Ceadas spoke through the wind. Those voices whispered, yet Clytemnestra could not grasp their words. So she let her mind wonder as she looked at the sun peeking through the leafy branches.

An eerie silence looms over the forest. Clytemnestra knows she is being followed. She quickly descends from the high ground leaving the ravine behind, trying not to trip on the slippery stones that form the hunting trail. The wind is getting colder, the sky darker. As she pants, she can see her breath spreading in the chilled air. She follows the same stream that used to guide her when she was little, an almost invisible trickle that wets the orange leaves on the ground. She slips and cuts her palm against the sharp edge of a rock. She clenches her fist; her bleeding hand will leave tracks for her hunter.

The forest, in the quiet autumnal evenings, is inhabited by roe deer, hares and boars, but also becomes a lair for bears, panthers and wolves. Spartan boys fight these beasts in pairs as part of their training. Clytemnestra once shaved her head like a boy and went to the gymnasium with them hoping to prepare for a hunt. When her mother found out, she did not feed her for two days. 'Part of the training is to starve Spartan boys until they are forced to steal,' her mother said. Clytemnestra endured the punishment; she deserved it after all.

The stream leads to a spring and a little waterfall. At the top of it, she can see a rift that leads to a cave, partially hidden by tall oaks. She starts climbing the mossy rocks on the sides of the spring. She feels like a predator, silent and watchful, though she knows she is the prey. Splashes of cold water hit her face as she climbs. She narrows her eyes and focuses on the footholds the rock face provides. Her hand throbs with pain and keeps slipping over the surfaces of the cliff. Her bow is slung over her back, and the dagger hangs loose from her belt, its handle touching the skin of her thigh. When she reaches the entrance to the cave, she stops to catch her breath. She wonders if her shoulders are small enough to pass through the crevice. The darkness beyond that fracture scares her. She tears a piece of her tunic off, douses it in the clear water of the spring and wraps it around her bleeding hand. The tips of the oaks blend with the impending darkness, and everything is blurry to her tired eyes. If only she could get a better view of the hill…

She climbs up the tallest tree, as splinters scratch her bare arms. She stops astride a branch and listens, holding her dagger tight. The moon is high in the sky, its contours clear and cold like a silver shield, its light reflected in the sparkling water. Everything is still, except for the whispering of the wind.

A silver shape on the tree in front of her is caressed by the moonlight, as it slowly slips away from the shadows. Clytemnestra remains still, blood pulsating in her temples, her wounded hand trembling against the bark. The animal looks like a lynx; it has a silver coat of thick fur with fading brown spots and pointed ears.

Before she can move, the beast jumps and lands on her tree. The impact makes her lose her balance. She tries to hold on to the branches, but her nails break, her palms slip. She falls and hits her back against the muddy ground. For a second, her eyes are blind and her breath is gone. I am paralysed, she thinks, but her hands are already moving fast to her bow and arrows, and, as the animal tries to jump down on her, she shoots and quickly rolls on her side. She feels a blinding pain and screams as the lynx's claw scratches her back. She stands up as the animal stands. Behind it, the narrow crevice that leads into the cave. She does not have time to take another arrow, so she throws her dagger, which sinks into the animal's shoulder. She runs, taking advantage of the predator's wound, seeking refuge in the cave. She hardly passes through the crevice, grazing her head and hips to get in. She sinks into the darkness and waits, praying that the cave has no other entrance, and no other visitor.

Slowly, her eyes learn to see in the dark. Her panting echoes in the humid air as if the cave itself were breathing. She has entered a living thing, a shelter, a mind that has thought and lived the lives of the creatures it has hosted over time. The cold rock is pleasant against her bleeding back. She waits for what seems like an eternity, until the moaning of the wounded animal moves further and further away. Her bow and most of her arrows are somehow intact and she holds on to them tightly. As she waits, gusts of wind become stories of nostalgia, puffs of breath turn into memories: dead heroes and warriors speak in cold whispers filled with regrets for everything they have lost.

The animal must be gone. Clytemnestra drags her body closer to the crevice and peeps out. It is night and the light of the moon casts blurry shadows on the ground, which is covered in muddy orange leaves and blood. There, close to the spring, lies the dead animal, its dark red blood spreading like spilled wine around it. Clytemnestra exits the cave with difficulty, her hips brushing against the smooth rocks. She limps closer to the dead shape and carefully retrieves her dagger. The animal's eyes are open, reflecting the perfectly round contour of the moon. Clytemnestra looks into them, as if to ask for forgiveness. Then she ties the animal's paws to her quiver and starts walking back hoping to be home by morning. Her mother will be proud of her hunt.

Chapter Two

Mirrors

Clytemnestra watches her sleeping sister Helen and breathes quietly, knowing that the slightest sound will wake her up. It is dawn. She lies on the large bed, wrapped in perfumed sheets, while the first light of the day enters through the windows.

Helen's hair, the colour of honey. It is so bright that it reminds her of gold when it is poured into stone cavities to make jewels. It spreads out across the white pillows, and, as the light of the rising sun kisses Helen's figure, its wavy strands sparkle like the sandy hills of a desert. When they were little, Clytemnestra was jealous of Helen's hair, and tried to cut it off with a knife she had stolen from the kitchen. Her own hair is as soft and wavy as Helen's, but darker. The colour of dirt, her sister used to say.

Helen's skin, smooth and fair, like a canvas ready to be painted. When she blushes, she lowers her head so that no one notices it. Clytemnestra carefully places her hand next to her sister's, comparing the tanned hues of her own skin with Helen's. As she does so, Helen's fingers move almost imperceptibly. What is she dreaming about?

Helen's eyes, their dark lashes casting long shadows on her cheeks. Clytemnestra thinks of her sister's irises, now hidden behind her delicate lids. They are the colour of seawater, and when the sun illuminates them, they remind Clytemnestra of the shimmer of light on the surface of the ocean. Helen's gaze is sweet and shy, but has become guarded with the passing of the years, and when Clytemnestra looks into her sister's eyes she sees a veil, carefully drawn not to let anyone in.

Helen's body, slender and beautiful. Her adolescent shapes are delicate and sensual, and Clytemnestra knows that soon Helen will have many suitors, and her beauty will be her greatest power. But now, as she sleeps half-wrapped in the white sheets, she looks frail and vulnerable, like a goddess stripped of her immortality, lying among humans by mistake.

The fresh breeze of the early morning quickly makes way for the summer heat. Along the banks of the Eurotas river, large brown areas, their shades ranging from burnt umber to bronze, blend into the yellowish green of the grass, where few blood-red anemones struggle to grow. Not far from the banks, a stripe of fertile soil, with olive and fig trees, is surrounded by dry terrains, rugged hills and rough mountains. The valley has a raw beauty, similar to that of its inhabitants. A land of warriors, both men and women, which outsiders often depict as 'lovely' and 'shining' because of the harmony of its warm colours that shimmer in the sunlight, but also as 'hollow' and 'broken' for its ravines and dryness. Clytemnestra looks at her naked figure mirrored in the Eurotas and thinks she is like her homeland, as her beauty is one with the resilience and strength of her body. If Helen weren't so perfect, would I be the most beautiful woman of Sparta? she wonders.

'Wait for me,' a sweet voice says.

Clytemnestra turns around. Helen is combing her hair. She is still wearing her sandals, while her tunic is lying at her feet.

'Why do you have to do everything in a hurry?' Helen asks, slightly annoyed, yet her voice remains sweet-toned.

Clytemnestra shrugs and patiently waits. To the world, Helen of Sparta might look like a goddess, but truly, she follows her sister in everything she does.

'Now move, it is too hot,' Clytemnestra says, before plunging her head into the river. The water is still cool, after the refreshing air of the night. This part of the river is protected by tall reeds that overgrow the banks, in a glade that feels more private than the rest of the valley. Sometimes, even on the hottest summer days, a soft breeze blows through the reeds and ripples the surface of the water. Clytemnestra remains submerged for a while, watching her long hair dancing around her like seaweed. When she remerges, Helen is still in the water up to her thighs. She always walks slowly into the river, wetting her body with her hands first, and once the water is running around her waist she shivers.

'Come on in,' Clytemnestra laughs. She swims towards Helen and hugs her waist. Her sister shudders.

'It's cold,' Helen moans, but keeps walking into the water, until her breasts are submerged. Clytemnestra keeps holding on to her with her arms, while letting her own body float, enjoying the contrast between the chill of the water and the warmth of her sister's skin.

'You are no Spartan woman,' she says with a smile.

Helen smiles back, 'Not as much as you.' She pauses for a moment; then she adds, 'If you were a man, you'd be the strongest soldier in Greece.'

'Perhaps not the strongest, but the smartest.'

Helen looks at her, her expression scolding her for her hubris.

'Don't anger the gods,' she says.

Clytemnestra laughs out loud, amused by Helen's innocent fear. 'If you're the most beautiful woman on earth, I might as well be the cleverest. I don't see why the gods should be angry for this, they'll always be cleverer and more beautiful anyway.'

Helen nods, thinking it through. Then, she arches her back, immersing her head into the river. When she stands up again, her hair clings to her shoulders. She swims towards her sister and hugs her from behind. The two remain floating in the water for a while, in silence, under the shade of a large tree that grows on the bank of the river.

The gymnasium is already filled with the smell of sweat and the familiar sound of gasping. It is still early in the morning, but the sun is strong, and in the large inner courtyard in the centre of the building the heat makes the sand burn. Only young girls are practising at this hour. Younger boys will practise later, and older men will take their place right before sunset. From under the shade of the southern portico, Clytemnestra looks at the tanned bodies running around the square, fully naked, drops of sweat trickling down their backs. At her arrival, some girls smile, but none interrupt their routine. She recognises most of them, daughters of rich families from Sparta, and smiles back.

It is very hot. Unwillingly, she walks into the Elaeothesium for her anointment. The room is a small, almost claustrophobic space that opens to the portico, where the aliptae anoint the bodies of the athletes just before they enter the gymnasium. Clytemnestra is not uncomfortable with her nudity. She has grown accustomed to it with the years and sometimes enjoys the subdued looks of excitement and appreciation that men cast on her. They make her feel beautiful, even though she knows it is only masculine lust, a desire that is probably cast towards most of the girls who practise in the gymnasium. Only a feeble light enters the room. Clytemnestra feels like she can barely breathe and closes her eyes until the procedure is over. The aliptae create a mixture of oil and sand, then spread it over the surface of her body and rub it into her skin. The rubbing is pleasant and the sand tickles on her belly and neck, but it will take hours to wash away.

When Clytemnestra walks back into the portico, the girls have finished running and are practising the throwing of the discus. They are forming a line and one after the other they take their positions, placing their right foot forward, bending their knee, and holding the discus in their right hand. In that moment of stillness, right before throwing the discus and turning their body towards it, they look like statues, mighty and eternal, with their muscles tense and stretched and the oil on their skin glowing under the rays of the sun. Clytemnestra joins them, and the girls keep practising their jumping, wrestling and running, as the sun gradually reaches its highest point and the heat its peak.

At last, there is the dancing. Helen has joined them now. She always misses most of the exercises, mainly because she is not as strong as the others, but also because she feels embarrassed as everyone's eyes scrutinise her naked body, their inquisitive gazes burning on her skin. Yet, she always appears before the dancing starts. It is a dance of freedom, of complete abandonment to a repetitive rhythm that gradually becomes faster and faster, as bare feet beat on the sand, pulsing through the sunlit, sultry air, and the dancers' hair moves like many tongues of flame. Clytemnestra's body is covered in sweat now and she is immersing herself in the primitive atmosphere that the dance and the heat produce, where desire, instincts and sensuality rule. Helen's movements mirror those of her sister, but are more composed and delicate, as if she were afraid of losing herself completely. Clytemnestra dances for herself; Helen dances for others.

The water of the bath is cold and pleasant on the skin. Only Helen, Clytemnestra and a few other girls, the Spartiates, are allowed to share the small room in one corner of the portico. Most of the other athletes, girls who cannot claim to be native Spartans, are washing the sweat away in a warmer bath in an even smaller room on the opposite side of the building. The stony walls are cool, and the girls rub their backs against them, while covering their skin in perfumed soap. In the shadowy darkness, they look like unsubstantial spirits to Clytemnestra, but then the contact of her skin with their skin, her body with their bodies, reminds her that they are flesh and blood.

She is too tired. She has not slept much in the past few days, thinking about the future with fear and excitement. She is sixteen now and will be married soon. Before marrying Tyndareus, her mother Leda had been an Aetolian princess, born in that arid and mountainous region in the north of Greece that is famous for its wild beasts and hunters. Leda was a huntress herself and used to tell Clytemnestra of the many boars she had killed with her arrows and of the perils and wilderness of the forests of Aetolia. When she told such stories, her eyes were filled with sadness and yearning. The tribes of Aetolia, the Curetes, were considered primitive by other Greeks, who circulated stories about them saying that they ate raw meat like animals. Clytemnestra never believed such tales as a child. When Leda, a tall, strong woman with raven hair and olive skin, gave birth to Helen – a light-skinned, blonde little girl – everyone in Sparta believed she was having an affair with Zeus, disguised in human form. The rumours became so popular that even Tyndareus, Clytemnestra's father, slowly came to hate his own daughter. He saw nothing of himself in her, as she grew and became passionate about music and dancing, and cried whenever she saw a wounded soldier. But Clytemnestra knows Helen is her sister. She knows that, even though Helen as a child looked frail and gentle, her will was as strong as her own. When they were little, Helen used to stand next to her and compare every tiny part of their bodies, until she found a similarity and was satisfied. After all, as Helen used to say, the eyelashes of both of them were thick, their fingers skinny, their necks long. On the other hand, Clytemnestra knows she has always been the exact copy of her mother. She wonders which husband Tyndareus will choose for her.

'The boys will be here soon.' Helen's soft whisper startles Clytemnestra. While she has been absorbed in her thinking, all the other girls have left. The tips of her fingers are wrinkly from the long time spent in the bath.

'Go ahead, I will catch up in a moment.'

Helen leaves the room, and now there is only Clytemnestra's silhouette, a still shadow on the stony walls. Without knowing why, she starts crying.

Chapter Three

The King of Maeonia

Clytemnestra cannot take her eyes off the stranger. In the bare dining room of the palace of Sparta, oil lamps cast flickering lights on the large table where Tyndareus's family and a few noble visitors are eating. The man looks young and different from every other guest. Clytemnestra notices that he does not devour the food with his hands, drink much diluted wine, nor does he laugh out loud at the men's vulgar jokes. Rather, he sits in his wooden chair with elegance and dignity and talks charmingly to Helen, who is seated next to him. His hair is black, and the dark, elegant brows that frame his turquoise eyes give him an odd and exotic look. He looks strikingly skinny, especially next to the other Greek men at the table, all of them muscular, sturdy soldiers whose bodies are scarred by war and hand-to-hand combat training. Her father introduced the stranger as the King of Maeonia, a land in the east, far across the sea. Clytemnestra wonders if kings fight their own battles in Maeonia, as they do in Sparta.

Now the stranger is looking at her with curiosity, as Helen whispers something to him. Clytemnestra wants to look away, but her eyes look into his. She hears her father's deep voice coming from her right, addressing the stranger over the loud chatter.

'Tell me Tantalus, are the women in your homeland as beautiful as they say?'

Is Tyndareus trying to arrange a marriage? Clytemnestra wonders. Sparta rarely has guests from such faraway lands, and the King of Maeonia must be a very rich man. Many men stop talking and look at the stranger with interest. He does not blink but smiles, and two small lines appear at the corner of his eyes.

'They truly are good-looking, but nothing like the beauty you can find here in Sparta.' For a moment, he looks at Leda, buried in the shadows next to her husband, and then at Helen and Clytemnestra. 'Your women possess the most precious beauty of all: strength of body and character.'

Leda lowers her eyes, while Helen smiles.

Tyndareus laughs and raises his cup. 'To the women of Sparta,' he says.

Everyone echoes his words, and the golden cups shine in the light of the lamps.

The sun sets late in summer. Standing on the terrace in front of the main hall, Tantalus looks at the mountains to the west and to the east. Their peaks are perfectly outlined against the orange sky and then slowly become blurred, melting into the growing darkness. When he hears quick, approaching steps, he does not turn around. Clytemnestra appears behind him. She has followed him, but now she doesn't know what to say. So she waits. Eventually, he turns, and his gaze gets lost staring at her heavy, golden earrings that swing, slightly touching her neck and shoulders. They are in the shape of big anemones and they cast clear shadows on her collarbones.

'Do you know about the origin of windflowers?' he says, overcoming the long moment of silence.

'We call them anemones,' replies Clytemnestra.

'Anemones,' he repeats. 'They were created by the goddess Aphrodite from the blood of Adonis, the boy she was in love with.'

'I know what happened. Adonis was slain by a wild boar.'

Tantalus looks into Clytemnestra's eyes. 'The boy dies but the goddess's love for him remains. It is a reminder of beauty and resistance in times of adversity.' His slight foreign accent is musical and emanates a sense of safety, of warmth.

'That is true, but Adonis is dead, and no flower can replace him.'

Tantalus smiles, amused: 'You truly are a strange woman.'

Clytemnestra does not reply.

'Your father says you are as wise as a mature woman can be, and when I ask your sister about you, she says you always know what you want.'

Clytemnestra thinks it isn't true, but does not contradict him: 'That would be enviable, even for a man.'

Tantalus reaches out for her hair. His hand sinks into her wavy locks until it touches the skin behind her neck. Clytemnestra opens her eyes wide.

The shadows are growing longer on the terrace, and the contours of Tantalus's face are blurred. Everything around her is soft, fading, as the skies merge with the earth, and their gestures and feelings dissolve like fleeting breath.

Housemates

Anna Maria Colivicchi

It was a writer's life, in which everything depended on writing, and everything – people met, observed, loved or disliked, houses, towns or part of towns – went into writing.

– Margaret Crosland

Filippo constantly tells jokes in a serious tone, but I've learnt how to tell when he's joking and when he's not. I always try not to laugh, I never succeed.

'We are similar, you and me,' he said. We were walking back home, our breaths like little clouds coming out of our mouths while we walked in the cold air. The way home feels shorter when I walk with him. It was dark already, even if it was only 5 pm. I thought that in Rome, where we both come from, the winter sun was just about to set at that time of the day.

To be honest, I think we have absolutely nothing in common. He drinks his coffee with two sugar lumps, I've always liked mine with milk and no sugar. At least when I make it. When he makes it, the coffee tastes burnt, but I drink it anyway. He studies finance and loves football – I call it an insane obsession of his. I study literature and hate pretty much every sport that involves a ball or running or sweating. The only sport that I've loved for my whole life is swimming. Are you joking? swimming is boring, he said when I told him. He does not see things if they are not right in front of his nose, I overthink everything I see. If I had met him during high school, I'm pretty positive I would have hated him. He was the classic has-potential-but-can't-be-bothered kind of guy. I've always been a straight-A student. I believe he has never read an entire book in his life, but he always gets offended when I say so. I've started bringing him my favourite books, saying, look, you need to read this, it's beautiful. At first, he didn't trust me. Last week he crawled into his bed and read the copy of *The Great Gatsby* I had taken out of the library for him. A few days ago, he bought his own copy of *Hamlet*.

'How can you say that?' I laughed, wishing he had a good explanation, wishing we really were similar.

'We are, you can't say we aren't,' he replied, looking straight ahead to avoid my gaze. I focused on the sound of our steps on the pavement.

I thought about the lyrics of one of my favourite songs, "both in equilibrium on the same pavement / I loved all of it / you only loved me / but you did it properly." That's how I felt, walking next to him, in equilibrium on the same pavement, in the cold air of November.

I woke up one fine morning and he had shaved his beard. I opened the door of my room to go to the bathroom, and he was standing there: the dark beard that used to cover his cheeks was now gone. It was the first time I saw him that way. I think that boys should tell you in advance when they want to shave their beards, so that you can be prepared and it doesn't result in a total shock. The point is that they look like completely different people, and you feel you have to learn all about their face once again. And their eyes look bigger.

When I was little, one of the things I loved the most was watching my dad putting shaving cream on his cheeks, and then carefully removing it with the razor, in front of the bathroom mirror. My dad used to have a very long beard, he started to work as a doctor in the emergency room when he was only twenty-six and the older doctors didn't take him seriously. That's why he grew a beard. I wonder if Filippo did it with the same purpose of looking older.

'What do you think?' he said, 'I don't like myself without my beard.'

He looked beautiful. I didn't say a word about it. 'Morning,' and I shuffled to the bathroom without looking at him in the eye. I realised I would miss the feeling of his beard on my cheeks.

His eyes are green sometimes, other times they are the colour of hazel. That morning they were green. And bigger. His shaved cheeks made me want to place one kiss on each of them. Or maybe one hundred kisses.

At night, when he's not back home yet, I lie awake and wait to hear his footsteps near the front door. I wait for the familiar sound of his keys. Sometimes I can't sleep if I don't hear that sound, if I know he's not home. Once I spent nearly the whole night awake, waiting for him. I know, pathetic. It was because we'd had a fight, and I wanted to make up. That was the first fight we'd ever had. And it wasn't even about anything serious, for God's sake, we had a fight about washing machine detergent. But still, I couldn't sleep, so I listened to the silence. I fell asleep and dreamt I was with him, on a train, going God knows where, his hand in my hand, trees and green fields out of the window. It could have been Scotland or Ireland. The sound of his steps on the stairs woke me up at 8.07 am. I opened the door of my room and he was sitting on the first step of the staircase, putting his shoes on. I was not sure if I was still dreaming.

'I could close one eye and fall back asleep, I'm super tired.' In the morning his voice sounds softer. 'I bought a new bottle of detergent, it's in my room. I'm sorry if I finished yours, I didn't want to fight yesterday, I was just tired.'

I did not want to fight either, who cares about the washing machine detergent, I was only desperate for your attention, I only wanted to spend time with you, even if we don't have much in common, but I like you, I really like you, because being with you feels natural, and I want your bad days and your good days, I waited for the sound of your keys, I wanted to say to him.

'I'm sorry.' It's all I managed to say. We hugged in the hallway, I was wearing my pyjamas and he was wearing only one shoe.

My room is just next to the front door, so I hear pretty much every sound in the house. I've learnt how to distinguish everyone's way of walking up the stairs.

I can recognise the sound of the kettle when Tom is making tea at 10 pm. I know that he likes to drink tea before going to bed, and that he can't drink it without soy milk. It takes ages for Tom to do his washing up, so we sometimes talk whilst he washes his plates in the warm water of the kitchen sink. 'Sofia, I've never had a sister, but I think that if I had one she would be similar to you,' he said once, during one of those endless washing up sessions. I've never had a brother, but I've always wanted to have one. I've always thought that having an older brother means having someone that can look after you. If I had one, I think he would be similar to Tom. He has a girlfriend, she studies Italian and has golden hair. She comes every Monday and spends the night at our house. Every Monday, they look happy. He cooks vegan food for both of them, lentil ragù and falafels, I hear them laughing in the kitchen. How does it feel to know someone so well? How does it feel to have someone that knows you so well? How does it feel to know you are irreplaceable to someone and that, in the same way, you can't replace the other person? That's what I ask myself every Monday.

I can recognise the sound of Violet's voice, when she is making dinner in the kitchen while talking on the phone. I know she finds it uncomfortable to sleep next to other people, and that she misses Mongolia, where she's from, even if she says that it's not a nice place to live. She has a boyfriend, back in Mongolia: we call him the-guy-that-wants-to-marry-her. I can hear her laughing sometimes when she speaks to him on the phone. She is twenty-six and has porcelain skin. Apparently in Mongolia she is considered old and she needs to marry soon. 'Sofia, look,' she told me once 'my hands are old,' she showed me the back of her hands. I wonder how she will sleep next to the-guy-that-wants-to-marry-her, if they really end up married.

Two nights ago, after dinner, I lay on the bed next to her. 'Violet, I have a terrible headache, I've been doing so many things this week, I'm dead tired.'

'Sofia, why are you so smart?' she replied, and then moved a bit on the mattress, to make some space for me. 'Are you sure you are comfortable this way?'

I nodded. 'I'm not smart Violet,' I said and closed my eyes, in a desperate attempt to calm my headache.

'You are a beautiful person. I think it's because you are in love.'

Am I really in love? I don't even know. Can you love someone that is so different from you? Does love make you beautiful, anyway? And when love finishes, do you go back to being ugly?

She has this way of talking, so blunt, so simple, that it almost feels like she knows everything about you, that she understands and you don't need to explain.

'Violet?'

'Yes?'

'Do you think you love him? The-guy-that-wants-to-marry-you?'

'No. But I will love him, one day, because he is a good guy.'

I can hear Alex talking to himself when he's writing essays. I can hear him swearing and sometimes I can hear him snoring: his room is right above mine. The other day he told me he is afraid he's going to fail his degree. I didn't know what to say, so I just hugged him and promised it's not going to happen, we are going to graduate all together. A few months ago, I did the same when his grandad died. He came to the kitchen, where I was having breakfast, and said, in a flat tone of voice, 'I'm going home. My grandad died,' and then left. I instantly thought about the day my grandad died, the worst day of my life. It was February and it was my first year at university. My mum had woken me up, tears streaming down her cheeks and I knew, she had not needed to tell me.

My grandad's hugs were solid, they made me feel like I could hold on to him. I had bought him a tag that said *grandads are for loving us and fixing things*, he hung it on the wall and he was proud of it. There is no better sentence to describe what he did for me, during the nineteen years of my life that I lived with him. He taught me maths, he read all of my essays, he could basically fix everything, a broken toy, an unglued book cover or a bad day. Sometimes his hugs were enough to fix everything that went wrong. Two days before he died, I cried in front of him and he still had the power to embrace me and calm me down. The day before he died, I prepared a soup for him, it was the first and last time I cooked for him. I said goodnight to him, he went to bed and never woke up. He was my rock, when I was little I believed he was immortal, that he was some kind of superhero with grey hair. That morning, I wondered if Alex's grandad was a superhero as well. 'Wait!' I shouted at him, and hugged him in the corridor.

Zara is definitely dating a guy. I can hear his voice coming from her room, which is right next to mine, but I never hear him entering the front door.

She does not want to talk about it. I hate it when people are scared to say their feelings out loud. Violet thinks he comes in through Zara's window, but at the moment we don't have any tangible proof of that. He has a car, I can hear the sound of the engine when it stops in front of our house to pick her up.

All of those sounds are now familiar to me, Filippo's keys and his way of walking up the stairs, Tom's kettle, the way Violet laughs, the way Alex snores, Zara's ghostly boyfriend. I don't like it when the house is silent: that is the sound of loneliness.

Two days ago, I realised I was looking forward to going to the supermarket. I couldn't focus on my reading, I was checking out the clock every five minutes. Filippo was supposed to come and pick me up at 4 pm, then we would walk to the supermarket and do the food shopping together.

I realised that when we had to take a flight together from Rome to go back to university before the start of term 2, I was looking forward to going to the airport. At the terminal, he paid for my cappuccino, we sat at a round table and talked for two hours without ever stopping. I wished I had arrived earlier, to spend more time with him, to drink two more cappuccinos while he talked about his up-coming exams, as we waited for our flight.

Before knowing him, I'd always hated flying and doing the food shopping.

In the supermarket, whilst he was pushing the cart around the frozen food department, I thought about George Orwell's essay *Why I Write*.

'Let's buy frozen mushrooms, you said you like mushrooms,' Filippo said, but I wasn't really listening.

What was it Orwell had said? That writers are often driven by 'sheer egoism'. It's a strong desire to appear clever, to be talked about and, mostly, to be remembered after they die. They share this characteristic with artists and politicians, and with successful businessmen.

Considering that he is an aspiring businessman and I'm an aspiring writer, Filippo was surprisingly right when he told me we were similar. We do have something in common. It's something that lies at the bottom of our being human: the desire to be recognised. I like to think that 'sheer egoism' is not only a desire to be talked about and to be remembered, but also a desire to be loved, to gain someone else's attention. I stopped in the middle of the aisle, he stopped the cart.

'What now? You don't like mushrooms.'

'Mushrooms are fine, actually,' I said, even though, before knowing him, I'd always hated mushrooms.

The Doctor's House

Anna Maria Colivicchi

Chapter One

1981

Sara arrived at The Doctor's House on a windy December morning. The trees lining the path to the manor had already lost all of their leaves, and looked as if they were shivering with cold. She parked her car by the main gate, because Giorgio said it would have been difficult to drive up to the House on that steep and narrow path. She was not sure whether he said it because he really meant it, or perhaps because he didn't have much confidence in her driving skills. In any case, the result was she had to carry her luggage – probably heavier than her body weight – up to the House, the wind blowing her scarf away. Her freshly washed hair danced around her face. She did not care about the luggage. After all, she was strong enough. She could even have driven up on the path if she really wanted to.

The country House was bigger than she expected, white-painted, with wooden doors and shutters. Where the path finished, three steps made of dark grey stones led to the main entrance. There were two big porches, one at the front of the House and one at the back, but there were no chairs or benches: she wondered if they ever sat in the porch to watch the sunset or to have breakfast in summer. She pushed a hand into the pocket of her jacket to find the keys Giorgio had given her.

The House smelled like every holiday home that has been closed for a long time: a mixture of dust and stale air. Sara could not stand that smell, it instantly reminded her of her parents' house back in Rome, of the claustrophobic feeling she could not get rid of when she spent time there. Her parents didn't know about her and Giorgio. She could picture her father's face, that severe and cold look he would give her if he knew she was in love with a married man. And what would her mother say? Nothing, probably, leaving the room without a word, relegated in her sorrow.

She stepped through the main door and entered the living room, where two bright yellow and uncomfortable-looking sofas took most of the space. How could they even think about buying two *yellow* sofas? she asked herself. She made her way through the living room and opened one of the big French windows on the back porch, in order to let in some air. In front of her, in the distance, the light blue line of the Adriatic Sea looked clear and sharp: it made her wonder how long it would take to get to the seaside.

Sara woke up the morning after her arrival, and Giorgio was there, sleeping next to her, as if that was the only place he should be. He looked peaceful, beautiful, and younger than his forty-one years. He must have arrived after midnight, when she was already asleep, tired after her journey.

She remembered the last time she saw him. Back then, he looked exhausted, a completely different person from the man who was now sharing that bed with her.

'She is going to kill me, I know it,' he had told Sara. They were sitting in a café not far from the Spanish Steps, two cappuccinos steaming in front of them. She had looked at him, leaning her head to one side, the way she always did when she was listening.

'You've done nothing wrong,' she had touched his elbow and he had taken her hand.

'I've just asked for a divorce, Sara! She isn't expecting it,' Giorgio could not look at her face, so he was staring out of the window. The traffic in Via Margutta was chaotic as always. 'She's not—'

'—Sane?!' she had said, perhaps too loudly. He had put a finger on his lips. 'You can't,' she had talked quietly this time, 'you can't keep on blaming yourself because she is not mentally stable. You can't keep on looking after her.'

Then, he had let her hand go, and covered his face with both his palms, and Sara had felt hopeless.

Sara had seen her only once and, luckily, Emma hadn't noticed her.

Emma, that was her name, even though Giorgio got used to never naming her. The importance of names: some people believe that if something has no name, then it does not exist. But Emma existed, had very long legs and hair the colour of gold. Sara had bumped into her one sunny morning of November, she was walking down Via Milano, it was a Tuesday. She was thinking about that transaction she needed to work out for Mr and Mrs Carotenuto, when Emma had come out of the building where Giorgio's office was, wearing a tight pistachio-green dress and high heels. Sara had thought she was one of those beautiful women with empty eyes. And empty eyes meant an empty soul.

Sara slipped out of the warm sheets, trying not to wake him up.

When she went downstairs – the steps of the staircase creaking under her bare feet – the living room smelt of the scented candles she had spread all over the house the night before. The two yellow sofas were still there, even though she had wished they would magically disappear during the night. 'We might have to do something about you guys,' she whispered to the pieces of furniture.

'Who are you talking to?' Giorgio said, appearing at the top of the stairs. Rubbing his eyes with his fists, he looked like a little boy who had just woken up, messy-haired and sleepy. The stairs creaked under his feet too.

'Oh no, I'm so sorry I woke you up,' she said. He put his arms around her waist and suddenly she was not so sorry he had woken up.

Sara made coffee for them both, while Giorgio was standing in front of the French windows, the sunlight on his face.

The first time he saw the field where the House now stood, had stuck in his memory like a recurrent dream. 'I think I've gone mad, but you have to help me,' he had said on the phone to his brother, an architect. And that is how they started, a few months later: a project in their hands and a lot of dreams running around in their heads. Giorgio had always wanted a place he could call his own, away from the traffic jams and the responsibilities of Rome. That hill, bare and wild, with a view of the Marecchia Valley and the Adriatic Sea close enough to be seen on the horizon, felt like the right place. The Valley had different colours in autumn, it would become orange, brown, dark green. Spring brought astonishing sunsets and new, bright leaves. Summer was chilly at night and hot during the day. But winter was his favourite time at the Doctor's House, because he would light up the fireplace, eat chestnuts and spend all day reading.

'What are you thinking about?' asked Sara, passing him a cup of coffee with milk, she knew he drank it with no sugar.

'Thank you,' he kissed her upper lip. 'I was wondering if you like it,' he said, pointing at the valley.

'I love it, I really do,' she replied. 'Do you want to sit at the table?'

Breakfast was Sara's favourite moment of the day: when everything started again, and she felt like a million possibilities were about to open up. She had always been a morning person. Mornings were everyday magic, how could you sleep in? She probably loved breakfast because at her parents' house they never ate anything before going to school or work. Her father only drank dark coffee, whilst doing his tie in front of the mirror.

'Actually,' she continued, 'help me, please, I want to move the table closer to the window. I want to see the valley while we eat breakfast.'

And they moved the table closer to the window, and they watched the naked trees being ruffled by the wind, whilst they ate jam on toast. The trees were shivering with cold again.

'Did you really buy those two?' she said and laughed, the coffee-cup held in her cold hands.

Giorgio smiled and reached for another slice of bread and jam. 'Do you mean the sofas?' he replied, 'no, it was *her* who really wanted *that* colour.'

'It doesn't surprise me that they are *so* ugly, then,' Sara said and stood up to get some more coffee from the kitchen, her white nightgown fluttering behind her.

Exit Plan

David Crowe

At most it looked like I was leaving a girlfriend, under a placid evening sky, cleansing her place of the toothbrush and clothes I'd left there. But really I lived alone, and I was leaving with all I cared to carry. I'd been alone since Alice left me.

I was nearly thirty and had spent the last decade in London. But I was tired of the place, so I booked a train north to Leeds. I knew a man there who'd made a lot of money selling computer parts. We were childhood friends, and I planned to leverage his nostalgia into easy employment.

But before all that, months before I left London, Alice caught a night flight to Hamburg for a conference on renewable energy, and the next morning I snorted a line of black pepper so that my nose burned and mucus flowed. I lay on the floor for a while with my face screwed up into the carpet. When my tears had thinned enough for me to see the numbers on my phone, I called Gary, the deputy head of the primary school I taught at, and sneezed down the line.

'Feels like another virus,' I said.

'You need to get some doctors to give you a real thorough looking at,' Gary said. 'I'm talking referrals to specialists and blood tests for everything there is. Nobody gets sick as often as you.'

'You're right.' I sneezed again, and snot lined with blood ran over my lips.

'The NHS will fob you off with bed rest and painkillers if they can, but you need to stand your ground. Make them work for you.'

'I will,' I said, pushing the palm of my free hand into my left eye. 'I just don't want to find out I have something major, something that'll age me fast.'

'Don't talk like that. Go see a doctor. Get some rest.'

'But I hate letting you down.'

'Stop it. We'll manage.'

I figured I'd bought myself the rest of the week.

That afternoon I met Duggan at The Red Duke, just off Kentish Town Road. He wore the same duffel coat he always wore. He hugged me, his bulk cocooning me. We sat at the bar, and Duggan shuffled a tarot deck he'd made himself that had Christ as the Hierophant and a mirror as the Fool. He followed a contrived dogma he'd learned from his wife Julia that wove Catholic ritual and European pessimism with continental divination.

The bartender, a young woman with a scalp-stretching ponytail, wandered over, and Duggan dealt her Goliath, Abel and John the Baptist while she picked at a scab on her elbow.

'They all died at the hands of their enemies,' said Duggan. 'Abel suggests a familial clash. Does your brother hate you?'

'I don't have a brother,' she said.

'Sister?'

'I'm godmother to her kids.'

'But does she hate you?'

'What do you want?'

'To help you.'

'To drink?'

Duggan picked up his cards from the bar, but his thick fingers couldn't peel off John the Baptist, who was stuck there with the residue of sugary liquids.

'This one doesn't want to leave your side,' Duggan said to the bartender, tapping the card. 'You should take his warning seriously.'

'What warning?' she said.

'Start by finding your enemies.'

'My enemies? That's easy. That's anyone who does card tricks and takes ten fucking minutes to not buy a drink.'

I ordered us a couple of dark ales.

Eddy – a tall lad with brown mutton chops, wearing denim and leather – walked in and racked up a game of pool. I agreed to play and staked a round of drinks. Eddy was on the black before I'd potted a single ball. But Eddy missed his next shot altogether when a rut in the table diverted the cue ball.

'Must be a new wound,' he said, stroking the felt.

'At least something in this place likes me,' I said. I was shooting stripes, and I sank the five and then the two. But I missed the seven and Eddy potted the black with a straight shot.

I gave my cue to Duggan, took a seat at the bar, thumbed the sticky corner of the beheaded saint and watched Eddy outplay Duggan, too.

Over the next hour or so, Duggan and I took turns losing to Eddy. We bought him drinks to pay our debts, cloud his vision and meddle with his coordination for the next match. We didn't care how much it cost us. We just wanted one victory.

But the bar started to fill with post-work drinkers who gradually hemmed us in closer and closer to the pool table, bumping into our cues and ruining our shots. So we gave up and set about drinking by the bar, except Duggan, who riffled his deck and played prophet for strangers. My stomach was bloated from the ales, so I switched to whiskey.

'Does he really think he can tap into the future?' Eddy asked me.

'Maybe. I know he wants people to think he can. He ever give you a reading?'

'Yeah. Something about patience earning deliverance or deliverance from patience. I know I got the archangel Gabriel.'

We stood in silence for a while. 'You need some help there, mate,' I said to a squat man with two hoop earrings in his left ear who'd been ignored by the bartender for a while. 'I can lift you up so you can see over the bar, if you want?'

'Fuck right off,' the man said.

'Hey hey hey,' I said. Eddy wanted none of this and moved off into the crowd. The man rose up on his toes and tried to wave the bartender over. 'Let me buy you a drink, to apologise,' I said.

'I never asked for anything from you,' the man said.

I looked around for another stranger to drag into conversation, but nobody else was alone, except for an Italian woman who tuned an acoustic guitar in the far corner.

I went and found Duggan dealing a tarot hand for a skinny, pink-lipped girl.

'Mary Magdalene was Christ's wife, lover of her teacher,' Duggan said. 'You're here to aid a wise man, to link body and soul with him.'

'That sounds convenient,' she said. 'What do the others mean?'

'The Knight of Faith embraces life. You must seize the Magdalene way – the beloved beside her prophet.'

'Has this ever worked?' she said, scratching at the knight's helmet and peeling it away.

'I can only tell you what the cards say.'

The squat man sat down next to her and said, 'Don't talk to these people.'

She stroked his arm, picked up his hand and kissed it. 'Jon, you should have a go,' she said. 'Do Jon's,' she said to Duggan.

'But I didn't finish yours,' Duggan replied.

'We've gone plenty far enough with mine,' she said. 'I think I know how it would have ended.'

Duggan dealt the man Nietzsche, Etteilla and Abraham.

I said, 'Nietzsche's cock was filled with syphilis. Where have you been sticking it, little man?'

'Shut your pal up,' he said to Duggan.

'Nietzsche shows independence, integrity and power. You're a powerful person. I can see it in your aura. A pioneer!' Duggan said.

'Lord of the dwarves!' I said, and I patted the man on the head.

He slapped my hand away and said to his girlfriend, 'What is this? I'm going to snap his hand off next time.'

'And Abraham,' Duggan said, waving the card in front of the man's face. 'A great man, disciplined in times of testing.'

'Didn't he pimp out his wife to save his own skin? Ditch this one quick,' I said to the pink-lipped girl.

'That's it. That's it,' the man said to his girlfriend.

'Great men don't bother with fools,' Duggan said when the man stood up and adjusted his shirt.

'That's right. That's right,' the girl said, tugging at his arm. 'Be my great man.'

He sat down, and I went to get another drink.

The Italian woman started to sing. Her songs were full of the horrors of love. Eddy sat up close, captivated, along with several other men.

And then Alice called me from Hamburg.

'Where are you?' she said.

'Hang on,' I said, leaving the pub to escape the din of the place. The cold evening air revitalised me a little.

Alice said, 'Hello? Hello. Where are you?'

'The Red Duke.'

'Are you drinking?'

'Of course not.' She wanted me to get her pregnant. Actually, I'd agreed to get her pregnant. But I didn't want to anymore, or I didn't know what I wanted. So I chewed nicotine gum and drank when I could.

'I miss you,' she said.

'I miss you,' I said. I talked about my day. I described how Graham May threw up in the Year Six assembly. He sat in the middle of the room, and the other children fled from him in a wailing surge.

Lying to Alice was easy.

Back inside, I saw the squat man go into the toilet. I followed him there. The room seemed empty, but one of the cubical doors was closed. So I knocked on it and said, 'Little pig, little pig, let me in.'

'Who's that? Fuck off.'

'Little pig, little pig, let me in.' I rattled the door.

'Fuck right off.'

'Then I'll huff and I'll puff and I'll blow your house down.' And I kicked the door. The lock gave a little, so I kicked the door again, dead on the red engaged tag, and it flew open and smacked the little guy's legs as he sat on the toilet fumbling with his trousers. But he did nothing back to me, just sat and stared, so I forced a laugh and went out to the bar.

The Italian woman sank lower in her chair with each song. She must have relived too many disastrous relationships through her performance, because she stopped mid-song and seemed hurt by the requests for more. Then she rejected the advances of several thirsty men, including Eddy's.

People emptied out after the music finished and soon there was space for me and Eddy to play pool again. The bartender kept looking over at us, and she made a few calls and cupped the receiver each time. Her wariness of us from behind the bar made us uneasy, so we played in silence. Eddy won and gloated through generosity by offering to buy the next round.

But the bartender said to Eddy, 'I won't serve you anymore. Not till you pay for that door.'

'What door?' he asked.

'In the gents. The cubicle door.'

'I'm just here playing pool.'

'You're just here drinking all day and thinking you can do what you like,' she said. 'Thinking you can smash the place up.'

'I wasn't… I didn't.'

'You look just like the man who did. Which means you are the man who did.'

'I don't do things like that. I respect this place. I love this place. I come here all the time because I love this place.'

I called to him, 'Have you calmed down yet, Eddy?' I walked over and rubbed his back. 'You still upset about that pretty singer? It's ok. If you need to be upset, just be upset in your heart.' Eddy turned red.

'Judas,' the bartender said. And sadness filled my chest.

'Can I get a drink?' Eddy asked.

'No,' she replied.

I wanted to apologise to Eddy, but I couldn't do it. He refused to play pool with me again, and then he left the pub.

I followed after him and called out, 'Eddy, come back! Eddy!' But he kept walking. Outside, a 9 Iron was propped up against the Red Duke's entrance. I swung it a few times, hitting phantom balls down the street, and then I took it home with me.

A few days later I picked Alice up from Heathrow. She was peckish and disorientated from a sleepless flight, and soon we sat in silence, drinking burnt coffee and eating greasy food at one of the tables crammed together in a motorway service station, surrounded by a ring of fast-food kiosks, each with its own queue of hungry travellers.

Alice listened to an old woman at a neighbouring table, who read poetry to her husband. The man – mostly bald but with white wisps above his ears and blue veins spidered across his nose – sat opposite his wife and stared at the book she held. I couldn't tell if he was concentrating or just too tired to pick his head up and look at his wife.

I tried to listen and memorise some lines to recite to Alice later, but I could only pick up a word or a phrase – evaporate, cartoon, empty iron bottle – before my focus would drift back to the woman's face, which was so wrinkled it looked like a rake had been dragged across her forehead, down her cheeks and over her lips. And then I couldn't look anymore, so I went and browsed the magazine racks of a busy newsagent.

When I returned to the table, the woman was reading silently while her husband slept. His head drooped to one side, and his body started to shift with it. I waited for the moment he would lean too far and lose his equilibrium. I wanted to see him jerk awake, to see him startled and then embarrassed. But he was too deep under, so he fell off his chair. His head whacked against the tiled floor.

Alice rushed down to him, lifted his head and slid her leg under it as a cushion. She stroked the tuft of white hair above his ear while blood ran from his head onto her jeans. The woman said, 'Douglas, Douglas. Carl's waiting for us.' Spittle bubbled at the corner of the man's mouth, and he murmured a few words that I couldn't make out.

Alice held the man until the paramedics arrived, and then, while they tried talking to the man, while they strapped him to a stretcher and bandaged his head, and while they wheeled him out to the ambulance, Alice held the woman.

That night, Alice and I slept badly, but the next evening I drank wine and watched her dance around the kitchen, cooking a red curry and singing along to a French ballad. She had this thing I never understood, where, because on the inside we're all blood and bones and organs and stench, she'd imagine she was filled with cotton stuffing, inoffensive as a teddy bear.

I picked up the 9 Iron, turned it over in my hands and asked her to hit me with it. She laughed, so I forced the club into her hands and pleaded with her to hit me. She dropped it on the floor. I sat down and ignored her when she stroked my back and kissed my face.

I don't know how long I sat there for, but she stayed with me and touched me the whole time.

Eventually she took my hand and led me toward our bedroom. But I blocked the door and asked her again to hit me with the 9 Iron. And this time she cried. I left and slept in my car.

We stayed together for a few more weeks because it took her a while to start listening to her friends, who were right about me. And then she was gone from my life, except once, when she returned to cough up something of her heart. But I didn't react to her words enough to really help her. Even now, I feel her disappointment.

One morning, after Alice had left me, I arrived at school exhausted and couldn't remember what I was meant to teach my class of eight-year-olds. I made them repeat the alphabet over and over again. After ten minutes they started to rebel, so I accused them of saying it incorrectly. The 'f' comes before the 'e'. They assumed it was a joke and laughed at my ineptitude. But I gave them no ground, no hint of doubt. And before the morning was through, they chimed in unison, 'a…b…c…d…f…e…g…' and beamed with new success.

I taught them small lies every day, and I sat in staff meetings waiting for someone to turn to me and mention anxious parents or question my health. I sat hoping someone would rebuke me totally. But nobody did. And then I stopped going to work. It was easy to ignore the answerphone messages.

But one day, two police officers came round my flat, a woman and a man. I'd seen a man just like him before. We were at a wedding. We'd shared the last of the free wine, and talked about pandemics and the necessary components of a great best-man's speech. By the end of the evening we were friends, but I never saw him again.

'Your employer is worried about you, so we're here to check on your wellbeing,' the woman said, browsing the tea-stained newspapers on my kitchen table.

'Could I have a glass of water?' the man asked.

'No,' I said. I felt powerful. He perched himself on the edge of the table and took off his cap. I said, 'Tell them I'm not coming back. Lie if you have to. Tell them I'm sick. Tell them I'm in jail for animal abuse or something. I don't care.'

'Sir, have you hurt any animals?' the woman asked. 'Can we look around the property?'

A couple of nights later, I booked my train to Leeds. I knew I had to purge myself and leave the city a different man. I couldn't just live somewhere else as the same person. So I met Duggan outside the Red Duke, the 9 Iron in my hand. He wrapped his arms around me and squeezed.

I went to enter the pub, but he held me back. 'We need to make a detour,' he said. 'Julia's at the Royal Free. She can't leave without a chaperone.'

'I'll wait here for you. I don't want to see a bunch of sick people.'

Duggan ignored me – a kind of unwanted graciousness. He opened the passenger door of his VW for me. 'Come on, let's go rescue my love,' he said.

As we drove west along dark London roads, swoops of light passed over us from the streetlamps above. With each pass I sank lower in my seat, my vision shifting from the road to the sky.

At the hospital, it took us a while to navigate the hallways. We found Julia, and Duggan went searching for a nurse who'd discharge his wife. Julia tried to hug me, but she pulled away in pain and sat down on one of the plastic waiting-room chairs. Her appendix had swollen and threatened to off itself and take her with it. So she got a doctor to hack it out and throw it away.

'There's a piece of me in some toxic waste disposal vat by now,' she said.

'Didn't you ask to keep it?'

'Why would I do that?'

'A memento of your time together?'

She looked around for Duggan.

'I'll go find him,' I said.

I wandered around awhile and found a wheelchair folded up outside a recovery ward. I sat in it and raced down a quiet corridor. I was surprised by the speed I could pick up. On my fifth run I didn't bother braking and I threw myself out of the chair just as I approached the wall.

When I came to, I was in Duggan's arms. He carried me out to his car, where Julia waited, and we drove to their place. While Julia went to bed, Duggan and I went out into their tiny garden and sat on its low stone wall. I told him about Alice and the 9 Iron, about how unfinished the whole episode was, and he knew what I was really asking him.

'There's just this thing I can't shake loose,' I said.

'You need forgiveness. You need grace.'

'I need an exorcism!'

'It won't work.'

'It might.'

Duggan went and got the 9 Iron from his car. He swung it at my stomach and that delicious swing doubled me over, like my stomach had changed for an instant into a beautiful bruise – shades of red and purple seeping into each other across a pale canvas. When I straightened up, he hit me again and I crumpled to the ground. Then he kicked my stomach over and over until the pain dispelled all my thoughts and memories and I lived a pure and present existence, drifting in some immaterial plane. But it didn't last long. And then I felt his boot stomp on my hand and a final kick land against my jaw and burst my lip.

I remember silence during the whole thing, but I must be mistaken because Julia came out and pulled Duggan away from me. I tried to wrestle him back from her, but she stumbled and sat on the wall. A few spots of blood marked her t-shirt, so I let Duggan check her wound and take her back inside.

On my way out, Julia looked disgusted, so I left without saying a word to her. As far as I know, Duggan never spoke to her about the beating. She must have assumed it was a punishment for something dark and vile.

At King's Cross Station, on platform eight, while I waited for the last train to Leeds, a man whose face glistened with sweat pestered me for money. When I ignored him and walked past he said something, but it took a while for the words to register. I think he said, 'You bitch dog.' And then I heard him yell, 'He tried to touch me! He exposed himself!'

And then the train arrived.

I sat in an empty carriage and waited, ready to be swept away, but the train didn't move. I was jubilant from the beating, so when the policemen escorted me from the train and quizzed me about the man, about whether I had exposed myself to him, I just said, 'I love all people. I love you and the justice you bring.'

The two officers didn't believe the man. But they must have assumed I'd done something wrong, or that I was wrong in some other way, because they left me in a cell overnight.

For a while after, I thought of that cell as all I needed – seclusion and a place to sleep. But after a few minor triumphs north of the capital, including a relationship that ended without my provocation, my desires grew beyond that tiny room.

I spent time in a police cell one other time, not very long ago, after I got drunk and tried to break into Birmingham Cathedral. I imagined the adjacent cells filling with all the friends I'd had and lost: Archie Barrett, who drank with me in The Queen's Stag every Thursday night during my time in Leeds, until I drove over his Red Setter and he wouldn't forgive me; the Corby family, Beth and Carl and their baby son, who took me in while unemployment bled a stain over a year of my life, until I stole their Toyota so I could start again some place else; Duggan, of course; and Alice, whose sweetness hurt me. There were maybe two-dozen people. That was all.

The real sadness though is that we never lived together like that, all in the same place, at the same time, all together for all of my life. I never had more than two or three of them around me at any one stretch, and never for very long. Sometimes, like between my failed months in Leeds and my time as a postman on the Isle of Man, I didn't have any of them at all.

Homeless

Eve Dashwood

Sing to me of the man, Muse, the man of twists and turns driven time and again off course, once he had plundered the hallowed heights of Troy.

The Odyssey, Homer

Johnno's dream was always the same. If he did but know it. His silhouette stood on the rim of the world, small against the night sky's splattering of malevolent, doubled stars. Unnavigable smudges of cosmic impotence, no guide to home. A searing universe of raw, psychedelic colours ravaged his body. A constellation of one. (Falling now!) An aurora-borealis swirl of burnt-up city neon, glimpsed, rain-blurred on the shimmered-edge of a fast, wet, fish eye. Johnno's eye. Myopic throbbing of fluorescent, night-vision goggle glare of bright, bright, emerald. This green and pleasant land. Red flares, white-rocket high, and blue thermal imaging of day-black sky, squinted through the smeared slit-eye of an army tank, like being in the belly of a great horse. Men, sardine-tin-tight. (Sweating now!) The tank tread trot. *Tick*. Each man's mind a clippety-clock. *Tick*. The tension of a time bomb. *Tock!* (Jump!) Rain spattered windows of timeless taxi cabs, or the bobbling, red-fringed tassel of rogan josh, *tuk-tuk*, rickshaws. Whirling, world-weary home-grown northern lights, 'With me little stick of Blackpool rock' wails George Formby through orange peel teeth and the incessant twang of the uke. (There now, back now!) Boy Johnno. The winter sea bursting over the kiss-me-quick-end-of-the-pier madness, the windy echo of the relentless Laughing Policeman 'Ha! Ha! Ha! Ha! Ha! Ha! Ha! Ha! Ha! Ha! Ha! Ha! Ha!' Gaudy illuminations seen smeared between the fish and chip heat haze on frozen windows, as he jostled along with Grandma Pen on the salt and vinegar wrapper, briny cockle, (that smell now!), Fleetwood Ferry tram. Waddling, winding its way on worn tracks, like a fat, boarding house landlady, bracing herself against the headscarf flapping wind. The fizz of the sparks flying overhead, sherbet high, flaring up into the dib-dab sky, a flashing cosmic sparkler, etching out his name in the darkness. Fisherman's Walk, Cabin, *ding-ding*, North Pier, Tower, Pleasure Beach, and then, at last 'next stop, end of the line!' at last, Starr Gate, at long, long, last. Home.

Johnno's dream was interrupted by a fluttering of wings. Now semi-conscious, the noise reminded him of Grandma Pen's black umbrella being flapped open and shut, on the black-leaded, scrubbed, 'within an inch of its life', doorstep of his childhood home. This movement felt like an ending, like a full stop on a sentence, punctuation in action, signalling, right there on the doorstep, an end to the world outside. Grandma and brolly, turning into the house with a 'Good riddance to bad rubbish!' flurry. (Christ! Johnno flinched in his half-sleep, spooked by the real noise and backdraft he felt off the wings of the bird.) Then, dreaming again, of the black, bat-like brolly that he remembered from that day, from that place.

'For as much as it has pleased Almighty God to take out of this world the soul of Angela, we therefore commit her body to the ground; earth to earth, ashes to ashes, dust to dust.' The foam of the sea, the soil of the grave. The white and the black – a monochrome liturgy of nature, which invaded Johnno the day they buried his mother, and swept over him now as he saw his four-year-old self, holding Pen's hand at the Fleetwood graveside. Two silhouettes sheltering under a shared umbrella, while the rain drove down in slanted, icy, javelin shards. Master Jonathan Doran: woolly-vested, snot-nosed, clinging to a hand-made teddy.

Johnno came to. No umbrella, but the *caw-caw* of the carrion crow that was picking at his leg. Black wings flapping, beak pecking, crow-claws gripping. His heart drilled an iambic artillery in his ears. He felt sick. He jerked his arm and the crow hopped away… A bit. As if to say, 'I am master here, I will do as I please.'

Johnno was too tired to argue. His eyelids heavy, his body motionless, save for his chest heaving with the swell of a great internal ocean. Needs must go with this flow...

Johnno woke fully, hand in hand with rose–fingered dawn. Through slitted eyes he saw, half buried in the scrub which was tickling his nose:

"Keep Off The Grass"

The crow hopped at his side, worrying the wrapping of a night-weary Kebab. (Jesus!) He had been dreaming, (what was it now?). He couldn't remember. He could never remember his dreams, but the feeling of them lingered with a queasy sense of something missing. A yearning, a sickness.

Johnno tried to lift his head, but he was too dizzy, so he lay still, waiting until the world stopped turning. SNAFU [Situation Normal All Fucked Up]. He looked up at the blue sky or was it down at the blue sea? As he braced himself against the solid block of colour he couldn't be sure which way was up or down. Moving waves or moving clouds? Is there anybody there? He tried to focus on patches of random whiteness as they went scudding past. Who the fuck says scudding? Poets, phoneys and piss-artists.

Mr Chapman, Blackpool grammar school:

'"Thro' scudding drifts the rainy Hyades,

Vexed the dim sea..."

Are you listening at the back, Doran?'

Or Professor Bateman, Oxford:

'"Then, scudding swiftly from the dangerous ground,

the deafen'd ear unlock'd, the chains unbound."

What do you think, Jonathan?'

He'd liked it well enough when he was a boy, but now he was a man he wasn't so sure. Now the vista was no longer wide and clear but peppered with dark clouds that invaded his field of vision.

The enemy has formed nuclear warheads, scud missiles,

and chemical warfare against me.

His plans are to take me out and destroy me...

He has set up camp on my ground...

He slides through shadows and attacks me in my sleep.

The beauty no longer carried, with terrors in heaven and earth. The army had a saying:

'Whoever said the pen is mightier than the sword obviously never encountered automatic weapons.'

It was all a bit of a trap anyway – poetry! Poems define life for you then you can't have the experience for yourself. No originality of thought, no freedom, not even in your head.

Happy with this logic, feeling it gave him a bit of solidity, he thought he could risk lifting the old grey matter.

Caw-caw, screeched the crow.

'Uck opp!' shouted Johnno, trying to make his mouth work and surprising himself with the dry, deep gravel that crawled out of his parched throat. The crow flew off. For now.

He lifted his head and looked around. (Where had he washed up?) A vast expanse of undulating, scrubby heath. He lay back down. What a fucking place to bivouac. No, not a camp, as he was totally exposed to the elements. He coughed. The effort damn near split him in two. 'Time for a fag', he thought, running his tongue over his cracked, caked lips. He sat up and realised there was a park bench to his left. A location! At his feet his faithful backpack MOLLE [Modular Lightweight Load-carrying Equipment] – bonus!

'Things are looking up', thought Johnno, 'someone must be looking down'.

He felt inside the pockets of his combat jacket searching for tobacco. Taking a mental inventory as he fingered each piece: Swiss Army knife; meds; compass; matches. He tossed them on his lap. Yes, he had legs – result! His shaking fingers searched inside the deep pocket of his combat trousers and felt the soft pouch of tobacco, along with the papers. He coughed again, this time releasing a little phlegm, which he spat out. (That was more like it!) He blinked, then stretched his eyes wide open – for clarity you understand, before the act of rolling the almighty.

He'd always rolled his own, even before he had to. He liked the kit and took his time setting out all the bits. (The skill before the thrill!) He laughed gently, fearful of over exciting his chest. Johnno unrolled the pouch and laid the papers and the matches on the slippery underside of the tobacco wrapper and then spread the ciggy-paper carefully on the clean surface. There was something soothing in rolling your own, allowing your body to take control over something you had done hundreds of times before, the muscle memory of your fingers, (like jerking off!). He took a tiny pinch of tobacco, the strands were like that golden saffron they sold in the Pul-e Khishti Bazaar and about as precious to him now. The dry tobacco trailed a thin gunpowder rill on the paper, (tight-arse!). He preferred it when it was new and slightly moist, sticking together in a nice bunch. Like soft, brown pubic hair still damp from the shower.

He made the tab – there had been a time he could have done this one handed, a trick all the squaddies admired, as he would gently and rhythmically roll the paper and contents together, like a nipple teased between finger and thumb. He felt a stirring. He thought of those big breasted black beauties in Havana, with a large, gaudy flower holding their hair back (Gauguin defined!), he smirked. As they rolled the fat length of the Montecristo between fingers and thumb. 'Maybe even across their thigh', he thought, as he ran the tip of his tongue along the edge of the thin tab. But he drooled too much saliva and ruined the smoke. (Fuck 'em!) He put the fag in the top pocket of his jacket to dry out for later. (Fuck!) He wondered what the chances were of getting laid? He ran his hand over his chin, remembering his scrubby beard was ginger. How had that happened? His hair was brown. Must be a kink in the DNA? He absentmindedly played with the hairs, 'at least it covers the scar', he thought, fingering through the fuzz to toy with the indent on his chin. No money, no prospects, and a ginger, (no, not much fucking hope!).

Suddenly, he heard a high-pitched noise, a squealing. (Shut it off, stop it!). He began to shake uncontrollably, so that his teeth were chattering, but his jaw was locked solid. He could see his legs trembling. (No, nooooo!) The arching whine of artillery fire over-head, the scorching heat and tutti-frutti sunlight, artificially bright yellow. The dust that blew all around, encasing him like a sweating cod in a salt crust, baking in his own juices. (Heeeee, juujju, he, hell!) 'Help!' he was finally able to spurt. 'Help me!'

Johnno's body jolted as if he had fallen to the ground. Perfect parachute landing fall (Balls of the feet. Side of the calf. Side of upper leg. Back of the hip. Side of the back. Roll. Arms in prayer). Only he hadn't just parachuted. He didn't have the sickness in his stomach and the pull on his lungs which he remembered from the drills. Or that feeling of military freefall, when he had jumped out of the army for good. 'Don't go there', thought Johnno, 'that way madness lies'.

Johnno felt his back being kicked.

'Hey!' said a man's voice.

Johnno exhaled one long sob, saliva dripping off his beard. He saw white Reebok trainers backing away from him, before he looked up. The man stared down at Johnno as if he had just excreted his entire body waste, instead of the morsel of spittle on the ground. Johnno's watch alarm was still beeping. He felt confused, but half sat up and moved his arm, feeling his elbow joint almost snapping in order to make this small movement. Hazily he switched the alarm off.

'Where am I?' he asked, rubbing his arm and trying to make his eyes focus.

'Hampstead Heath,' said the man. 'The Vale of Health.'

Johnno smirked as he sat up.

'Oh, you get the irony then? I'd ask if you want anything, but it would only be cigarettes and alcohol.' Johnno silently looked the man up and down. He was wearing everything Nike, a fitness tracker on his wrist, shiny blue sunglasses hanging off a cord around his neck and he gripped a bottle of fancy water.

'Or worse.' Said the man. 'There are too many of your sort round here, you should be trying to do something for yourself, why aren't you selling the Big Issue?'

'Why aren't you less of a wanker?' said Johnno.

The man made to kick him again, but Johnno grabbed his trainer and held it firm.

'You like that? Kicking a man when he's down?' Johnno released the trainer and the man ran off.

Anger was good. He could combat that. He could counter-punch it with equal measure. What he couldn't stand was pity. That he couldn't handle.

With shaking hands, Johnno made a grab for MOLLIE and ran the zipper around. (Please let it be as it was, don't let anything have happened!) His hands plunged inside, sliding past the green tarp, over the plastic edges of the first aid kit, snagging on the sharp teeth of his waterproof, until finally he felt the softness at the bottom. His stomach relaxed, his breathing calmed. It was alright. He pulled the teddy up to the top of the bag. (Thank Christ!) His thumb stroked the blue teddy's knitted head – he was not alone. Now he was strong. Now he was solid. Johnno lay back, the bear on his chest. He focused on his breathing, exhaling through his tears and snot, wiping his nose on his sleeve.

The alarm meant meds. Johnno sat up, got the tablets from his pocket and twisted the lid off, tipping the last pill into his palm. (Shit!) He scanned around for something to drink and saw the top of a glass bottle lying further off – he hauled himself across the scrub towards it. Whisky. Empty. He chucked it, remembering he had cast it out the same way last night, after draining it dry. He recalled the tune My Bonnie Lies over the Ocean and singing:

"'Some mothers have sons in the Army!
Some mothers have sons overseas!
Some mothers have sons that are cowards…'"

He looked around again and saw a tap next to the park bench.

"Not Drinking Water"

(What was it for then – dogs? Hampstead fucking Heath!) He crawled across to it and turned it on, the water gushed into the indented mud underneath, releasing a smell of sulphur. He slowly got to his feet, letting the water run, but the shaped black earth ('earth to earth'), quickly filled up and the water ran recklessly in random rivulets across the dry scrub. Fast and free it flowed over the ground, not stopping to wipe its feet. He cupped some water in his hand and took the tablet, then splashed his face, allowing the coolness to revive him. He needed to piss, so he added his own juices to the baked soil. (Scorched Earth!) He smirked at this deliberate destruction of resources, watching as the dark yellow urine ran its own acidic stream over the barren land – what a fucking libation! Johnno spotted the half-eaten kebab, which he picked up. He removed the feathers that the crow had left behind, scattering them to the wind as an offering.

Who begat crow?
Screaming for blood, grubs, crusts, anything
Trembling featherless elbows in the nests of filth.
He shuddered at the image. And his prospects. He ate the kebab.

It was time for his ablutions. He washed his head, neck and hands under the tap, trying to cleanse himself from the food and gulped handfuls of water. He sat on the bench and took out the fag from before. Good enough now, he lit it and inhaled the smoke. Hacking dryly, he waited for his lungs to settle, but in case anyone was watching, pretended to admire the view. He began to worry that someone was, but when he looked around there was only the crow again. It was eyeing him, its head tilted to one side. It hopped to where he had thrown its feathers and began to pick them up, with sharp, fast movements, deliberately pecking them one by one into its beak. When it had re-captured them all it stood sentinel for a moment and then flew off towards a bank of trees.

Johnno saw a woman cross in front of the woody area, chatting on her mobile and walking two spaniels. One of them looked like the stray Grandma Pen had taken in when Johnno had first gone to live with her. Pen said he was to name him and they decided on Argos because he had been found wandering outside the store. As the spaniel bounded around the mounds of grass he remembered Argos leaping in and out of the banks of sand dunes, chasing imaginary rabbits – his ears flying around his face. Johnno played with him on the beach in all weather's. Then they would return home wet, dirty and tired, to wolf down sardines on toast in front of a blazing fire. Johnno felt a softness against his hand and looked down. The other spaniel nuzzled against him as if it knew him. Its face was grizzled, its eye-lids drooped low beneath their sockets and its fur was matted. A living shade of Argos, that made Johnno start. How long ago was it? Where had he been? But the dog's ears were pricked and its brown eyes gazed at him with a look of devotion that seemed to say 'welcome back'. Maybe it was the traits of loyalty and faithfulness that he recognized in the dog. Qualities

Johnno admired, even now, but that were in short supply – 'except maybe in the army', he thought.

The dog's hind quarters hung low, as it sniffed around the legs of the bench, before moving stiffly to the water tap. It balanced and cocked its leg up the post, pissing into the murky pool. Johnno blew out the smoke from his nose and mouth in acknowledgement of what dogs and other animals know, that it only takes one small thing to turn a fountain spring into a cesspit. Hope into despair. The dog came up to his leg and he petted it, enjoying the soft warmth of its fur as he massaged the bushy ear in his hand.

'Leopold!' shouted its owner. 'Come here, boy!'

He saw the woman staring across at them – her body tentative, waiting to see what he would do. (What the fuck did she think he was going to do?) The dog stole a last look at Johnno through bloodshot eyes, before finally hobbling off. Johnno was alone.

Suddenly he felt the familiar stinging on his finger, where the fag had gone so low it burnt again the already sore spot on his skin. Who calls anything Leopold anyway?

He knew a Leopold once, at RMAS [Royal Military Academy Sandhurst]. Leopold Van Klap. A proper MUPPET [Most Useless Person Pirbright Ever Trained]. What a half-pint hero! No backbone. When they did their Basic he would always be the last one into the drill square, with the colour sergeant shouting: 'I'm going to stick this pace stick through your ears and ride you round this parade square like a shagging motorbike.' Then when it was their turn to do the log race as part of their BFT [Basic Fitness Test] he literally biffed it. No metal. Not fit. Johnno threw the tiny butt down and squashed it into the ground with his heel, ('ashes to ashes'). Not like Johnno FOC [First Of Class]. Standing, he took a few deep breaths before he began jumping up and down on the spot, did some squats and attempted a few bench presses on the seat. To see if he would pass the CFT [Combat Fitness Test] now. (Jesus!) He felt dizzy, so cut short his usual 40 rounds. But he mustn't lose his tone. It was all about discipline. ('Serve to Lead'). He could see the bank of trees where the crow had gone beginning to sway. He wondered about the crow and saw other birds coming home to roost.

The wind was beginning to pick up, with dark clouds scudding. (No, they were moving fucking fast!) That's another thing animals know that poets don't, if the shit is about to hit the fan you tuck your head in and don't stand admiring the fucking view.

Thus thou, Ravine of Arve – dark, deep Ravine –
Thou many-coloured, many voiced vale,
Over whose pines, and crags, and caverns sail
Fast cloud shadows and sunbeams: awful scene.

The fucking sublime couldn't match up with the real horrors he'd seen. He knew all about being a man standing on the edge. And look what happened to Byron. Interfering where he didn't belong – didn't come home. Oh yes, he's remembered as a hero, but he was a fool. No training, no idea of a military life – he was a ponce. At some point, as Mr Chapman always said, you have to decide which way you are swaying. A thinker or a man of action, a hero or a coward, alive or dead. Johnno knew he shouldn't have come home either.

To the left of the trees a swathe of London stretched out.

Like a patient etherized upon a table.

Suddenly Johnno was back there.

Through the smoke, the shrieks, the shrapnel he was carrying the boy in his arms. Tommo still firing rounds at his side. Johnno's blood, from where a shard of metal had embedded itself into his chin, was pouring across the boy's body, running into the ravine of the child's chest. He smelt the iron of the blood and saw the two red rivers of gore dark and deep, merging. The bright yellow of the tangy turmeric, the ripe red of the peppered paprika from the many-coloured bazaar, danced at the outer edges of Johnno's eyes then, as he ran. Amidst this chaotic, awful scene, he heard the many voiced screams of the market-place, but all the while, over and above all else, all the while, he heard the cry of the child. It merged now with the *caw-caw* of the crow soaring overhead, as Johnno stood transfixed, silently crying and drenched in sweat, looking out over the skyline. (Civilization!) The modern sublime. This was not for him – he was not ready to face it yet. He splashed his face with water from the tap, washing away the memory, re-filling his water bottle he willed the water to run faster. He wanted to get away now. RTM [Ready To Move] – it was no longer safe. He didn't feel at home here, the park bench was no comfort, the tap was a sewer, and civilization was too close. He needed to get away, to try to stay one step ahead. He took a swig of water. (Fuck!) He needed a proper drink. He began bouncing on his feet, moving them up and down, lightly on his toes like a prize-fighter. The Ali Shuffle. Sparring with an imaginary opponent. 'Peace was no good for a mercenary', he thought, and by peace he only meant the absence of war. He hung the water bottle off MOLLE. He needed to keep moving. Besides there were the tell-tail signs of a storm brewing.

Johnno zipped up the backpack and hauled it on his back, then grabbed his tobacco pouch. He shoved it into his trouser pocket, but felt something else. He pulled out a fragment of paper: Homelea, 83 Endell Street, London WC2H. Northern Line.

Where the fuck had that come from? He re-read the address. No alarms went off. He wasn't sure if this was a good or a bad omen, but the name sounded nice. Homelea. He turned the paper over in his fingers. What did he have to lose? He would set his compass for north.

Everybody Sees the Wind Blow

Luke Dean

Chapter One

Did he take the zip wire or the stairs? Well, the zip wire, duh. Halfway down he let go of the handle and cannonballed backward in silent slow-mo – though full-speed and with the handle still rattling down the wire, but you can imagine – plunged thorax-first into the foam pit, from which he was then obliged to clamber while the auto-winch hauled the handle back up to the nest. It took longer, all in all, than descending the staircase and hence the need to choose (but come on, not really).

The 10 o'clock news had shown footage of the wreckage on Barbuda and Anguilla, and of Miami Beach homeowners sandbagging doorways and taping up windows in a futile effort to prepare for the coming winds. Outside the Holborn office of the Dursten and Orville advertising agency clouds skated across the skyline at an unnatural rate. The same footage was shown on the 11 o'clock news, and again at 1 o'clock, each time re-running the governor of Florida's request: 'Pray for us.'

So Zed had walked along the gallery and climbed the spiral stairs to the nest to do just that. He'd sat cross-legged on the flat wooden floor in the centre at first, palms pressed before chest, eyelids closed. But back ache had soon set in and he'd lain down on the woven heather that curved up into the dome of the ceiling.

New Orleans, he thought. Which was of course not the place they'd just been newsing about, but images of neighbourhoods underwater with residents awaiting rescue from their rooftops had so branded Zed's memory that as far as he was concerned, that was where hurricanes happened. He addressed his prayer to no one. He prayed that the death toll be low and the casualties few. He prayed that power outages be brief, the damage to road networks mild, and that the great arm of the state be fleet and efficient in its repair. He prayed that the people be neighbours to one another in this desperate time and hereafter, and that they not grasp too tightly the sorrow they were bound to endure. He prayed for fine weather and a forgiving economy. And once his prayers were over, he lay a while longer against the heather. It was always hard to leave the nest once you got down on the heather. It was much easier to have a little snooze and wake up at 16:23 and then look at your watch and say 'fuck it' and then snooze a bit longer and then cast yourself down the zip wire on your way out. Cos how much work would you get done before seventeen oh oh, anyway?

'Fuck all,' said Zed, 'fuck all,' and he flung himself down the wire.

This was not Zed's usual routine. He did not as a rule spend afternoons snoozing in the nest, nor even turn on the news at work. Not that anyone would care, for the Bowline campaign would be ready by October come rain or shine. It was rare that he should clock off before seven and it made little sense to do so today, since Greta would be with her parents in Marlow all weekend. But this is what he did. Must one always pretend to rationality?

There were no clocks displayed on the creative floor at Dursten and Orville. Instead there was a huge sundial in a sky-lit square, whose gnomon's shadow fell on mottos in place of hours. Zed watered his Aloe vera plant Frank, and Frank's babies, Alice and Hyacinth.

'It's the weekend,' Zed announced and with a wave bade adieu to Holly and Simon, who were still jobbing away in their respective corners. He caught up his coat and hat and gave a half-bow to the sundial before heading for the door. *'It's later than you think'* read its present position. 5 o'clock.

Outside, the sun was busy drying dark patches on the pavement and removing people's jackets so you could see more of their skin. A pair of spandex-clad legs emerged from the rush of foot traffic and entered The Health Club as Zed was reaching the bottom of the stairs. The leggings were printed with little pictures of blue and white mosaic squares, pink cherry blossom, and monarch butterflies, all smushed together between paisley chains in one delicious figure-hugging menagerie that made you glad to be alive. Zed passed her in the reception area of Dursten and Orville, which it shared with The Health Club on the ground floor on account of Dursten and Orville owning The Health Club. It was an employee benefit disguised as, and fully functioning as, a public gym, which employees were encouraged to use by the simple fact of having to pass it on their way out of work, and they were encouraged to value it by having to pay for it out of their salaries *after* receiving said salaries. They had to insert their own bank cards and enter their own pins to pay the monthly subscription – for most employees less than an hour and a half's pay, which if you think about it isn't too dear for an attractive body, not too dear at all.

People passed along the street holding collapsed umbrellas or coats slung over their arms, the odd madman still sporting a fully fastened North Face down as they squinted to navigate the rush hour parade. Outside the post office stood a group of teens all wearing clompy leather ankle boots and knee-length camel coats that they would, for the most part, have to grow into. Each was holding a phone in front of themselves and periodically glancing at the screen, waiting for the icon to turn blue. A well-known Pokestop, High Holborn Post Office was often host to such a group of youths stocking up on Pokeballs and Revives and such. Outside the tube station a tatty army fatigue with its hair in a dread sock was requesting financial assistance from passers-by.

He was obviously unemployed. Un-em-p-loyed.

Zed gave him a five pound note and wished him luck. He was a saint like that.

The sky was again black by the time Zed emerged at West Norwood, and rain was falling with such ferocity as will make a body prefer waiting in a train station to a speedy return home.

'Is it gonna be this crazy all day?' Zed shouted at the sky.

A clump of commuters clogged the thoroughfare between the stairs and the station exit. Fortunately for Zed, though, the station and the rain were not the only options, for the Great North Wood was at a distance of feet and its kitchen was a veritable hive of creativity and passion.

The bar contained a fine selection of precision-sculpted beards as well as a smattering of cable knits and sparkly dresses. One really could not complain of a lack of visual stimuli.

Zed found a seat at the bar and ordered a carafe of red and a ramekin of olives. And as he sat there perusing the room and eating his olives something firm and wet entered his left ear while his right was taken entirely into a mouth and bitten a little too roughly for a greeting. It was Tom, and Tom was already drunk.

'You really are a swine, you know Tom.'

'Zlattko, I've missed you,' Tom said. Still standing up, he leant over Zed's shoulder, set his glass down on the bar and served himself from Zed's carafe.

Zed took a good look at him. 'You're receding,' he said.

'And you're expanding,' said Tom.

'I am *not*.'

'No, you're right, you're as ripe as you ever were. You're just a bit rude, that's your problem.'

'*I'm* a bit rude?'

'And a bit tetchy, too. God Zed, who pissed in your cornflakes this morning?'

'Oh well never mind my cornflakes,' said Zed. 'Suits you anyway, a bit of hair loss, goes well with your round face.'

'There you go,' said Tom, stroking Zed's neck and behind his ear, 'I bet you feel much better.'

'You're going to try to fuck me, aren't you?' Zed grasped the lapels of Tom's mackintosh and brought his face up close to Tom's. He misted up Tom's spectacles with his breath and then leaned in close to his ear and said, 'You'd better get me drunk first.'

They drained the carafe and drank three carafes more. They ate pollock and lobster and spätzle with chives. They cancelled the cares of ten thousand ages. Tom pointed out that the wine was full of essence. Zed agreed and they raised a toast to essence. They gave thanks for the food and toasted to lobster. They told tales of victories and drank them with wine.

Then Zed pointed out that he'd become sleepy. Tom agreed, Zed was obviously sleepy. Then Tom revealed he had some ching and they took turns visiting the toilets. It was mostly novocaine, though, and something else that caused them both a complete evacuation of their bowels. Soon thereafter Zed became aware he no longer wished to remain. The novocaine had ruined his taste for wine.

But it was only just gone eleven, there would be no one at home and now he was all booted up on coke. It would have been miserly not to stay until closing.

They sat a moment without speaking. Each drained his glass. The suit sitting next to Tom got up and headed for the door and Zed reached over for the empty Brixton pale ale left on the bar. He peeled the label off the shoulder of the bottle and folded it into a little nubbin of paper he could roll between thumb and forefinger. Tom ordered another carafe of wine.

'So how's life at Durvin and Mooster's?' said Tom.

'You've been waiting all night to say that, haven't you?'

'I wanted to leave it long enough that you might believe I'd forgotten asking you earlier.'

'It was worth it,' said Zed, and he gave Tom a congratulatory wink.

'So?' said Tom. 'Working on anything interesting?'

'Just finished this TV slot for butter that's not bad,' said Zed.

A slightly chubby couple, both with thick West Country accents and front teeth that whistle a little on esses and soft cees, stand in a kitchen together in their pyjamas waiting for a crumpet to toast. When the toaster pops, the man says to his wife 'corr bet you want a noice bit o' butter on there, don't you?'

'Ooh yeah a noice bit o' butter, 'atta sort you out,' says the woman and there's a cut to a short clip of them each biting into a buttered crumpet on another occasion. Cut back to the present scene where the woman is now buttering her crumpet.

The man gently elbows her arm as she's spreading the butter. 'corr I bet you dun' arf like a noice bit o' butter, though,' he says.

'Corr a bit o' butter, 'ass alright ennit?' says the woman and she bites into her crumpet. And then the two gaze into the camera as if into the distance and there is silence, save for the sounds of the woman chewing her crumpet.

'Corr I tell you what, though, I dun' arf like a noice bit o' butter,' says the man.

'You'll see it. There's gonna be a billboard follow-up,' said Zed.

'Oh god yeah, it's about time someone got us eating more butter,' said Tom.

'Tell me about it,' said Zed. 'Dairy farmers are on their knees as it is without all this olive spread shite and everyone turning vegan.'

'No you're right, it's dreadful,' said Tom.

'I mean it. That's money from the land. How're we ever going to make up the deficit without looking after our primary industries?' said Zed.

'It's hard to tell if you're being ironic,' said Tom.

'It is, isn't it?'

'You're a good man, Zed. I'm glad to see you landed right, anyway.'

'Shall we have another nosey?'

Tom slid the baggie into Zed's pocket and Zed went to the toilet for quite a generous razz on the old schnozcumber, stashing his fiddly paper in his pocket for later use. Then he slipped out of the cubicle and stood at a urinal to take a leak. But he wasn't paying enough attention to what he was doing and he ended up urinating on the wall a little. He didn't know if the wall had a regular spot in the cleaning schedule, but it seemed unlikely to be a daily task. Who knew how long his fluids or their salty residue would remain?

He took out his notepad and wrote *Piss* on the top page and then tore the page out. He smoothed the paper against the wall where he'd pissed on it, but the paper wouldn't stick the way he'd imagined it would. There wasn't enough moisture left on the wall; the piss had all run down the tiles. So Zed took the paper over to the sink and wet it under the tap and then he brought it back to the urinals and this time it stuck. The water made the ink run a little so that the letters came out blurry, but the note was still legible. Then he washed his hands with soap. You should always use soap.

The conversation turned to fruit. Which were better, melons or pears? Zed was backing melons, while Tom advanced a theory that a pear, when peeled and sliced, was at least as good as, but most likely better than a melon. Further, he argued that most people were eating kiwis wrong, digging the flesh out with spoons, like cavemen, as if potato peelers didn't exist, as if you couldn't eat a kiwi in two bites if you went about it right.

'Do you remember when Dom ate that banana with the skin on?' said Zed.

'He knows how to entertain, that boy, doesn't he? Do you remember when Simon ran himself over with his own car?' said Tom.

'Oh man. Do you remember that time we spent all afternoon reminiscing?' said Zed.

'What a day!' said Tom.

'What a day.'

The paper nubbin Zed had been fiddling with finally derailed and Zed stood up and peered at the floor around his stool searching for it until Tom laid a hand on his shoulder and promised to buy him a new one. He retook his seat and found that the barstool's leather cover made for pretty good rubbing to a restless thumb.

'So how's Greta?' said Tom. 'Where'd you say she was?'

'Greta's okay. Her dad's lost his marbles.'

'Oh, shit. How?' said Tom.

A bartender in a baggy jumper with a vaguely pukey pattern rang the bell for last orders. 'We'd better grab another,' said Zed and he gave the order.

Tom twiddled the wispy little soul patch he had going on. 'What happened to him?' he said.

'He got old.'

'Shit man, I'm sorry.'

'Yeah well,' said Zed.

'How's Greta coping? Fuck man, how're you?'

'You just gotta get on with it,' said Zed. He fumbled around inside his jacket and found the washing label and started rubbing the two halves of silky fabric over one another. These were easily the nicest things to fiddle with. As a young child, Zed had been such a clothes label zealot that his mother had collected as many as she could and sewn him a blanket with them, and still he'd woken family members in the night, digging fingers under their nightwear to get at the labels. 'Shall we have another nosey?' he said.

Tom passed him the baggie. 'Have the rest,' he said, 'I've got plenty.'

'You're a bit old to be dealing, aren't you?' said Zed.

Tom assured him he was still gainfully employed. 'Life hasn't been *that* unkind to me,' he said.

'So how come you're carrying extra?' said Zed.

'I just happen to have two.'

Then the pukey-pattern jumper came around collecting glasses and – you know what it was like? You know those mats from PE class with the vinyl stretched over the top and underneath they're like tons of crumb-sized bits of different kinds of foam all glued together. The jumper was like that – he came over and said that they were clearing up now and if Zlattko and Thomas could finish up and fuck off pretty soon that'd be great.

So they drank their wine and wiped their chins and doffed their caps to the establishment at large before heading out the door. Outside Tom offered to walk Zed home.

'You could've bought yourself a prostitute for what you spent on wine and shitty coke this evening,' said Zed.

'You know, one of these days you're gonna lose me if you don't learn to treat me right,' said Tom.

'Oh fuck off you creep,' said Zed and then blew Tom a kiss before turning homeward.

'Give my love to Greta, won't you.'

In his hallway Zed stopped to check himself in the silver gilt mirror and congratulated himself on his chequered waistcoat. He looked pretty sharp, debonair, if you will. Time was treating him well. He had a five o'clock shadow that spoke kindly of his jawline, and his tousled hair bestowed him with a boyish charm that might in times of need be relied upon to bring home the bacon. But his chest hurt and his forehead felt tight like old leather, bereft of all moisture and somewhat divorced from the body. He needed hydrating, that much was clear.

So he guzzled down a kale and cranberry smoothie, with half a lime thrown in to stave off the scurvy. After that he felt brand new. Then he fixed himself a night cap and an aspirin to suck on and wasted no time getting under the covers. He found Greta's baggy tank top underneath her pillow, pressed it to his nose and breathed deep. Boy did she smell good. He curled his knees up under his chest and brought his other hand in to seal Greta's top around his nose and mouth. He could never get enough of this. She smelled the way your mouth tastes after crying, all mixed up with wood smoke and wet clay, the smell of ripe figs and the taste of lavender honey. Boy did she smell good. If you could condense it somehow, he'd have poured it on everything, sweet or savoury, and he'd have carried a hip flask of it stashed in his pocket for between-meal top-ups. Boy did she smell good. Even first thing in the morning, even her morning breath tasted better than fresh air.

After an hour or two Zed figured he ought to try another tack, and since there were no downers in the house besides alcohol, he pulled out his willy to have a tug.

Chemistry was not in his favour, however, and the satin sheets wherein he lay were little help to his stale imagination, so after a few minutes' fondling he went and rooted around in the laundry basket and came back with a pair of panties. He lay on the bed again with the gusset draped over his nostrils and resumed his fondling. It didn't take him long to get it up now. This was his favourite smell in the universe and he breathed deeply while he beat off, trying to fill his lungs with it. He even licked at the little trail of dried mucus, gingerly at first, but then with his whole tongue spread across the gusset, still flogging away, but making little progress. Eventually he stuffed the panties right in his mouth and chewed and sucked on the cloth, swallowing great gobfulls of saliva infused with Greta's fluids. But it was no use. He beat himself raw before he finally gave up. When he did, he heard the morning birdsong getting under way and before long gave up on the idea of sleep altogether. And since he was in it for the duration now, he went and fetched Tom's chalk and fed his nose a morsel. If he was being honest he'd have preferred some sleep, but life was for living and it wouldn't do to squander the morning in drowsiness.

He made a cup of tea and had a go at YouTube, but he wasn't very good at that either and the longest he watched of anything was an unbroken minute of rain on a lagoon. My kingdom for a splif, he thought. He switched off the screen, poured a glass of champagne and opened the living room window, the better to hear the morning choir. But the champagne churned his stomach, and with the sounds of traffic down on Knight's Hill steadily encroaching on the good vibrations, it soon became clear Zed would have to leave London.

A shower, a bus, and two tubes later Zed stood at the counter of the West Cornwall Pasty Co inside Paddington station, having decided that some greasy pastry filled with gristle probably was the right thing for his ailing tummy. Once on board the train, though, things really started to come together for Zed. He finished his pasty and shared a moment with a baby who was facing the opposite direction, each unabashedly staring at the other. And then he went and fetched himself a gin tin from the buffet car, which he took in sips, feeling like a king as the indifference of London gave way to the indifference of England.

Carter's Folly

Will Francis

They began as pranks. Little messages written to one another in crossword puzzles, or down the horizontal lengths of published articles in the newspapers. Take the first letter of every new line, write them out, and then rewrite the message as a whole. A simple rail-fence-cipher – though sometimes they would use a classical cipher to make the code harder, embedding the code word of the previous puzzle to prove they were keeping up with the game. To miss even a single code would see you get left behind.

They had started out with five members, but one of them dropped after a year – he had gone abroad for a half-year on an archaeological expedition in Egypt, leading a team to dig out a newly discovered Pharaonic tomb, plundering some ancient crypt. He returned lacking the time to read through six months' worth of embedded article puzzles and ciphers. The five still met up regularly, the fifth not excluded from the circle; only from the inside jokes, left buried in horizontal lines down the columns of published academic papers and encrypted article headers. Now only four of them exchanged the codes.

When the four discovered a new columnist had appeared, using all the same encrypted messages and code-keys as themselves, an unknown author writing under a pseudonym – don't the papers just love those? – none of the four were too concerned. Neil found it first, showing the others the little message spelt out down the horizontal column of lines. Together, they assumed the fifth had finally caught up! The game continued!

But the fifth had no knowledge of the new columnist – that hidden sixth presence – the fifth had not noticed the new articles at all. Ever since returning from Egypt he had noticed little, and spoken less each time the group met. After several weeks the answer became clear, falling into all of their laps like another puzzle: there was a new puzzler among them.

The sixth was a presence only in spirit. The four columnists still met together, with their fifth friend oblivious to the looks of suspicion that now cloaked their gatherings and meetings. Any one of the five could be playing a joke on the others: writing twice as much to jostle the group. The four still writing decided to entreat with the sixth puzzler: they accepted the new code words and included him in their cryptic circle. Encrypted simple letters applauded his effort and ingenuity, invited him to their meetings, to come and have a drink, and share in the joy of a secret kept. From his little London desk, Neil found himself looking at pictures in the papers, imagining the sixth staring back. The sixth did not respond to the four's published entreaties in kind, only escalating the difficulty of the puzzles. Under the sixth's purview, the ciphers grew in complexity, toying with the boundaries and rules of the game. And once a week the code word, in continuing the circle across code-breakers, would pass to the mysterious sixth member. As the key to solving the next cipher, the new code word was held hostage, should the sixth choose simply not to respond, or make their code indecipherable. The four began to worry: would they be locked out of their own game? Would it be cheating, or a loss of honour to ask for the code word from each other? Would it be a submission to exclude this new member? Create a new codeword and lock out this intruder – for that is what they had come to consider the sixth – from their puzzles? This one who had caught their game and possibly even followed it from its inception?

They decided not to. Pride overtook anxiety and caution. It so often does. The intruder remained among them, their anonymity preying on the four, until paranoia and doubt spilled out into the printed word. As the sixth had begun to create extra puzzles, jumbled together in additional columns in other newspapers, using repeated pen-names to lead the others along, the four reacted by writing more to one-another. Together the frequency of codes spiralled beyond control, everyone writing to one-another constantly (the papers themselves delighted in the attention their Letters section received) and in further weakening difficulty. In the rush to print, the five writers grew too lethargic for complexity. Codes became simple, almost easy – they dropped the code-word in their desperation to be seen and shared. A weakness that inspired the sixth: he promised that in deciphering the puzzles he printed, lay his identity. The challenge was set before the four: the first to uncover the identity of the sixth could surely prove his mastery above the rest.

> It is no secret that the
> newest expedition in
> returned from Egypt c
> statue, long thought l
> is being held alongsid
> Museum. The exhibit
> open to the public pe
> The statue is of black
> inlaid with gold, and s
> mastery over the Red
> divided Kingdom. The
> Egyptian mythology a
> myth. The role of Set
> is noted to have inclu

> sands, and storms. Se
> Nephthys, the godde:
> Young (2003), sugges
> into question. Insteac
> religion, now calls ne
> revised status as 'hou
> Sutekh in various dep
> years, with the head c
> animals, the 'Set anin
> 'Typhonic Beast'. In m
> mythology and cult. T
> rests in the British Mu
>
> \- Dr. Sebastian Nifosi

A simple three-rail rail-fence-cipher, now became the most commonly used between the five players. At his desk in his little London apartment, Neil took the first letter of the first word of each line:

INRSIMOTIMDEMISNYIRRSYATMR

He drew out from the article the letters used in the cipher, and counted the total number of letters: Twenty-Six.

With the three-rail cipher (as Neil suspected it would be) Neil took twenty-six and divided by four. Four went into twenty-six six times, but it left two numbers that did not fit. 6.2. With two numbers left over, Neil rounded down: 6.2, became 6, and the answer to how many letters make up the bottom layer. He took the number and rounded up: 6.2, became 7. Seven, and he had worked out the number of letters in the top row. Finally, twenty-six take away thirteen (add the top and bottom layers, seven plus six), and that leaves him with thirteen: the number of letters in the middle layer of the decrypted code.

Tiredness tugged at Neil's fingers, but he soldiered on, writing out the necessary grid, marking out the first seven letters of the cypher to make the top layer, and the final six letters to create the bottom layer:

[INRSIMO] TIMDEMISNYIRR [SYATMR]

Finally, Neil was able to decrypt the code:

I	•	•	•	N	•	•	•	R	•	•	•	S	•	•	•	I	•	•	•	M	•	•	•	O	•	•
•	T	•	I	•	M	•	D	•	E	•	M	•	I	•	S	•	N	•	Y	•	I	•	R	•	R	•
•	•	S	•	•	•	Y	•	•	•	A	•	•	•	T	•	•	•	M	•	•	•	R	•	•	•	•

It was not just the work that had been keeping Neil awake at an unreasonable hour. The deciphered message was now haunting his thoughts. Nervous fingers tapped out a familiar rhythm on his desk, as he absently re-wrote and deciphered the string of letters. A beleaguered hand passed through fine white hair, and his pen came to rest – the nib leant at an unusual angle, pressed too hard into the paper.

Who had written this one? He knew the 'author', *'Dr. Sebastian Nifosi'* was an alias of one of the four – but they had stopped writing recently (stopped answering their calls, and simply vanished in fact), and it had re-appeared under the use of the mysterious sixth. Was the sixth now playing more games? Taunting them all about their missing friend? Or was their friend trying to reach out to them, in a manner less convenient than text or the post? Dry eyes blinked, worn fingers furled and unfurled. His hands reached into a desk drawer for heart medication, strictly one-a-day, but it had been pushed to the back of Neil's mind for too long, and he could feel his chest begin to tighten.

When he had begun working the light still fluttered in through the window above his desk, catching what rays could shine out over compacted

London roofs. Now it had long been blocked out by the city. He checked his phone on the desk and was shocked to realise it was close to midnight. Neil smiled weakly, putting his phone down, and lowered his head into his hands. The desire to keep working was strong, he had other articles to decipher (there were always too many lately!), but it was late, and sleep was clouding his mind.

For weeks now Neil had slept poorly, always waking up the next morning unrefreshed, chasing the tail ends of forgotten dreams. Ever since he and his friends had all begun decrypting the latest codes left by the sixth, with their strange lettered patterns and words which made little coherent sense to them, every one of the four had mentioned a lack of sleep, and memories of strange dreams.

A feeling of forgetting. They laughed about it, each one of them admitted to being enthralled by the new codes, captivated by the idea of decoding the sixth's identity first, and each had been working too hard trying to keep up with one-another. But no-one was going to be the first to relent. So Neil kept working hard, and kept feeling each morning as if he hadn't slept at all. But he knew he had.

Neil stretched languidly from his chair, stood, and began to flick off the lamps in his little converted office. The house was old, rickety, and almost as worn as him (he smiled), so the lights were slow to react. The rest of the house was quite asleep, and Neil lived alone. He staggered into his bedroom, placed his glasses in the case beside his bed, and prayed dully that he might fall asleep quickly. That he might have pleasant dreams for a change.

The codes still undeciphered littered his desk, fragments of secrets uncovered. Some from friends, others a stranger.

With Stevens' ne
examining the na
suggested urgen
gives no real indi
Lessons in attent
action had been
rendered futile. I
negated the effe
instead. Whethe
suspect, or if inst

nasty character ie
characterisation
lewd beekeeper
morbidly leaving
remember home
makes no attem
is already too lat
act. Fate, or mor
example of the g

- Felix Wright, aust

[WESGL]ARNISNCLM[RMIAE]

Garriers, in his ess
dramatizing the tr
ridiculous suggest
actual curse. That
unrealistic. Wheth
relative sense, or
your own conclusi
understudy comp
dreams which we
every turn. No rec
measured or prov
actuality, several
obvious. In time
real or otherwise
simply fictional.

- Dr. Jeremy Alwis

[GDRA]URYUDEM[AORS]

The poetry of
Dream: A Frag
finished in 179
less than expe
death, it never
maturity that
hypocrisy. Tho
years after pu
opium, though
the quote fails
excel at. Whet

lucidity. In bre
intransience ar
examples in th
Regardless of t
after the react
seemed, ironic
every critic has
noted that spe
each time. To
Kubla Khan ha
ending with th

[TDFLDM]HYOTELIERAS[ENEKE]

He stood in a familiar place, wondering where he was. All around him were burning sands, glistening golder than gold, and stretching as far as he could see in every direction. A multicoloured twinkle stole his attention and he followed the light above him to see a thousand-thousand stars glaring balefully down, the weight of their brilliance reflecting off the burnished sands and blinding him with colour: ruby red and sapphire blue blending together in a malicious rainbow. Above them all soared the sun, larger than he knew, a huge disc which towered over the sky and scorched the atmosphere. The light burned behind his eyes, clustering his vision, so he covered his face, and tried to peek between closed fingers, as if fighting snow blindness. No sooner had Neil hidden his eyes, but the light had changed. Dimmed. He lowered his hands. No longer were there the endless sands, but the crest of a hill, carrying above it the weight of the horizon. Beyond it the sky was being drained of its magnificence: a storm cloaked Neil's sight, and he realised that the stars were being strangled by sandy winds. It was coming closer. Spanning miles in moments. It flayed light and darkened the sun. Neil looked where he was bidden. Unable to run, move, or cry out. A passenger in his own mind.

And on the crest of the horizon, stood a figure, wearing the storm as a cloak. The dark winds lapped lovingly at his shoulders, but never covered his face. The figure was a man, naked to the waist and with dark skin as bronzed as the sands. His head was that of a snouted beast Neil didn't recognise, black skin, boxed ears. His eyes gazed down on Neil, blacker than the darkling sky, and Neil stood petrified. From all around him, seeming to echo across the world, the figure mouthlessly gave a silent scream, and the storm grew in fierce intensity until climaxing in a peal of thunder that split the sky.

Neil woke, gasping for air, his lungs hungry, his heart beat in his chest, a drum, a clamour in his head, the room shifted, a soft light from the window, a thinner light peeking beneath the doorway, and familiarity began to descend over him.

He was sitting up in bed, his heart still beating relentlessly, but he could see again, move again, and he looked around his room. He brought a hand up to his chest, feeling it reverberate with his own pulse, there was a tightness, a pressure on his chest, a now-lifted weight. He willed his already-weak heart to be still: he couldn't take that much excitement during the day, let alone allow it to run away with him in his sleep. But he could move again, no longer paralysed by the dream.

What had woken him?

The thunder came again. It was quieter this time, but not from outside – the soft and familiar sounds of traffic had not woken him, and the open window told him it wasn't raining. The sound had come from his apartment: a bang. Something hitting the floor, made louder by old and frail floors.

Neil stared out at the closed door. A light was shining underneath the crack. Had he not turned them off? The light was not the yellow of a home bulb, but white like a lamp or torch. Dawning realisation and tension rose as one... And the light moved. Someone was in his apartment.

Willing himself to silence, Neil raised a hand to his mouth, even as his pulse began to quicken again. Wide eyes looked around the dimly lit room; at his bedside table Neil found his phone wasn't there. Had it been taken? Had someone been in here too? No, he thought, he had left it on his desk in his study... which someone else now occupied. In the corner, against the door, an old set of battered golf clubs in a bag. Neil snorted softly – he was a book critic, and not built to fight an intruder – and kept scanning the room. The window was open, but even if he did catch someone's attention outside, no-one would get here in time. He could hear noises from his office. The clattering of things being moved.

The bedsheets were slick with sweat and stuck to him like grease paper, but Neil shuffled to the edge of the bed and swung his legs down to the ground, distractedly sweeping off of his leg a trace of fine golden sand that had gotten caught in damp bedsheets, and made to stand up – only for the floor to creak beneath him. Wincing, and damning the old floors, Neil kept an eye on the door, watching for any sign of light, or the sound of approaching footsteps. After a minute had passed, he slowly began to make his way towards the wardrobe – a potential hiding spot? – and from there to the door, pulse quickening. Leaning against the wall, Neil raised a hand to his wrist and took measure of his pulse. After a minute it was high, but not dangerously so. That was fine, he—

—stopped, and turned his head to the door. In that minute the apartment had been quiet, save for the occasional moving car coming from outside. Neil reached out to take a golf club after all, taking a moment to choose which golf club to use – as if that mattered.

He put an ear to the door: beyond it, the apartment was still strangely serene. Utterly still. Where was the intruder? Had he heard the floor creak? Was he even now approaching the door – having mastered the art of crossing the weathered floorboards silently – with gun or knife in hand? Was he now drawing back a leg to kick down the door that divided the two, or just standing on the other side, ready to pounce?

Neil could feel his heart racing again, tightening, and the questions flooded his mind, bogging him down, he paused, waited, decided he could wait no longer, and threw open the bedroom door, striding out with golf club in hand, doing his utmost to look for all the world to see as a warrior striding into battle, armed with sword and pyjamas.

Beyond his bedroom door the apartment was empty, and dark. Neil stood nonetheless, golf club raised above his head. His hands shook. His eyes darted this way and that. They flickered into open doors and skirted over potential hiding spots – he had not known his own apartment was so dangerous – and Neil followed. Nerves pushed him around corners and along the edges of walls. Dark corners became menacing and every shadow concealed violent potential. The gloom of half-light peering from behind closed curtains cloaked his apartment and inside it he felt a stranger in his own home. Finally, he reached his study and desk, risking the strategically dangerous decision to cross the empty room – leaving his back exposed to the dark! His phone sat on his desk unmolested. Untouched. The desk itself however looked at him with a foreign look. It seemed alien to him now.

Neil looked around, knuckles white from clutching the weapon at his side, a sand-wedge never used. The room was still. Unmoving. It still seemed menacing in the dark, and something still put Neil's nerves on edge... but nothing moved. He broke the stillness and crossed into his living room. The T.V. was on standby, the dim non-light of the black screen basking the room in a perpetual twilight. He shivered. He moved to turn the T.V. off and snuffed the light out. In the dark, Neil breathed deeply, and stepped back into his office, feeling for the light switch.

In the light the room looked different, and Neil felt more secure. He looked around. Nothing had been taken. Nothing disturbed. He checked the other rooms of his apartment and it was the same everywhere. It was like nothing had happened. Was an intruder still inside with him now? Neil walked to the front door, he clasped his golf club still, but his grip was not so tight now. His fingers tingled. The front door was still firmly locked from the inside – the chain still pulled across. Neil found himself looking at that for some time.

What burglar locks the front door behind them?

What intruder would cut off their only exit upon being caught?

Neil checked the chain was secure, and in exasperation rested his forehead against it. Tiredness clutched at his muscles. This was nonsense. An aftershock of his dream.

He went back to his office – turning on all the lights as he went – and sat down at his desk, idly pocketing his phone, and breathing deeply. The familiar weight of his chair went some way to bleed the tension that was gripping him. His pulse slowed. His chest relaxed – and only now did he realise the tightness that had come back. He reached into the top drawer of his desk and took another pill, swallowing it without water. It was strictly to be taken at certain times of the day, but surely in all this excitement...

The dreams were only getting worse, and now they were apparently staying with him after he'd woken.

Neil laid his head back and let his mind wander, still swimming in adrenaline and sleep. He thought to the puzzles he had been trying to decipher, pouring over as if they were the key to progressing through to the next day. No wonder he was seeing things, he laughed, he'd been working himself half to death. As if the identity of the sixth mattered any more. Let the others lord their discovery over me. Let me fall out of the circle, out of the game. It wasn't worth the excitement. Still smiling, Neil moved to push the sheafs of paper and newspapers cuttings that he had been working on, before catching himself and looking closer at the desk. And he saw it. What it had been that made the desk appear so hostile in the dark.

The papers he was working on had been disturbed. He stood slowly, looking over every detail of his desk. He was sure of it. They'd been moved. One newspaper was weeks old, thrown out for sure, and here, a clipping balancing on the top, not tucked inside a different drawer? Trembling fingers pushed paper apart, perhaps this was still confusion from the dream, where were the notes he was just working on?

He found them, defaced in wet ink by his own handwriting.

Neil whirled around, and almost fell over in trying to grab his golf club in doing so. He staggered, gripping the club handle and holding it out in front of himself, trying to force some distance between himself and—

—the room was empty.

Shaking now, Neil turned back over the desk, hoping to make out the writing. He plunged his other hand into his pocket for his phone, beginning to dial for the police. The wet ink was a dark blue, a hue that for some reason brought to mind sapphires and stars.

To his horror, the writing was gibberish, utterly jumbled up, no words of warning. It was just a string of letters, scrawled across the page. A dark thought unbidden; 'gibberish unless you took the time to decrypt it…'

RRASEEUNHTATKNTWWA

Neil didn't. He ignored it, finished dialling the police, and swung back around with his golf club. This was the moment an intruder would sneak up behind him – he wasn't going to wait to be jumped.

A figure did stand behind him. And Neil dropped his sword.

The man in his apartment was naked to the waist and with dark skin as bronzed as burnt sand. His head was that of a snouted beast that Neil knew well, black skin, and boxed ears. The eyes were an endless black, and their silent stare was paralysing. Neil looked down and watched numbly to see its feet had tracked fine golden sand onto the carpet – a small mound had appeared to meet it. Human toes never touched the ground. There was no sound – indeed Neil could hear nothing, even as he fell back, away from darkling eyes. His chest ached. Tightened.

He staggered backwards against the desk and thought only of his sandy carpet (touched now by gold), as he clutched at his chest.

Cecily

Annie Garthwaite

Prologue

June 1487

He, and whatever news he carried, had been already more than twelve hours under her roof. He had ridden through the gates of Berkhamsted yesterday evening, clattering across cobbles and setting the dogs barking, while in her quiet solar, the light of a waning sun turned the golden thread of her rosary to fire. Her ladies had broken in upon her to tell of his arrival.

'Ladies, I am telling my beads.'

'But it is Master Lavenham, my Lady. He brings news of your grandson's strike against Tudor. Surely you will see him?'

'I see to my soul mistress, I am at prayer, as you see. Now is not the time. Tomorrow. Let him wait upon my audience.'

So, they had housed him in the north tower and all night, as she lay restless, she had thought of him there. She was sure he did not sleep. If he'd ridden to her straight from the battlefield then joy or despair would keep him wakeful. By now, she supposed, the whole household would know. Robbed of the chance to tell it to her, his tongue would have clacked its story into the open ears of her servants and men.

Would she see it, she wondered, in her chaplain's face, when he came to her for matins in the morning? Would it be written in the lines of her maid's brow when she brought her breakfast bread and ale? She could remember times when she had run headlong down winding stairs, heedless of tripping hems, to hear news of the battles of her house; could remember pacing the rushes to dust in night time vigils before Wakefield, St Albans, Towton, Barnet, Tewkesbury. A bloody list that had ended at Bosworth Field two years ago.

She crossed thin arms across fleshless breasts and willed herself to sleep. Whatever news he carries, she told herself, it will mean no change to me.

She had last seen Lavenham six months ago. He had come to bid her farewell before sailing to Ireland. She had touched a finger to the running hound emblazoned on his shoulder. 'You wear the badge of Lovell,' she said. 'My dead son Richard's faithful dog.'

'I am Lovell's man now and go to fight with him for your grandson.'

She took her hand from him, clasped it to the other in the hollow of her sleeve and frowned.

'Have courage, lady,' he urged. 'I am not alone in daring to name him king.'

'Tudor is king, and my granddaughter his queen.'

'Against all honour, lady, surely! Your grandson was crowned last week in Dublin. I go to him now and the loyal Irish will fight with us to bring the Tudor down.'

She had turned from him impatiently. 'This is dangerous talk Thomas. And foolery. Whatever poor wight was crowned last week in Dublin it was no kin of mine. George's son lies at Tudor's pleasure in London's tower and God keep him there.' And she hoped God would. For the weakness of mind that had shown itself in George was more than manifest in his son. Sweet but simple. The face of an angel, but a head as empty of thought as his father's was full of malice. No. She hoped he rested still in the Tower and knew in captivity some semblance of peace.

'Do I go with your blessing, lady?' he had asked her departing back.

She turned to him from the door. 'My blessing? Well. If you have the strength to bear that burden I've not the heart to withhold it. Go with God.'

Now he was back. And she must, at some point, hear him out. But not yet. Not yet, she thought, as rosewater washed away the heaviness of a sleepless night. I must hear mass first.

When her chaplain entered her chamber, she blessed him for the plainness of his face. No tell-tale signs there, just the calm devotion that greeted her every morning. The steadfastness of his strong voice intoning with hers and, after matins, the comfort of the sacrament; the bread breaking dryly on her tongue. His hand, weighty with blessing upon her head, sending a surge of peace through old bones.

And after.

'You've a visitor, Lady.'

And peace was gone.

'I give audience this afternoon.'

'He has ridden far, in some danger and waited long already. Can you not see him now?'

'My day is ordered, as you well know.' She paced to the window, looked out into sunlight and closed her eyes against it. He knew her pattern better than any other; her morning devotions, her public worship, her frugal meals. She received visitors for one hour in the afternoon. They were few these days and she preferred it so. Then evensong and private prayer, confession, compline, rest. The austere cycle from which she has not deviated these two years past.

'He may need to leave quickly.'

She was growing impatient. 'I must to prayer.'

'You must to duty, Lady.'

'I have no wish to see him. Why do you of all people press me to it? I have left the world he comes from and hope soon to leave this. Against that longed-for day, I must to prayer.'

'You are of this world, Lady. When we fail in our duty to our fellow Christians because we devote ourselves only to contemplation, it is as if we would adorn the face of Christ and keep it fair but leave his suffering limbs untended.'

She could not stand against her god. She drew down the papery lids of her eyes and sighed. 'Send him to me.'

She knew Lavenham's story before he opened his mouth. It was written plain in the redness of his eyes, in the pallor of his skin. And, surely, to her it could be no surprise.

'Come,' she beckoned him into the room. 'Tell me of my dead, Master Lavenham.'

And he wept on his knees as he told her how the armies of York and Tudor had met outside Stoke. How her daughter's son, Jack, Earl of Lincoln, had led the vanguard. How they had been pushed back and back by sheer strength of numbers. How the Irish, and the Burgundian mercenaries her daughter Margaret had paid so dearly for, had at last turned and fled, throwing down their weapons to run all the faster, only to drown in the river that cut off their retreat. The would-be king, who Lavenham had learned in Dublin to be nothing more than a puppet-pretender, was Tudor's prisoner, God save him.

And now, at last, he listed the dead. She heard their names with dry eyes. Old men that had fought beside her husband in another age. Young men who had been their sons and grandsons. The last of York. Leaves before winter. And Jack, yes, of course, Jack, hacked down on the river bank, sword in hand.

As he spoke her eyes gazed beyond him to the tapestried wall behind, where John the Baptist's gory head was endlessly offered up to a troubled Herod while Salome, dark eyed and sinuous as a snake, danced and smiled.

How many times, she wondered, has a woman's sin led men to their deaths?

'Enough, Master Lavenham.' She stood. 'I thank you for your news. I leave you now.'

Startled by her abruptness he looked up through his tears to see her walking, straight backed toward the door. 'Lady, I go from here to your daughter who has lost her child. Have you no word of comfort for her?'

She turned. She was tall still and held herself erect. She looked down upon him, her eyes tiny in the folds of her face. 'No. None.' And then she paused. 'Only that she has no other sons.'

She stepped away. The door closed soft behind her.

The household mass was over, the chapel empty. With a difficulty that appalled her, she eased her body down until she lay outstretched before the altar, before the shivering candle flame of God's presence. The stone was mercifully cool against her cheek. 'Holy Mother,' she began. The tremor in her voice shocked her; it flickered through pillars and arches and returned to lick at her ears.

She shivered and prayed on. Into the deep darkness behind her fast-closed eyes she began again her endless novena; the names of her dead children. 'I have built, oh my God, an abbey in my soul. From there I cry out to you for their repose. For Henry, William, Ursula, Thomas and John, the fortunate dead who came to you from their cradles. For Anne. For my beloved lost sons; for Edmund, Edward, George and Richard. For Margaret and Elizabeth who live yet and mourn.' For all their dear dead children. Their names were ashes on her tongue and she ate them, a bitter sacrament. Her penance.

Chapter One

Sunday, 16 December 1431

Dear God in heaven, thinks Cecily, is this how kings are made? The vast spaces of Notre Dame, brought near to glory by incense and spangled with glass prismed sunlight, fall silent on a breath. Among the kneeling ranks of England's nobility, she dares to raise her eyes. Through trembling, prayer-steepled fingers she watches as Uncle Beaufort, the towering scarlet cardinal, lowers the long-contested crown of France onto the child Henry's head. Henry himself is a shimmer of white; his ten-year old arms outstretched, his bare breast sheened with chrism, his face tear-swept and rapt. She sees his mouth fall open in a small round oh as the weight of this second crown and kingdom falls upon him. She watches as he raises his head in a shaft of sun; sees his dazzled eyes strain heavenward as if to meet with angels, only to alight upon another crown. That of England. It has been his by right since he was six months old and is held now, fast and firm before him, in the hands of his kinsman, John Duke of Bedford. The Duke's voice rings out over the bowed heads of three hundred English dukes, earls, barons, knights and their ladies, who crossed the channel at his call eighteen months ago to witness this miracle. 'Henry, the sixth of that name, by the will of God, king of England *and* of France.' They had not thought, when they set out, that it would take so long.

Lowering her eyes again Cecily feels her husband Richard, his body pressed close to her side in this jewel-weighted crowd, draw in a great draught of air. 'By the will of God,' he whispers. The silk of his sleeve shushes against the velvet of hers as he raises his hand to touch his bowed head, to cross his heart, to be kissed by his lips. 'By the will of God,' she echoes, mirroring his movement and bringing her hand to rest upon his. As he turns towards her she sees that his face, beneath the fall of black hair, is pale and shining, his eyes alight with wonder. It is no less a marvel for you than for I, she thinks, though you have seen Henry made king once already in Westminster.

But that was two long years ago; that first coronation that made Henry king of England. It was before the hope-filled sea voyage that brought them all to France and the fretful months of waiting in Rouen, while the tides of war had turned against them then turned again. It was before that peasant girl Joan d'Arc, the self-appointed saviour of France, over-reached herself, led her army to Compiegne and was captured. It was before capture became trial and the good Duke Bedford, vehement in triumph and hatred, swore to see the heretic witch dead by any means. It was before Joan burned.

Then too, Cecily had been at Richard's side in a sunlit crowd. She had watched unflinching as the thin girl, hair shorn and head bloody, was brought to the stake and bound. She had made fists to still the trembling in her fingers as Joan raised bruised and half blinded eyes to seek out the crucifix, held aloft in the straining arms of attendant priests. There followed, it seemed to Cecily, an age of preparation, as faggots were laid and re-laid, torches brought and prayers garbled. At last the fire had been set and its first flames, almost invisible in the bright light of a May morning, rose up to lick like dogs at Joan's feet and thighs. In the first row of watchers Cecily felt their heat against her own cheek and heard the girl's voice, as strong as any man's, ring out, 'Everything I have done was by God's order.' Then, more urgently, 'I pray you; hold up the cross of Christ that I may see it till I die.'

Cecily had stiffed her spine. She had not turned aside as flesh burned, blossomed and fell away. Narrowing her eyes against the heat, she had fixed her gaze determinedly on Joan, this girl who had lived only three more years of life than her own sixteen, as the fire roared, consumed, was sated and, finally, died. She stirred only when she felt Richard, who had stood no less firm than she, shift his feet and begin to turn. 'Come,' he coaxed her. 'It's done. Let us be gone from here.' He had moved to wrap an arm around her waist, but she stalled him, placing instead her fire warmed fingers on the back of his gloved hand. Comprehending her signal, conscious of her dignity, he raised their lightly joined hands and took his place beside her. With a sword's length of distance between them, he led her through a crowd that parted before them like water.

Later that evening she had learned that Bedford, that good, kind man, had ordered what little remained of Joan to be burned twice more and her ashes given to the waters of the Seine, so that no shred of her could be redeemed by grieving friends or venerated in martyrdom.

Everything by God's order, thinks Cecily, just as Joan herself had said. And now, today, and after nearly one hundred years of war, England has a king in France. Among the slow moving coronation procession Cecily passes out through Notre Dame's great west door, beneath the great tympanum, where Christ Triumphant, serene and indifferent, presides over the judgement of the dead. Emerging into sunlight she feels the sanctified glory of the church fall away as the world, sharp with frost and conflict, rises up to meet her. She knows that today's crowning does not mark an end to war. In truth it is little more than a gesture, grand and provocative, tit for tat. For France has a king already. The mad king's Dauphin, the last remnant of the Valois line all had thought finished at Agincourt. Two years ago he finally gave off licking his wounds and rode on the back of Joan's holy vision to his crowning in Rheims. Thence their coming into France.

Bedford growls into Richard's ear, 'What we do today sends a clear message to Charles the pretender, Charles the bastard, Charles the thrice cursed bane of my life. And with his peasant bitch burned, he will surely tremble to hear it; England still has a stomach for the fight and the heir of Agincourt comes now in person to stake his claim.'

Cecily thinks, but does not say, that the message might be more convincing if the heir of Agincourt was not a puling child who had thrown his insides up over the ship's rail in the first hour out from Dover on a calm sea. Or if he went to his weapons practice more enthusiastically or more often than to prayer. But perhaps Charles and his spies do not know these things. She hides a smile behind her sleeve. Richard, seeing it, looks away, though not at Bedford.

Stepping into the carriage that will take them from the cathedral to the coronation feast, Cecily pauses a moment. She looks ahead to where the shimmering king, on a horse well chosen for a sovereign, but towering for a ten-year-old boy, is moving off through a banner waving crowd. All most splendid. Then she turns, looking back to where the business of the day already reclaims the cathedral square. She narrows her eyes against the pale winter sun and stretches her sight further still. Beyond the encircling river lie the unfathomed byways of Paris. England's hold there, she knows, is tenuous and challenged. Beneath the cheers that ring out around her, it seems she hears, subdued and distant, low French voices, surly and resentful, biding their time. She wonders about Charles down there in Rheims. Is his courage burned to ash with Joan's bones, or does she walk in his dreams now, urging him on? She draws up the weighted velvet of her gown, steps inside the enclosed interior of the carriage, takes a seat opposite her husband and crosses her long white hands.

'So, it is done, Cecily,' he says. 'At last.'

'By God's will,' she answers. Granting him a small smile she leans back against the cushions and closes her eyes. In the darkness behind their lids she calculates the value of all she has learned since coming into France; that the will of God, which has called all things into being, might turn a child into a king, a girl into a warrior or a body into ash. And that any man, or woman indeed, may, according to their courage or their power, shape it to their purpose.

Chapter Two

That night the royal company dine listlessly on roast goose. No one is hungry, though they've barely eaten all day. They'd all been too nervous to break their fast well that morning and the food at the coronation banquet, though impressive to look upon, had made poor eating. Pungent sauces masked fish dishes that were overcooked and cold when brought to table. Glistening pastries hid meats grey with fat. The French lords had complained among themselves, muttering under their breath about the incompetence of English cooks. All show and no substance, thought Cecily. It would not have happened at home. In her mother's household, the language of food spoke through the senses to the heart: see what we have, how we can sustain you. Don't you want to be one of us?

It had spoken to Richard, certainly. He had wanted very much to be one of them since, in his twelfth year, orphaned and adrift, he had been brought north through the foulest weather December can bring, into the warm brilliance of Raby's great hall at dinner. The royal courier, who had ridden graceless and hunched ahead of him for the two week journey, now pushed him forward, full of smiles. 'Your new ward, my Lord,' he said. 'I bring him and the season's greetings from the Lord Protector, the great Duke of Gloucester.' Richard raised his eyes, ready to be resentful. But then his vision was filled with the sight of Ralph, the Earl of Westmoreland, rising from the table and striding towards him, tall and smiling with his arms thrown wide. 'Ah, you're in now out of the cold, Richard. Get that wet cloak off you and come eat. Formalities later.'

It was the day he first saw Cecily. From the space hastily cleared for him by bustling servants, and with the sharp blade of his hunger blunted, he dared to raise his eyes from the hanap of warm cider that soothed his chilblained fingers. The Earl was talking, bright and fast down the table, to men who seemed hungrier for his attention than for the food before them. Nearer, a young girl, no more than nine, stared fixedly at him from beside the chair of a lady rich in silk who, with her hand lying soft on the Earl's sleeve, stared likewise, as if measuring him for clothes. The girl blinked her grey eyes, reached up to whisper behind her hand into the lady's ear, then returned to her staring. The lady smiled softly down on the girl's head then turned another smile, less loving, more knowing, on him. 'You are welcome, Richard. My daughter Cecily says so. Be at home.'

Richard came, in time, to idolise Cecily's father. Ralph Neville replaced the uncertainties of a childhood shadowed by treason with the reliable virtues of life in a well-governed household. Between his own father's execution and Ralph's acquisition of his wardship, Richard had spent eight precarious years between pillar and post, uncertain of his welcome or his future. Among Cecily's brothers and the other young men drawn together under Ralph's affinity, he had found a place within a finely ordered discipline, where loyalty and good endeavour brought a series of rewards he understood and knew how to value. The rules were simple. He found he could keep them.

He had learned early enough that he had been brought into Ralph's household by a business transaction, but as time fostered his understanding of it, he found he was content with its terms. By the mercy of King Henry V, who had brought the axe down on his father's traitorous neck, he retained rights of inheritance to the headless Earldom of Cambridge. Through his father's brother, who had died three months later fighting at Henry's side in France, the dukedom of York.

Ralph had bought Richard's wardship from the crown to tie that inheritance to his own family. Richard found himself married to Cecily, the youngest daughter of Ralph's house, within months of his arrival among them. He had stood beside the grey eyed girl in the castle's gilded chapel while the priest muttered and his bride, stiff in her finery, listened earnestly and, when asked, repeated the words put to her with certainty. 'That's done then, Richard,' said Ralph, leaning down to look him in the eye and laying a steadying hand on his shoulder. 'You're one of us now.' He had watched over Ralph's shoulder as his young bride was led away by her nurses. When she turned and smiled slowly at him from the doorway, he felt his heart settle.

Cecily has come to be no less content with the exchange than he.

Especially since, only two years after that day, Richard's maternal uncle had died childless, adding the rich earldom of March to the treasury that would unlock for them both when he reached his majority. From being the youngest daughter of the house, who might have expected to have to make do with slim pickings after husbands had been secured for her ten sisters, she found herself married to a man who looked set to become the richest noble in England. A man who, behind only today's boy king and his two royal uncles, would stand fourth in line to the thrones of England and France.

Each of those uncles, the dukes of Bedford and Gloucester, sit opposite her now, picking at the cooling carcass of the bird and passing the wine jug between them as they talk. Their wives, and Cecily's sister Anne, have their heads together at the far end of the table. Cecily doesn't know if they are planning a skirmish or comparing the skills of their dress makers, and doesn't much care. Like Richard, she is watching the two dukes, wondering what their next move will be and what it will mean for them. Ralph is already six years dead, but Cecily's mother, as she packed, preened and prepared her for this journey into France, schooled her to think ahead. 'We have given you a good husband, Cecily. It's up to you now, what you make of him.'

These are the opening chapters of a novel that deals with the life of Cecily Neville, the 15th century's most powerful dynastic matriarch. *The mother of both Edward IV and Richard III, Cecily is a royal power broker operating at the heart of English politics during one of the most tumultuous periods of England's history; the Wars of the Roses.*

Elephant Breath

Steve Gay

It's merciless, the tube at Oxford Circus. It steals your life one commute at a time, sucks you through its vessels, then blows you onto the streets with the discarded handbills. Blink and it's another day. The alarm goes, and you're throwing on your make up, hurrying down the tubes once more. In, out, in again. Over and over. Waiting for that day when it breathes you somewhere different.

'I'm scared!' he said. Not quietly. Bellowed it actually, the poor man. 'I'm scared!' Half way up the escalator this morning and we're packed as usual. He couldn't have looked more alone though, standing sideways, half crouching, gripping the rubber handrail with bloodless hands. I'm perched a step down, and behind me is Colin, lost in the advertising of course, powers of observation blunted to anything real.

I wasn't surprised that no one acknowledged the man. It's how people are on the tube, sealed, zoned, focused on getting where they're going. There's no room for distraction. Unless you're competing, pushing, elbowing, you're wasting your life. That's how it is for my husband too. 'The unforgiving minute, Jen,' he says, fingers held as pistols. 'Sixty-seconds of distance run.'

The escalator man, though. I put my hand on his arm, try to calm him, tell him to breathe slowly. Everything will be fine. We'll be at the top soon. He nods, but his jaw is shaking, and I know he can't hold it. His face has this feverish sheen and there's a drip, just quivering on the tip of his nose. He's dressed for business, but that isn't what the day has in store for him. I know what's coming, and there'll be no stopping it. Inside, his heart is banging away, lungs going at full tilt, mechanics are wrapping rags around groaning pipes, shouting to the bridge through tin funnels. And then he's off again, his panic hitting new heights. He reaches over the rail to slap at the metalwork between the escalators, stainless steel squealing under his palms. Then his hands stick fast, and he's dragged backwards, eyes wide and glassy. And down we all go.

Colin thinks you can prepare for such things, thinks I am complacent, that I tempt providence. He'll have advice on it no doubt, how I shouldn't have stood where I did, the precautions I might have taken. Flats, not heels, my cycle helmet perhaps, a baking tray under my coat. Sometimes shit just happens though, doesn't it. He won't accept that, and he won't accept there's a cost for not accepting it, that your body keeps tally, yearns to breathe slowly. 'Be a moving target,' he says, 'Who dares, wins.' Well, I can't deny it works in his corporate world, and I do share the benefits. He's advancing us, raising us up. I'm improving a little every day.

Anyway, we're stuck on the escalator, not hurt but piled on each other, head down going upwards. The man is still terrified. His shirt is clinging damp to his skin, and he's breathing compost and things gone off. Then he turns his face towards me, flesh drawn tight to his skull, and his mouth opens in a silent scream.

The escalator stops, and the stillness brings a change upon him. He's apologetic now, horrified, loathing himself in stabbing phrases. Beneath me, Colin is restive, as impatient as all the other tin soldiers. He can hear the drumbeat and time is wasting. 'Just get a grip!' he snaps, and a touch on my shoulder tells me who the comment is for. It's for both of us, the man for his frailty, and me for my quiet endurance.

That's what I do, you see – I endure. In a very British way, I like to think. But I should take on all-comers, apparently. I should rage against the system, the NHS mainly, so taxing on my dedication, but so sparing in its appreciation. As if that was the problem though, the obstacle to my happiness. For Colin, it's the principle. Keeping my mouth shut is meek acceptance. It disappoints him.

'You know what they say about the meek, don't you?' he says.

'That they shall inherit the Earth?' It's better to endure the punchline, than steal it.

'But not the mineral rights!' And then he looks at me, brow raised, expecting the sort of response the quip might have received on its first outing, half a century ago, at an oil barons' ball. In any case, I'm not meek, I'm resolute. My quietness is an act of discipline, a decision not to make things worse.

Toby thinks I'm a soft touch too, and I suppose I am as far as cats are concerned. This morning he was purring in my face when the light was hardly striping the blinds. Colin won't get up to feed him, and Toby knows Colin as well as he knows me. So down I go to the kitchen while action man dozes through a few extra batches of sixty seconds.

Colin's meeting with himself didn't go well this morning. That's what he calls his daily appointment with shampoo and water. The Stay-dri rainforest, Puddle-hops, some great advertising campaigns were developed in our shower. Meanwhile glaciers advance and retreat. I turned on the kitchen tap just to hear him shriek.

He comes down frustrated. 'Sorry hon!' I say. 'Forgot.' Bright and breezy.

'Again, Jen. Again!' In fairness, I have done it before, and it's rarely an accident.

'Making you a cup of tea.' I say, and nod towards the kettle. Then I turn my attention back to the square of colour I'm painting on the wall. I suppose you could call it colour.

Colin looks over my shoulder. 'Magnolia,' he observes. 'You've got to be kidding.'

'Beige of some sort,' I say. 'We've got five litres left over from the garage.'

'That's it? That's your reason?'

'It's a neutral tone,' I say, 'a blank canvas.' And then, 'It's waiting to be complemented, to be lifted.'

He looks at me askance. He doesn't know it, but the decision was made while he was in the shower. Who paints, wins.

'There's a Rainbow World out there,' he says. 'You need to get a life, Jen.' A bit harsh, but it's a throwaway. He's just warming up for a day at the sharp end.

'So, a new client then – a new campaign?' Colin's go-getting world will now be powered by emulsion. I can't help myself. I say 'You wouldn't know the colours on our walls if your life depended on it. Your job, even.'

He rubs at his chin for a moment. 'Well, I know the palette of the moment is grey,' he says. He pats at his pockets, suddenly afraid he's been separated from his phone. 'But you're on the right track.' He pauses, actually lowers his voice. 'We're pitching to develop RW's new range.'

'Of grey? A secret grey rainbow?' I resist glancing over my shoulder, but I'm whispering for some reason.

He sighs, looks at the ceiling.

'Are you developing the paint, or just the names?' I ask, keeping my face innocent while he searches it. I might have upset him.

'Paint is just paint. It's what it represents that matters.'

'Oh,' I say.

He wants more from me. For a moment, there's a trace of the old insecurity around his eyes, a faint imprint from the days when he valued my opinion, when he was lower on the ladder and holding tight. He won't ask me now. He can't. I reach for his hand, but he's turned for his cup of tea. 'Yes, it's what it *means*,' he says. 'Most people don't get that. Just met with myself about it. Had something on the tip of my tongue when the water went cold.'

'Sorry again. My mind was a bit beige there. Sort of choked with "Cairo Dust".'

He shakes his head. 'Like that would sell.' Still, I can see from his eyebrows that he's working with it.

I pull a face, looking for a smile. '"Camel Dung," then. What do you think?'

His mouth turns upwards, acknowledges the humour without any amusement. 'I think you should stick to your own job.' His fingers are tapping imaginary keys at the edge of the work surface. They're typing, 'Leave the creative stuff to me, Jen.'

'My own job?' I hold my brush up, let the paint drip into the pot. Then I'll call this shade "Operating Theatre".'

He sips his tea, regards it as if noticing its shade for the first time. 'Beige is timid,' he says. 'The whole point of it is to be inoffensive.' Perhaps he's right. Maybe that's all it has going for it, that it can exist unnoticed. It's a colour for camouflage.

I told Colin about the symposium: *New Horizons in Pulmonary Care*. I don't know, maybe it was just to see his reaction. I wasn't intending to go, not really. He was looking at his phone, so I told him again. 'It's in Bath,' I said. 'This weekend. I thought just for once…' He looked at me squarely, caught his lip between his teeth as he does when his mind changes direction. Like the time when he first saw me, at a bus stop on the Strand. Under the Christmas lights. In the pouring rain.

'Symposium,' he said. I thought he might ask to come with me, suggest mixing work with pleasure, dinner perhaps, soaking together in the spa waters. Then he repeated it, rolling the word around his mouth, and I realised he was just considering its colour.

'We've always meant to go to Bath,' I said.

He held my gaze for a moment, then his phone made a tone, stole him back. I waited, stirred the paint. 'Weren't you going to that thing a few months back?' he said. 'Then in the end you didn't.' I didn't have an answer, and he didn't wait for one. 'Don't worry,' he said, 'I'll be on the RW pitch this weekend.' He adjusted his collar, pinched the knot of his tie, a greyhound sensing the chase. 'You know what they say…'

I pressed the lid back onto the tin of paint and we said it together. 'If you snooze, you lose.'

*

The Underground staff had us quickly back on our feet, lifting and pulling as if they were disentangling garden chairs. I don't recall anyone saying much; perhaps they did, but all I could hear were the loudspeakers, apologising for any inconvenience caused. People were dusting their sleeves all around, inspecting themselves for scrapes and laddered tights. I didn't feel I could just leave the man. It wasn't a professional thing, I just felt I should escort him down, make sure he was alright. Colin looked at me hard, as if the workings of my mind were quite unfathomable. He tugged at his coat, buttoning it with a brisk finality that brought his participation in the incident to a close. While I was drawn into a vortex of sentiment, he would ascend to the lobby. So off he went with earnest steps, examining each advert along the way, reaching the summit without ropes or oxygen. And with a silver sweet wrapper stuck to his heel.

The man didn't thank me. Sometimes people do when you help them, sometimes they don't. I like to think they appreciate it later, but that's not why you do it. I found him a corner and he sat slumped there, suit jacket over his knees and a blood pressure cuff squeezing his arm. A paramedic tried to make conversation, but he just stared straight ahead, drained, monochrome, hands loose at his sides. Even his wedding ring failed to shine. I see this at the hospital all the time. It's familiar, but somehow down there it was different, down in that underground hall, with heels echoing all around, and in the background, drifting from a distant cavern, the faint drawl of a saxophone.

With the escalator running again, I left the man and went up to the lobby. Colin was waiting there, his ruthless minute invested in the posters around the station. I found him standing in front of one for Air India, framed by the exotic fauna of the sub-continent, feet apart and arms folded, like some big game hunter.

'Well, that was something,' I said. 'He was in a hell of a state. Poor man.'

'Elephant breath,' he replied, his face in work mode, and not an ounce of sympathy in his voice. I suppose they consider it an attribute in advertising, to be able to capture a person with a bare expression, a playground taunt. At the exit, he kissed me on the cheek and we went our separate ways. I turned at the junction with Regent Street, and stood looking back. I could still see Colin striding away, walking in the road to avoid the congestion on the pavement, the sweet wrapper flashing with each step. I texted him about it, thinking that I should, and I found my hands were shaking.

'Elephant Breath.' It wasn't until I got to work that I realised what he meant. But by then, it was too late. My meeting with myself had adjourned. There will be time enough to reflect on it at the Thermae Bath Spa. There, in the steam room, I'll let my lungs fill with liquid air, and flex my feet on the biscuit softness of Cotswold tiles.

'I'm scared,' I'll say. Quietly of course. And then, when I am asked why I am leaving him, I will simply tell them that I need to get a life. But it isn't like that really, it's the other way around. He left me. On an escalator at Oxford Circus. For a particular shade of grey.

Concrete and Roses

Steve Gay

Our house stood out from the others on our street. It wasn't because it looked unusual from the front, although the flowered arch over the gate was certainly pretty, but because my family had a reputation. It was my dad who made the little council house so well-known, notorious in fact, if you were one of those who had stood against his militancy at the engineering works, or were scandalised by his atheism. But to those who knocked at our door for the surgical boots he made in his shed, Dad was a saint. Whether he would have appreciated the term, or not.

My dad could do anything. His enthusiasm for concrete brought children from all over, marvelling at the creations in our back garden, hauling themselves onto the back of the ornamental elephant, their laughter flying over hedges when a hose up its bum sent a rainbow arc spraying from its trunk. He even set my leg once when I broke it sliding on the ice. I just sat up on the kitchen table, and he did it. I can't remember if it hurt, just that I never doubted that he would fix it. Because he said that he would. He was like that; few people questioned him, and those who did invariably lost to the force of his will, and the strength of his argument.

Of all of us, I was Dad's favourite. Actually, I don't know that, I just felt it, or assumed it on account of the year of my birth. His favourite number: prime, sum of consecutive squares and, of course, the atomic number of copper, that most wondrous of elements for an electrical engineer. Somehow twenty-nine was all around me, wrapping my childhood in mathematical significance. It was the number of paving stones down to the gate, and having counted them, I would sit under the rose arch waiting for the coalman to come up the street, stopping it seemed, every twenty-ninth step of his old mare. And when it unburdened itself of its precious manure, I collected it for the flower beds, before the neighbours seized the opportunity.

I took the number with me over the street to the recreation ground. Once the war started and the rec lost its iron railings to the factories, the green expanse was thought a prime site for a glider invasion. So, the Home Guard came with spades, and up went a battalion of defensive posts. The men had hardly left, before I was out there with my cricket bat and a piece of chalk. I didn't really need to count as I paced between the posts, and perhaps I altered my stride to make the number right. But I announced a different one to the lads – the exact length of a wicket. And I marked the stumps on the wooden posts with my chalk.

It wasn't long before Mr. Peabody showed up, striding chest out from his hut by the pavilion to tell me off for being there on a Sunday. Some of the boys ran off to their Christian homes. The others took a step behind me, relieved that the brunt would be taken by the heathen they mocked on school days.

I knew what was coming, but with right on my side, and my dad's instruction, I wasn't going to flinch. Mr Peabody knew it too, and that only raised his temperature as he approached. By the time he was standing in front of me, his face was properly red. He needed two deep breaths before he could speak, though in the meantime his arms did the talking for him. 'Off you go!' was the gist of it.

'Now then, Master Brown,' he said eventually. 'Do I have to say this again? Haven't I told you the recreation ground is closed on a Sunday?'

'Doesn't look closed to me,' I said. 'Gates aren't locked.'

He stepped closer, arms clasped behind his back, leaning toward me as if he was inspecting an insect. 'Do not test me, Brown,' he said, stressing his consonants almost to breaking point. 'The gates are not locked, because there are no longer any gates. If there were gates they would be locked, but there aren't, so they ain't.' He stood tall again.

'Why is it closed on a Sunday?' I said.

'You know that very well, Brown. It's because today is a day of rest for decent folk, the day that the Lord Almighty rested as an example to us all. After he had created heaven and Earth and everything else.'

'Is it closed for Jews?'

'You are not a Jew, are you Brown? So, don't play Einstein with me.'

'Einstein's a Jew. My dad says so.'

'Your dad,' said Mr. Peabody, and sighed.

'My dad says I can come here to play on a Sunday.'

'Well, you can tell your dad...'

'Says you should tell him yourself. He'll be happy for you to call on him.'

'Again.' said Mr Peabody. He smoothed his moustache, tucked an imaginary baton into his armpit and strode off towards our house, where Dad was pruning the roses. His arm was swinging up almost horizontal with each stride.

'He'll have someone's eye out like that,' I said, 'That's what my dad says.'

We watched the two of them discussing the matter over the garden gate. Somehow the exchange seemed more amiable than it had been with me, but that was the effect Dad had with people. Eventually he put his hand on Mr. Peabody's arm, who then turned and walked off up the street. Dad stood with his hands on his hips and watched him go, then looked over at us and waved.

'We've got ten more minutes, lads.' I said.

'How many times has he had that argument with your dad?' one of them said, making the crease with his bat.

'Twenty-nine,' I said.

'Concrete and Roses' is the first scene of a completed historical novella, 'The Birds that Do Not Sing.'

That day changed everything for Jim. Coventry burned on the horizon, neighbours were missing, and faces were grim all around. It was a day when childhood turned to adolescence, when family and establishment collided, principles were challenged, and sides taken. A day of choices, and their devastating consequences.

Unsinkable

Katie Margaret Hall

The letter arrived on an otherwise unremarkable day. The letter sat waiting for me there on our doormat, waiting for me to come home and find it. A single sheet of paper that contained words with enough power to shatter my life into pieces.

That day had been filled with more meetings than emails and a rush of productivity – a rarity for me following an uncertain few months of chronic pain that seemed never to just go the fuck away. Fifteen years of keyhole surgeries, stop-starting the pain, creating more pain and problems, leaving me wanting to stay far away from anything that involved my sexual self.

The plain white D5 envelope caught my attention, with 'first class' red-ink-pressed in the top right corner, innocently placed next to the faded blue stamp of University Hospital Lewisham. My stomach dropped as though free falling on a funfair ride, adrenalin-surfing feelings of curiosity mixed with a little fear. Hospitals never send letters first class, unless... I shook the doubts forming in my mind and with cautious care, stuck my finger in the tiny gap between fold and body and tore at the paper, a tortuous sensation of rugged paper caressing my skin.

Slowly unfolding the page, I procrastinated to prolong the blissful ignorance I was sure would be coming to an end. The letter informed me an appointment had been scheduled with the gynaecology oncology team at the hospital for the following Monday, just five days away. I already had a surgery follow up appointment booked, I thought, so what did this appointment mean?

My brain rushed to panic state, as is often the case with my anxiety-challenged mind. My experience told me they only handed out appointments like this when it's serious, when they need to tell you something quickly. I didn't recognise the name attached to the appointment, it wasn't my usual trusted consultant. I put the piece of paper down and tried to stop catastrophising, halting the thoughts sprinting through my neural pathways before they settled in some worry centre that had been languishing while I had been returning my life to normal.

'This must be a mistake,' my rational mind tried to reason, 'you know how many the hospital administration have made this year, there will be an explanation. Nothing to worry about.' I stepped away from the letter after dropping it on the hallway table and decided to carry on as usual.

This turned out to be harder than I naively expected. As I sat down the silent sheet of paper shouted at me, demanding to be read again. I buried it under a sofa cushion to stifle the noise. I exhaled long, jagged breaths to stop any sobs excavating their way out. I turned the TV volume to extra loud, ate my dinner and waited for my sister to get home from work.

She sensed that something was wrong as soon as she walked through the door. I oscillated between desperately wanting to tell her about the letter, and wanting to protect her from its implications. We had lost our grandmother to leukaemia just four months previously and we were still in the early stages of the grief cycle.

She looked at me, questions filling her eyes. I lifted up the sofa cushion slowly and passed her the tell-tale document. I waited as she furrowed her brow to a frown the way she always does when she reads. Her pragmatic approach took over before we even talked about things, there she was on her phone tapping away at the screen. She had googled the doctor named in the letter, having also recognised he was new to us.

'He's listed as the gynaecology oncologist for the hospital, the only one.' She said.

Thoughts I had been trying to suppress began to race wildly and chaotically around my mind; so many questions formed and unfurled.

'It's the biopsy result from the polyp removal. It must be.' I said, mostly to break the despairing silence. My sister took my hand, and asked me what I wanted to do, how I needed to be comforted, reminded me we didn't know anything for certain yet. I was lost, I had no idea what to do in this situation. My anxiety on the other hand, knew exactly what to do, and took full advantage of the opportunity to run riot.

As I lay in bed that night, I started to fantasise about what I would do if I only had a short time left to live. How I would give up work and travel the world and do all the things I always said I wanted to. I began to plan my funeral, choose songs that I would want dozens of mourners sobbing through in the remembrance of my life cut short. In the days that followed I wrote lists of people who would need to know, and prioritised them in order of who would need to be told first. I had spent my working life creating communication strategies, never imagining one day I'd be writing one for my own news. I exhausted myself every night until I fell asleep and dreamt about trying to run away, running but always getting lost and having to come back to the start. My sister tried to remind me of all the other things it might not be.

Half an hour before the appointment, walking to the bus stop on my way to the hospital, a nurse rang. She introduced herself and said without a breath, 'did you get the letter for the appointment, are you coming and are you bringing someone with you?' If I wasn't already anxious enough, my mind started to spin, the call confirming everything I was hoping might not be true.

My sister joined me in the cold, grey waiting room at the end of the Women's Health corridor. We sat in uncomfortable chairs that struggled to stay level on the squeaky floor. I read posters about smear tests and domestic violence to stay distracted. Twenty minutes after the appointment time, I was called into a room by a nurse in dark blue scrubs. We sat in a tiny space, not big enough for four adults and the elephant in the room. There was no air to breathe. The middle aged male consultant, dressed like every other consultant I'd ever met – open collar shirt and suit trousers and a suit jacket hung lopsidedly on the back of his swivel chair and grey, grey, grey – swung awkwardly back and forth between us and the notes in my yellow-pages-sized medical file.

'Can we do an examination?' he asked. I nodded. 'Just go behind the curtain and undress fully from the waist down. You can keep your socks and shoes on. Lie on the exam table when you're ready.' I de-robed, shedding my clothes and dignity behind the paper curtain and lay knees apart on the cold bed. He came through and slapped on a beige latex glove. I tried not to tense as I knew from experience that would make the ordeal hurt a lot more.

'Just relax, yes?' he said. Easier said than done when a stranger is foraging around inside you. The pain was immediate and sharp, it drew my breath inward. He didn't continue for long. I got dressed, pulled back the curtain and sat back down with everyone.

He spoke the diagnosis without introducing himself and without ever saying the word 'cancer' preferring medical jargon euphemisms: 'Abnormal cells were found. You know what this means, yes?'. I'd figured that bit out thanks. How many though, and what are we going to do about them was what I needed to know, but I couldn't speak the words.

'It is likely we have caught it early,' he said, trying to reassure me, 'that's normally the case for women your age. This means you will have surgery to remove everything, your womb, your remaining ovary, your tubes and your cervix. That should get rid of the abnormal cells and all the pain you've been having. You've been having pain, yes? First, we do scans to get a picture of whether the cells have escaped outside the womb through your lymph nodes. Were you planning on having a family?'

The information, delivered with well-trained doses of empathy balanced with pragmatism, was thrown at me so quickly there was no chance to digest it all. But, unless the doctor is saying 'you do not have cancer', the words just bounce off the walls, useless and rejected. My sister sat unusually quietly, scribbling it all down in her notebook, coping the only way she knows how. The nurse, who was probably the one who phoned me earlier, sat with her head tilted, watching me. She reached out to stroke my hand when the consultant finished speaking. I felt saturated with pity, and invaded by the impersonal tones and tenses of the consultant's delivery.

Barely ten minutes after I'd entered the room a Macmillan handbook for womb cancer was handed over, and the nurse suggested I read the whole thing carefully as it contained all the things my new 'team' did not have the time to explain during the target-driven appointment lengths. The handbook was retracted then returned to me in a brown envelope. For the sake of the other patients, I thought. Then, without ceremony, I was shooed out.

We sat in silence upstairs on the bus home. I wondered what the upcoming scans would show, visualising fluorescent cells lurking in little pockets throughout my entire body. I felt connected to yet consumed by the body that should be protecting me. We attempted to delay the shock by following the carefully drawn up communications plan; there were so many people to call. For a second I wished that I didn't have such a large extended family. Telling people over and over became a masterclass in learning how to manage other people's reactions to the news as they filled every hollow of my body that hadn't already been occupied.

That night, with sleep just out of reach, I started to draw up my game plan. I'd have to dig in, find the strength to get through this. Questions about what I was really made of hung in the air, threatening to choke me. But from somewhere inside, somewhere previously unknown to me, I felt a power kick in, a fighting instinct I'd never had to draw on before, reinforced by the humbling display of love and support from the people in my life.

Step one was figuring out how to get through the day. I worked hard, using days of solving problems for other people as a distraction from my own insoluble problems. Then came the appointments, desperately trying to fit themselves into each two-week window of the cancer treatment pathway, competing with each other and royal mail. The hospital appointments administration team, a mysterious group of people responsible for making all the important things happen, booked my first two big scans for exactly the same time. Several phone calls assured me that radiology would be able to figure it out on the day. I drank a litre of barium solution, intent on following all the orders to the letter.

On arrival for the appointments it was quickly clear that the receptionist could not handle the clashing appointments nor the idea that I needed to be in two places at once. My sister was allowed to sub for me at the check-in stage. With the barium sitting uncomfortably in my stomach, I was keen to get the appointments started as soon as possible.

I sat in the waiting room next to a bald woman nearly twice my age who was waiting for a scan which would tell the doctors if the third type of chemotherapy she was undergoing – the type that gave her hair loss and weight loss but not optimism loss – was working to a measurable effect. Despite her situation, all she wanted to say was that I was too young to be there. I sipped on the second litre of barium and thought about what my scans might reveal. I wondered when I would be back to measure my progress.

After an hour of lying alone, near naked and stock still in one mechanical tunnel then another, full of large quantities dye, my newly acquired tower of strength began to crack. Out of coping strategies when it was just my mind and body and silence and nothing to hide behind, I wondered why I was the one lying there. The questions I had been suppressing suddenly rose up to the surface. 'Is this happening to me because of...? What about the long list of things I regret in life? And what about the list of things I haven't done, or important things not yet said to people? Have I left it too late?' They whirled around my mind, with nothing to shield me from them, not even the magnetic field, as I passed in and out of an industrial machine on a mechanical table. The questions refused to leave, eating at the rationality that had been balancing my heavy weight of doubt. Now they started to multiply like the abnormal cells vomiting inside my womb.

*

At work the next day, in an important meeting about income targets and budgets, the weight of the situation hit me, and I started to slur my speech. Words I wanted to say wouldn't come out in their normal way, and I did not have the energy to help them. My cheeks flushing, I excused myself, and with seven sets of eyes staring at me, left to hide in the toilet stalls. When this happened the next day, and the day after again, I begrudgingly decided to reduce my working hours. Despite being desperate to maintain my normal life, I couldn't bear the look of pity on people's faces. On the outside, of course, I maintained the smiles. The phrase 'best case scenario' adjoined almost every conversation I had while I waited for my scan results.

Ten days that felt like ten years later, it was D-Day. It had been explained that 'the staging and treatment process goes like this: you will have two appointments booked, one for Wednesday and one for Thursday – depending on how bad the results and therefore where you will be treated, as decided by the cancer review board. Wednesday means surgery and chemo, Thursday means surgery only. If you get a call on Wednesday morning it is good news and the less serious outcome. If you don't get a call you head off to the Wednesday appointment fearing the worst. Got it?'

A painfully slow morning with my sister and father, who invited himself along for moral support, trying their best to entertain me until finally my phone rang. My stress-filled body sat stuck in shock at the positive outcome. That the cancer had been caught early enough failed to penetrate my tightly wound muscles and bones, the news washing off as though it didn't even matter. Somehow, I caught the nurse's words just before they hit the floor and conveyed them to my sister and Dad. They cried for me.

The scuffed magnolia walls of hospital waiting rooms became a double-edged sword, offering me protection against my enemy invasion, but at the same time sucking the humanity from my soul. I've never understood why these rooms are some of the most depressing places on earth, surely that can't be good for wellbeing? 'If I never see the inside of a hospital again it will be too soon,' I thought, sitting on a cold, hard, chipped-grey metal seat, reading posters about smear tests and domestic violence refuges yet again.

This scan results appointment was even shorter than the initial 'abnormal cells' appointment. Another new consultant, even-voiced and pragmatic, told me that the scans were favourable and I should expect to be treated by surgery only, that I am lucky. I won't die of cancer but I will never be able to have children. A reasonable price to pay, when those are the only options on the table and it's not a hypothetical parlour game. Didn't I used to say 'I don't want to have children, my biological clock is not enslaving me'? I'm sure I did, when I had a choice.

Instead, I could look forward to preparing my body for major surgery, with lifelong side effects I can't do anything to treat, no hormone replacement therapy because the hormone is what causes the mutation and 'abnormality', followed by a six-week recovery period, all going to plan. The waiting list gods gave me two weeks, time to plan a handover and tie up loose ends at work – 'just like going on maternity leave, yeah?'

Two weeks became five became three as my consultant and the hospital administration danced a tango; together, apart. I waved the red flag between their moves to remind them I was there, a person, underneath all their bureaucracy, and then it all dissolved to nothing when the date finally arrived, seven weeks after an innocent-looking envelope changed everything.

*

On the day of the surgery, I was given an appointment for mandatory talk therapy with a dedicated psychotherapist trained to talk to cancer patients. I turned up thinking it might be an interesting way of killing an hour until my roll call for the surgery conveyor belt. What I didn't expect was to be offered a space to say everything I hadn't been able to say anywhere else. On peeling back the protective layers I'd been using to hold myself together, we revealed that what I termed as 'dealing with' or 'processing' was perhaps a bottling up of feelings about things that had been pissing me off. We sat facing each other, the therapist and I, and from the moment he said 'How are you?' everything I'd been pushing down took its moment to escape and be felt. The release felt good and reassured me that it would feel good when the surgeon would do the same to my mutated cells.

I told the therapist about the pressure I felt having been ill for most of my adult life, with a seemingly never-ending buffet of gynaecological wonders caused by the fact I naturally over-produce oestrogen. I gave into the ill health for a long time, I told him, passively taking whatever came next, adjusting to the chronic pain and lethargy, the multiple surgeries, the short respites between reoccurrences. I reflected that this time it felt different, there was a sea-change I hadn't expected. I started to change my perspectives on many things, given a new lens to view the world, powered by what my instinct told me I needed to do to survive and beat this deadly disease. Issues that until recently I had allowed to become murky and cloudy I was now seeing with great clarity. I started to feel power in making choices and decisions about my life and the strength to do so without the interference of opinions that did not have my best interest at heart.

I was drawing on the loving support offered to me, and I felt lifted by it; the reactions that drained me I could discard with a new-found assertiveness. There were people that wanted to make my illness their problem, to take the social freedom a status like having cancer offered. It was the first time in my life I had a single, clear vision and purpose, and as my therapist reassured me, I was not being selfish because tough decisions suddenly became much easier. As I talked I realised how appealing this strategy is, a trustworthy system separating the wheat from the chaff, liberating me and teaching me what I wanted my post-cancer life to be.

I left the cosy arm-chaired therapy room a little lighter on my feet and ready to face the next step towards my post-cancer life. The surgery ward was in the newer part of the hospital, where the walls were less scuffed and instead adorned with colourful paintings to break up the magnolia atmosphere. It was time to take the surgery and recovery seriously, so I listened quietly and patiently to everything the nurses, doctors, anaesthetists had to say as each in turn promised they knew what was best for me. I'd been there many times before, in the cotton gown that doesn't quite close at the back, but this time was different, bigger than all the previous times put together.

I didn't even reach seven on my count back from ten, and then I woke up and it was over. I'd been treated and most likely cured. An indelible mark was left even though it's not in the form of mutated cells, but locked away in scars on my belly that will never fully heal.

Lying in the hospital bed, new questions formed – the kind that health care professionals don't talk about, the embarrassing questions left to self-help support groups and online communities. As my focus shifted from survival to recovery, I scoured the Macmillan messageboard to see how other women had dealt with the changes. I found women willing, comfortable to share their experiences of how they found the changes in their bodies, how they had to rediscover intimacy with their sexual self, following the permanent alterations made by the miracle of the laparoscope and stitches. The freedom from no more monthly, intra-monthly tenderness, pain nor blood that accompanies the loss of being able to bear a child. I liked how none of them felt less of a woman despite losing some of their fundamental female biology. Their words comforted me as they told their stories of how their bodies accommodated the changes thrust upon them and how they grieved for the loss of what gave birth to their pain.

During my short diagnosis to treatment to recovery period, two people I knew died of cancer. One was given a terminal diagnosis a year or so before, and treated right up to the last few days of her life before she was told there was nothing more that could be done, the tumours had advanced too far. Less than a week later she was gone, leaving behind a husband and two daughters. Another was diagnosed after I received my news, with the prognosis of a few measly months; terminal. Within a week this had been recalculated and she was gone before she really had the chance to process her situation. I don't take for granted that I am one of the lucky ones. I get to live out the rest of my life and do all the things I don't want to regret not doing...a survivor, surviving, unsinkable.

Poetry

E. A. Jane

Christopher

I once met a man
Who had been struck by
Lightning—
And I think I understand
The flash of light
Across frightened eyes
The marks upon his skin
And with nervous patience
We wait for the
            Thunder.

January 18th

Bitter cold and blue
The sky this day is empty
Waiting to be full
Blank canvas of spilled, wet ink
Begin my day, end my night

Nice Boys

And he poured blood on my white hands to forecast the near end of me.

And I did not lie quietly, I spoke and pleaded reasonably.

And he looked down and glanced at me, like that loose latchkey

And I walked to the door, we hugged, I walked back carelessly.

And he will not remember me.

Ritual

Circle daubs on a double bed sheet
We talk over topics I would often glance
Finding me where the folded edges meet

Out in the street, we laugh and play sweet
Pianist tunes in remembrance
Of those circle daubs on my double bed sheet

We were children with hidden blistered feet
Marching to tunes not yet romanced
Finding ourselves where the folded edges meet

We kept our hands clasped and our hair neat
I think I fell in love with your ceaseless trance
Between orange circles on this double bed sheet

Your understanding was an unrelenting treat
And your words meant never to enhance
The story we cultivated in the springtime heat

So, come back to me, take your seat
Exhumed in sombre circumstance
With circle daubs across a double bed sheet
Sinking into creases where the folded edges meet

Door Number 12

I find relics in those past lives
And will never know what compelled
Me to forgo those empty embraces
Lipstick marks, black hair, golf clubs still
Lingering in my head's periphery
While my eyes can focus on nothing
And my hands pass over that memory
One endless hour of bruising and bluffing.
Still. The sky is greyer than charcoal
It rains because it wishes to
And your key lost its omnipotence
I wait to be half of that whole
Technicolour of gold and green and blue
Safe, knowing I am loved in your absence

Wordsmith

I am a dictionary
A thesaurus
An etymological illusion
With pages mixed
(Falling from the spine)
Out of all sense
A swell of words
(Seeing no vision)
With no direction

No inspiration
I was a dictionary
Once

Mojave

"Watch out for tortoises"
Scrawled across the arid hills
And distant mountains
And displaced dunes

All life looks like stone here
The sand is thick and heavy
Holding firm at the back of my throat
And clasped upon my feet

I saw no tortoise
Perhaps that is why we must watch?
Stone can turn to anything here
As quickly as sun turns to night

Tecopa

Face back in a flatbed truck. Sun painted legs
Wedged against the side. Hair in eyes, in mouth
Yet sight greater than clarity. Kick the dirt from well-walked boots
And scuff the heels. From dirt to sky
To salt down below. Wire sprouting limbs
Pressing out from the earth. Dried crisp by the melting sun
Grazing past fingertips. Thick with dust and sweat
Keeping them alive. And moving

Vital

How can I say goodbye?
A meagre fable in comparison to you birth, your existence
I spent the night wandering the streets. My mind—
Racing.
Should I have known you better?
Life will happen as swiftly as it is taken
Tears do no justice to injustice, as my heart
Beats.

A letter to my Mother which I never sent

These sheets of paper
Will never change
Just how beautiful you looked
On your wedding day

And if you ever think
That paper can dictate
Your life, your love
Then you are misguided
And I am misinformed
You are my heart
My spirit, my reason, my mind
And you need not him
Nor any other
But your own Blood
To hold you in safety

Just remember the day
That your son told you
Never to worry
Because soon he would return

And take away the sadness
When all you could have wanted
Was for him to know
That his home was no longer warm
And you could not promise comfort

And when he left
And the key sat turned in the door
So that he could not return
Know that I was that key
And your son was that door
Keeping you safe
And keeping you warm
Shutting out the shadows
So that you could see again

Greek Gods

We were Greek gods
Before being divine was something
Worth being
All capable
  /knowing
  /powerful
All things she has never felt
For some great time
And from some great—
Distance
The gold in her hair is faded and Bronze
And the leaves of her victory are withered and
Gone.
We were Greek gods
The goddess thought
From her crop above the world

Watching
        Watching
And we were never strong enough

Bleached Earth

E. A. Jane

The night fell swiftly and heavily west of Shoshone, a heavy veil of blood orange staining the jagged horizon. Clare had come to know this place well. It takes mere days to understand the pattern of this land, and after weeks she had come to enjoy witnessing the gentle cadence of the evening light. However it was not the sort of display to which one could easily become accustomed. Her auburn hair had been bleached at its tips from overexposure to the sun. Her skin was flaking across her shoulders and her nose was ripe-red after another day amongst the hills. She reclined in the water as the last line of light finally brushed past the summit of the distant painted mountains.

James had told her about these hot springs just outside of Tecopa. Her bedraggled host had driven her out here two weeks previously. His dog, Scout, had taken the front seat of the rusted Chevy pick-up and James simply shrugged. 'It's Scout's seat.' He climbed onto the threadbare driver's seat and turned the key, which was all but welded into the ignition. Clare looked the vehicle up and down; even the rust had rusted. There was no front bumper, the paint was chipped off and the suspension had been lifted almost comically in some backyard garage, so the truck could take some off-roading.

Clare walked around to the rear, planted her foot behind the closed tailgate and swung herself up into the bed. It was carpeted with ropes and tarpaulins in shades of blue and black among which she settled herself. She knocked the window into the cab and gave a thumbs-up. Scout looked around lazily and James nodded into the rear-view mirror. The truck jolted forward, stalling instantly. James hit the wheel with one palm and Scout barked enthusiastically. The truck kicked back into life and the truck roared once again. Clare pushed her legs into the side of the bed, wedging herself in place as they began to rumble across the yard. James' raised shack of a house glowed magnificent in the sunset hues of red and ochre as they picked up speed and met the dirt road.

It had been a steady twenty-minute ride down from Shoshone to Tecopa. They turned from the main stretch of road onto the Old Spanish Trail. Clare looked back down the road, through the cloud of dirt kicked up by the wheels. The dry earth was a sheet of rock and small bushels of foliage. Up ahead on the horizon came a sign for China Date Farm. Some trailers and wooden raised houses began to appear through the dust-haze. They followed the road around a natural curve in the landscape and down a slight incline. James pulled up next to an old wooden gate. Behind the gate and a triangular sign that proclaimed 'Flash Floods' there was a vast bank of dried-out mud. It wasn't as harsh as the usual earth, instead it was darker and stained through with moisture. At the foot of the bank there were large curtains of wild rushes skirted in a wide half-moon meander.

'Meet you back here when the sun has gone down,' said James. He began to ascend the bank, followed by Scout, until he disappeared from view. Clare raised a hand to her forehead and gazed at the height of the sun. She calculated she had about half an hour, and set off steadily along the base of the bank, her beaten walking boots slipping into the mud. A thin ribbon of dark water arose from between the rushes and grew wider as she continued away from the truck. Soon there was a trodden-down landing, which acted as a natural access point into the water. Clare took one sweeping look around before kicking off her boots and removing her sweat-stained clothes. She squatted and dipped one foot into the water, noticing the soft current that fuelled it. It was hot, like a freshly-drawn bath or a mug of slowly steeped tea. She slipped from the bank into the soft mud below the shallow stream. Lifting handfuls of mud out of the surface, she took the grey sludge tentatively to her shoulders and worked it in until the flaking skin had calmed and disappeared.

She had returned to the stream alone almost every night since, riding the short distance in an old Jeep that James had lent her in place of her fragile rental car. On occasion she found herself drawn to other, smaller springs and outlets that were hidden off the main tracks. Now though, two weeks after James had taken her out there on the back of his truck, she had walked further towards the source of the stream. Eventually she settled in the hotter water and watched. Every day followed the same ritual of cleansing her bare skin and watching as the night drew in. She was just like any other fixture in the water, silently guarding the mountains until the stars came back to pepper the sky.

This is the beginning of Bleached Earth, a novella which follows the experience of an artist named Clare as she spends time in Death Valley. *On her exploration, she comes across a strange, uncharted commune of individuals who show her the vitality behind a place that she saw as so inhospitable. Together, they await the flash floods.*

Don't Thank Me Yet

Ellen Lavelle

A while back, I was stabbed in the chest by a man called Robert Gower and it looked as though I was going to die. I was unconscious for a couple of days and so I missed most of the action. I had to rely on my grandmother and Greg, my boyfriend at the time, to tell me exactly what happened. My journalistic skills were invaluable. Once I was conscious again and able to speak, I asked them both to recount the events as they remembered them. This process brought two things to my attention. First, that I was extremely lucky to be alive. If there had been a different surgeon on duty, if the ambulance arrived a few minutes later; apparently, it didn't bear thinking about. The second revelation: Greg had been having an affair with a girl called Rebecca Marris, with whom he shared a desk at work.

It all came out because he was at her apartment when he got the call from the hospital, saying I was in the ICU and that I probably wouldn't make it through the night. I remember him sitting in the chair next to my bed, his face tear-streaked, dark shadows smeared under his eyes, miserable with guilt. A part of me was impressed; I had never thought he had it in him. Greg and I had met at the first paper I worked on. He was only able to talk to me after weeks of emailing me repeatedly to ask if I would lend him office equipment: paperclips, staplers, he had borrowed them all.. The idea that he had successfully seduced another woman was stunning, let alone the fact that he had managed to sustain and conceal this affair over a prolonged period of time.

I stared at him through a fog of painkillers from my bed in the ward. In my lap lay a sweaty cheese sandwich provided by the hospital; it curled up at the edges, growing staler by the second. Greg's lower lip trembled and the hand holding a plastic cup of coffee shook with guilt and exhaustion.

'You've barely been around lately,' he said. 'I just feel like we don't know each other anymore.'

I had to acknowledge the truth in this. Over the last few months, I had spent more time with a private detective named Tristan Allen than I had with Greg. Allen was an ex-convict in his fifties. He'd been inside with my uncle Terry; we met at Terry's welcome home party. Beer in hand, speech slurring, Terry had slapped Allen repeatedly on his chest as he relayed to me a condensed history of all the times Allen had saved his skin.

Allen and I had been watching my attacker, Robert Gower, for a while. A fifteen-year-old girl called Danielle McEllroy had gone missing, last seen walking home from school. The police were closing in on her Maths teacher, who had been meeting her after class, supposedly to go over past exam papers. The police thought they had their guy, but Allen, whose sources were best left anonymous, knew better. Gower owned a chip shop and worked as a Fence for local gangs. One of Allen's acquaintances had heard something – not the whole story, but enough to make him pass on what he knew. For the best part of a month, we'd been watching Gower from the comfort of Allen's battered sedan, sharing packets of minstrels, listening to late-night radio. All this had come to a dramatic climax when I'd seen Gower, a single man in his forties, buying tampons from the minimarket next door. Allen broke into the flat above the chippy that night while Gower was down the pub. I watched from the car outside.

When it was all over, Allen told me he found Danielle in the back room, trying to sleep sitting up because her wrists were tied to the radiator. I didn't witness the rescue, the relief, the thankful tears. I only saw her later, screaming while I bled onto the linoleum. Gower had forgotten his phone and came back to the flat to get it. Without thinking, I followed him inside, unarmed, untrained, without a plan. Later, Allen outlined all the ways in which this was stupid. Early in our stakeout sessions, we had agreed that I would leave all the potentially dangerous activity to him. I had ignored this agreement – I would never make it in the army. Allen had been on tours in the Falklands and Iraq before he'd been inside and told me from the plastic chair next to my hospital bed that I would make a crap soldier. I followed Gower into the flat, disobeying a direct order, and, when he reached the door to the living room where Danielle was tied up, I tackled him from behind. In the ensuing struggle, Gower stabbed me with a kitchen knife that had been lying on the counter. Allen, having heard the ruckus, threw Gower to the floor and pinned his arms behind his back but it was too late. As I faded into unconsciousness, pain ripping through my chest, I saw the packet of tampons lying open on the floor by the radiator.

And so, I couldn't contradict Greg; over the last few months, I hadn't been a particularly present girlfriend. As a result, he had found Rebecca. I often found myself wondering what they were doing when he got the call from the hospital. For some reason, I got a kick out of imagining Greg tied up on the bed, trussed up in leather, jolted out of lustful mania by the sound of his jaunty iPhone ringtone. As they hooked me up to IVs, stitched me up, sorted me out, I thought about that a lot.

'I never liked him,' my grandmother said, tapping her yellow fingernails against the metal bars at the end of my bed. The non-smoking rule was non-negotiable and she found this difficult. When I began to get stronger, she would often suggest we get a 'breath of fresh air' as, after all, no one could possibly deny the good it would do me. She would roll my wheelchair over the hospital threshold and, the moment we were clear of the automatic doors, she let go of the handles, leaving me to roll a few inches while she lit up a Marlboro. I was probably well within my rights to object to this but, as the smoke wafted over me, it took me back to my childhood in my grandmother's pub: peeling the plastic covers off coasters, laminated menus sticky with beer and gravy.

'I never liked him,' she said. 'He was always full of it.' Greg was from the South; something else my grandmother found difficult.

There was no point pretending Greg and I stood a chance. Once discharged from the hospital, I went to recover at my grandmother's in Yorkshire while Greg packed away the things I had left in the flat we shared in London and mailed them North.

I stayed at my grandmother's flat for eighteen months, alternating between watching daytime television while stretched out on the sofa and watching daytime television stretched out on the bed in the spare room. My grandmother lived in a flat above her pub. I had grown up there and I now realised that the space that had seemed perfectly adequate before had probably only seemed so because I was used to it. With the cardboard boxes full of my belongings stacked around me, labelled in Greg's handwriting, I felt as though the walls were closing in. Once the screaming agony in my chest had become a constant dull ache, uncomfortable but possible to endure with medication, I began to plan my escape.

It came in the form of an old friend from university. While I had been spying on the owners of chip shops, Camilla had been taking over the world. In class, she had always been bossy and controlling. She'd earned herself the nickname 'Hitler' after one particular group assignment in which she made another classmate cry. Her focus had paid off, however. Now, she ran her own online platform, commissioning freelance journalists to cover articles. She'd won awards – I'd seen the pictures on Facebook: Camilla, squeezed into evening gowns, her makeup dewy in the spotlight as she held various oddly-shaped trophies. She was the big deal everyone had expected her to become.

She sent a get-well soon card to the pub. On the front, it had a picture of cracked egg with a bandage on its head. 'Heard you had an egg-cident!' the caption read. I had no idea what Camilla intended to communicate with her selection of card but I appreciated the gesture all the same. She'd filled the inside of the card with her large, rounded handwriting, expressing how sorry she was to hear about my injury and asked if there was anything she could do to help. When I was fully mobile, I sent her an email. My chest ached but I was able to deal with the pain. My psychologist was proud of my progress. My gran no longer allowed me to abstain from washing-up duty. I was on the ascent.

I arranged to meet Camilla in London. November hung heavy in the air, making the sky dark and the streets gloomy. By that time, I'd been in the city a month already; I was staying in a hostel while I tried to find an affordable flat. That morning, I had to take a Swedish girl's phone charger out of the wall socket in order to plug in my hair straighteners. I even took extra care while applying my makeup but had to rely solely on the flickering bathroom light and a pocket mirror. I made sure to plug the girl's charger back in afterwards.

It was lunchtime. I marched into the restaurant, medicated and faint with hunger but happy to be there. The windows were rain-streaked, the décor minimalist. The smell of garlic and fresh tomatoes made my stomach stir. I had bought a second-hand bike and my back pricked with sweat from the ride. There had been no point straightening my hair. The cut was new and looked terrible – I could feel the ends of my bob curling, cringing in the damp atmosphere – but it was too late to do anything about it now. I shuffled between the tables, bulky with my parka and rucksack, trying to avoid hitting people with my bike helmet. It was my second helmet in three weeks. I had stopped leaving helmets with my bike, which was often chained to anything vertical and narrow. In this city, if you didn't nail a thing down, people would quite happily help themselves.

Camilla was sitting at the back of the restaurant, filling up most of the booth with her bottom. She stood up as I approached the table. Her face was fleshier than before, her tight shift dress struggling against the swell of her bosom and the curve of her hips. Her neck seemed to have disappeared in the few years since the last time I'd seen her, consumed by her chin, dissolving into her shoulders. It was as though as she'd become more successful, she'd expanded. However, her hair had always been beautiful and was now tucked obediently into a French twist.

'It's not an exciting assignment,' Camilla said, as we sat down. 'Just a museum opening.'

I shrugged off my parka and dropped my bike helmet onto the floor, scooting it under the table with my foot. 'I'm all about toning down the excitement,' I said. 'Something boring would be great.'

She'd already ordered a glass of wine and she took a swig. Her nails clinked against the glass. They were long and pastel pink, a minute picture of a rose painted in the centre of each. They would have been impressive works of art were it not for the fact that most of them had been bitten and the ends were now ragged. 'Your hair looks nice,' she lied.

'Thanks,' I said. 'I really do appreciate this – you meeting me.'

She shrugged her meaty shoulders and stifled a burp. 'It's cool,' she said.

A slick-looking waiter with coiffed hair and tattoos stretching up his muscly neck asked if I'd like anything to drink. I ordered a coffee and turned back to Camilla, who was smiling at me. It was a smile I'd seen deployed several times over the last year; sympathetic, but not too pronounced, in case a display of strong emotion broke me.

'I'm just glad to see you back on your feet,' she said. With another weak smile, she drained her wine glass in one gulp. Catching my expression, the smile broke into a genuine smirk. 'Weird morning. Percy woke up with a rash so I was like, Fuck, this could be meningitis, but I had a meeting at eight thirty, so I told James to take her to the GP but he was due in court. So, of course, I was like 'well it's a good job I don't have anything planned for today, darling'. Consuela was late, so I had to take Zara with me and she's an absolute nightmare at the moment. I had to send Lucy, the dippy new PA to the meeting and she's not texted me yet with an update. I have to keep checking my phone. Sorry, I'm not being rude.' She swiped at the cracked screen of her phone. I had been to Camilla's house, years ago; I had seen the expensive, custom-designed worktops in her kitchen, piled high with miscellany, waiting to be tipped onto the floor by a child, cat or flailing limb. It appeared as though her phone was the latest casualty. 'Still nothing. Fuck's sake, Lucy.'

'And Percy?' I asked.

Camilla blinked at me. 'What?'

'Is Percy ok?'

'Turns out she's allergic to Radox shower gel. Absolutely bloody typical. But anyway, how are you?' she asked, panicky, as if she'd just remembered my situation and realized that I ought to have the monopoly on pessimism.

'Good,' I said. The slick waiter arrived with my coffee and asked for our food order. I chose a pizza at random and Camilla placed her own, very complicated, obviously rehearsed, order.

'They do a really good Calzone here,' Camilla explained. 'I came with James and his parents a couple of weeks ago.'

James Harmston: barrister, Winchester alumnus and father of Camilla's two small daughters. His aftershave smelled of fresh pine and competence. At Camilla's thirtieth birthday party a few years ago, he got so drunk that he fell asleep half way through removing his clothes (apparently in order to get in the hot tub) and I had found him, outstretched in the hall, his Armani slacks knotted around his ankles, a string of drool hanging from his mouth. I was now unable to hear his name without also seeing his pasty white paunch with its dusting of dark hair, and hear Camilla, in a similar state of inebriation, shriek that he had ruined everything, including her *life*.

'So, this exhibition opening,' Camilla said. 'It's at *The International*.'

One of the biggest museums in London; I had the feeling Camilla was being more generous with this assignment than she was letting on. I raised an eyebrow.

'It's honestly not a big deal,' she said, sweeping her fringe out of her eyes. Rings gleamed on her squat fingers. 'They're just opening this new exhibition. There's some sort of new technological element – something to do with smartphones. Honestly, you're doing me a favour covering this. Maggie's in LA and Laura's on maternity leave. We're a bit thin on the ground at the moment, so your help is much appreciated. It's on Friday, ten until four.'

'I'll be there,' I said. 'And thanks again.'

'Where are you living?' she asked, suddenly.

In the kitchen, someone dropped a plate and I stood up, heart hammering. Camilla stared up at me and I laughed quickly and sat down again. That sort of thing had been happening a lot recently.

'I'm in a hostel,' I said, taking a sip of coffee to give my hands something to do. 'It's fine though,' I said, hastily. 'You meet all kinds of people. And I've made friends with the cockroaches now.'

Camilla's face screwed up. Then she stared somewhere over my left shoulder for an abnormally long time.

'I was joking,' I said, as the seconds stretched on. 'There aren't really any cockroaches. At least, there weren't any this morning.'

'This might sound a bit weird,' she said. 'But I have an idea.'

She knew someone, she said, that needed a flat mate. However, as she spoke, she seemed to be asking herself a series of questions. Our food arrived and we began to eat, Camilla talking herself in and out of the idea with every bite.

'I mean,' she said. 'It sounds as though your situation is actually pretty perfect for you at the moment, anyway. I probably shouldn't get involved.'

I chewed silently on an anchovy, watching her.

'But you might get on really well. And it would probably do her as much good as it would do you. She doesn't like to admit it, but I think she's lonely…' Frowning, she sawed at the crust of her calzone.

'Where's the flat?' I asked.

'It's not that she's difficult,' Camilla continued, ignoring me. 'She can be great – she's actually a real laugh. She's just not always *present*, you know what I mean? Not that you'd have to see her all that often – I know people that live together and barely speak to each other within a week. Hell, I've seen James conscious only twice since Tuesday and that was only because we had Percy's parents' evening yesterday. He's got a really tough case on at the moment.'

'Where is the flat?' I asked again.

'Bloomsbury,' she said. My eyebrows shot up. 'But she might have already found someone,' she said. 'I haven't spoken to her in a while.'

'I don't have that kind of money,' I said.

'That might not necessarily be a problem,' Camilla said, winding a strand of mozzarella around her fork. 'It's complicated. I should probably let her explain. That's if you're interested.'

'Are there cockroaches?'

'She's never mentioned them.'

'Then I'm interested.'

'Ok,' Camilla smiled, but it wasn't entirely convincing. 'I'll give her a call.'

Camilla demolished her calzone while I pushed my pizza around on my plate, transferring the crusts from one side to the other and then arranging them like a stack of logs in the centre. The hunger that earlier had burned in my gut had waned slightly. Instead, my stomach now danced with nerves.

My chest was also aching, as if it had remembered to take me down a few pegs. But I was there now – I was moving on, whether it liked it or not.

Once she'd finished, Camilla stepped outside to make the call. She was back in a couple of minutes and settled herself back into the booth with a sigh.

'I've left a message on her answerphone,' she said. 'I gave her your number, so she can give you a call back.'

'That's great,' I said. 'Thank you so much.'

'Don't thank me yet,' Camilla said. 'Let's just see how it goes.' Then, sticking an arm in the air to hail a waiter, she ordered another glass of wine.

I had found a temp job in a bar and took shifts a couple of evenings a week, to help make ends meet. I had to tie my hair up, which had become difficult post-bob, and wear a previously-owned t-shirt with the bar's logo – a panda smoking a cigarette – emblazoned on the front and back. The previous owner of the t-shirt had been several sizes larger than me and unacquainted with deodorant. I had washed it several times, silently fuming as I watched it spin in the hostel's four-quid-a-load machine. Still, I felt the need to douse myself with body spray pre-shift and sometimes even mid-shift, depending on the temperature of the bar and the number of patrons.

It was a quiet one that night. I'd made three pitchers of piña coladas for a group of girls now sitting in the corner. One of them, with the telltale red eyes and quivering lower lip of the recently-dumped, was being consoled by her friends. Their hushed conversation in the privacy of a booth was occasionally broken by a round of hugs and a chorus of 'Fuck you, Gavin!' as they clinked their pitchers together. An older couple swayed, completely bereft of rhythm, on the dance floor to DJ Dan's charts mix; over by his decks, Dan eyed them glumly beneath his backwards-cap. They were obviously not the audience he'd anticipated when he'd assembled the mixtape. A group of workmen were drinking lager around a table in the centre of the bar. The younger members of the party laughed along with the jokes of their elders, while surreptitiously eyeing the piña-colada-drinking girls in the corner. In some ways, it was pleasant. I was able to switch off, polish glasses, clean lines without thinking, anxiety drowned out by the thump of the bass. In other ways, it wasn't quite so great; the music wasn't loud enough to drown out Stacey.

'If you had to lose a limb which limb would you choose to lose?' asked Stacey. She was twenty, taking a year out from her sociology degree in order to find herself. I set the glass I had just been polishing back on the shelf.

'Well I'm right-handed,' I said. 'So I'd probably keep my right arm.'

'Yeah but which one would you lose?' Stacey rolled her nose ring between her fingers. She had been told not to do this by our manager, Nigel, because in the dim light of the bar it looked as though she was picking her nose.

'I think I'd go for my left arm,' I said. Nigel appeared behind us, from the direction of the office, clipboard in hand. He started to scribble on the paper, in a futile attempt to disguise the fact he was eavesdropping. Nigel was big on health and safety and customer service that was 'second-to-none'. The spotlights reflected off his bald head, which, helpfully, made him easy to spot from any location in the bar; his head glowed like a beacon.

'Safe,' Stacey said. Still twisting the nose ring, she seemed to think for a second, her wide eyes staring off into the darkness of the bar. Nigel's pencil paused on the clipboard. 'I'd definitely keep my left arm and lose my right,' she said, after a moment. 'I'm right handed, but my all favourite tattoos are on my left.' She stretched out her arm. A dense sleeve of ink crept out from under her t-shirt. The pattern was difficult to discern in the dim light but, intertwined in loops of what looked like lace and barbed wire, I could just make out the shape of a zombie-squirrel and, in the crease of her elbow, an angel weeping onto a guitar.

'Those are pretty special,' I said.

In order to avoid the impending bollocking from Nigel, I stepped out from behind the bar and onto the dark dance floor. I wiped the tables, collected a few of the empty glasses from the table of workmen and, after Nigel floated away, his disapproval drifting like a cloud in his wake, re-joined Stacey at the bar.

'It's wrong to ask people which limb they'd prefer to lose,' Stacey told me as I stacked the dirty glasses onto the trolley. Her tone was serious, her eyes wide, as if I was the one that had misbehaved. 'In case we get a customer that has actually had a limb amputated.'

'I'll remember that,' I said.

The Incredible and Amazing Adventures of Kintsugi Boy

PS Keynes

Chapter One

The first time I died, I was eight.

I don't remember much about it, to be honest, although Jake loves telling the story. He makes it sound totally dramatic and like he was the hero of the hour. I suppose he was, because if he hadn't run to Mrs Poole's house and called the ambulance, then I wouldn't be here at all. But it's hard to think of someone else as the hero when you were the one who was lying sprawled out in the park with your heart stopped dead and your blood pooling in your veins like the thick jam Nana makes.

Like I say, though, I don't remember it at all.

The second time was when I was eleven. I'd been taken into hospital because things were getting really bad and Dr Cam said that even walking around could be fatal to someone like me. I could keel over at any minute. *A devastating event*, he called it. Mum and dad certainly looked *devastated* when he told us. Their faces went this grey, blotchy colour and mum reached for dad's hand like she had suddenly gone blind and couldn't find her chair. I just felt numb. I remember staring at my reflection in the monitor by my bed and rewinding to this random moment from when I was a kid and I'd had this wooden sword in my Christmas stocking. I'd wanted it for ages, and I was so totally made up to have it that I went everywhere with it. To the shops, the toilet – everywhere. Mum and Dad started calling me Sir Callum like I was one of those oldie worldie knights from fairy stories which was quite lame but I didn't mind at the time because I was only, like, four, and being a knight when I grew up was what I wanted most in the world.

And then one day I was using my sword to poke a hole in a cardboard box and it just sort of snapped in my hand. I guess I'd been thumping it around so much that the wood just gave up, or something. I dunno. Anyway, it felt like the worst thing. I had this feeling of total misery, like I'd been hollowed out by an ice-cream scoop.

I did the best I could to mend my sword with bits of cardboard and a shed load of sticky tape from the desk drawer (which I wasn't supposed to go into *on pain of death* but I figured it was an emergency) and when I'd fixed it I finally took it to show mum. When she saw it with this massive ball of tape and cardboard stuck round the end her eyes went all round and swimmy like she was going to cry or something stupid, so I said *don't worry mum, I've fixed it.* And she said, *Oh Callum, you loved it so much.*

And that's what I was remembering when Dr Cam told us about the devastation.

Anywho. Now things are different and mum and dad don't have to worry about being devastated because I am fixed. Thanks to Dr Cam I have a new heart that will last me, if not forever, then *for a fair old while.* I suspect that means I should be grateful for having got a bit more time, but all I can think is how I should have had a *fair old while* to start off with, thank you very much.

So don't tell me I should be grateful.

Fast forward to now and we're in English when Mrs Kirk announces we're doing this Shakespeare sonnet which starts *Shall I compare thee to a summer's day.* I reckon love poetry should be banned from school. It's just not fair. Straight away, I get this prickly feeling which starts in my feet and moves up my body, like thousands of killer ants are crawling all over my skin. It's totally horrible.

As soon as Mrs Kirk begins reading the poem we all start groaning and Shona Atkins at the back makes these retching sounds like she's about to be sick. Mrs Kirk rolls her eyes and carries on anyway, raising her voice over the groans. Eventually, the class settles down and she's actually got silence by the end, which is pretty good for 9B.

Mrs Kirk smiles, puts down her book, and looks at the class over her glasses. She is sitting on her desk at the front, swinging her legs so her trousers ride up and we can see her purple Converse with multi-coloured laces. She's nice and everything, but she's definitely one of those teachers who try too hard.

'Does anyone want to have a stab at what the poem's about?'

There's some shuffling and whispering and then Shona Atkins shouts out 'Sex!' and everyone starts laughing, even Mrs Kirk a bit. I can feel my face start to go red because, of course, I'm now totally thinking things I don't need to be thinking in front of twenty-eight of my classmates. I poke my pencil into the palm of my hand to try to distract myself.

'Actually, it's about a bit more than that.' Mrs Kirk is starting to hand out worksheets. 'Let's try looking at the poem in more detail. Shall I pair you up?'

There's a couple more giggles, then Mrs Kirk says '9B' in her serious voice. So we all start to talk about who we want to work with, but of course, when a teacher asks a *shall I* question, it's not really a question at all. Mrs Kirk divides us up and I realise, with a wobbly feeling, that she is pairing me with Joe. When Mrs Kirk says our names together, I sort of jump and the lead on my pencil shoots into the skin of my palm. I feel sick.

I try to think of a convincing reason why I need to be paired with Latiyah Shenley or Toby Mountford or anyone else, but I can't think of anything quickly enough and I find myself making room for Joe's book and planner.

He throws himself down into his chair and I feel a flash of irritation as his feet kick mine. He's so tall, he takes up loads more room than I do and I hate the way I have to squash into my seat to make sure we're not touching.

'Well, this is boring.' Joe grins at me and shrugs, and I try to match the tone, kicking back on my chair to show how much I totally *do not care.*

'Yeah, dead boring.'

'I don't even know how someone can look like a summer's day, anyway.'

'No. Me neither.'

I sneak a look at him as he hunches over his poem. This is the thing about Joe Rickman: he might say something is boring but he still does it anyway. He never gets into trouble in class, because he does as he's told. He's not like Connor Miles, who's dead popular but spends half his life in isolation. Joe is popular *despite* being good.

As if that weren't annoying enough, whenever Joe walks into a classroom all the girls flick their hair and do that stupid thing with their lips like they're ducks or something lame. Even the teachers go a bit gooey over him, although not in a flirty way, cos that would be totally gross. But there's something about his black, wavy hair and green eyes that has everyone smiling at him like he's God's gift to humanity.

As if.

Joe has started scribbling stuff on the poem. I watch as words like *rhyming couplet* and *metaphor* are scrawled on the paper in big, looping curls. His writing is flowing and easy to read – more like a girl's than a boy's. I cross my legs and cough noisily. I really need to get on before Miss comes over.

The words of the poem swim in and out of focus and a line catches my eye: *too hot the eye of Heaven shines*. Suddenly, the classroom feels really warm, and I'm totally regretting the jumper mum made me wear under my blazer this morning. I shift in my seat and accidentally bump Joe's arm. His pen swerves across the page and I cough again. 'Sorry.'

'No worries.' Joe flashes me his perfect grin and goes back to his writing. I glare at my desk. I hate doing stuff like this – it's just embarrassing. Love poetry sucks.

When I was nine, I'd just got into my pyjamas one night when my parents came into my room looking shifty. They both sat either side of me on the bed, like they were there to catch me if I made a run for it. I had this sense that they were about to impart something truly amazing, like, *Callum, you are adopted* or *Callum, you once had a twin*. But the reality was far, far worse.

'Callum, we need to talk to you about sex.'

What followed was the most excruciating ten minutes of my life. And that includes the 32 times I've been in hospital. Like, I would honestly rather have all my heart surgeries again than listen to my mum and dad talk about that stuff. I thought I was going to explode with embarrassment. To be completely fair to them, I got the impression they weren't exactly enjoying the experience either.

At the end of what seemed like a decade, mum took my hand and looked me straight in the eye. 'I know it's probably all a bit of a shock, sweetheart, but we'll leave this here for you to read.' She put down a book she'd been carrying, called *How We Are Here*.

'Do you have any questions for now?'

I shook my head, willing them to go. Of course, I could have told them that I had known most of this stuff since I was seven and Tommy Morgan brought a dirty magazine into school. Practically all of Falcons Class had taken turns to look at it round the back of the mobile hut on the playground. But there are some things that it's best not to say to my parents. They can get upset easily. So I put *How We Are Here* at the back of my bookshelf and got it out occasionally to stare at the pictures when I felt like it, if you know what I mean.

It's one of those pictures that I'm thinking of now as my eyes take in the text of the poem. I really need to focus.

'Everything alright here?'

Mrs Kirk is standing over us, peering at the crap notes I have scrawled on my sheet. I nod, and duck my head down to add another meaningless phrase. *Emotive language.*

'Come on, Callum, don't leave all the hard work to Joe.' Mrs Kirk gives me a friendly grin and moves on, because teachers don't tend to tell off the boy with a new heart too much in case the stress means he drops dead in front of them. It's a small perk of dying twice. I nod, and look sideways at Joe. He's frowning at his paper in concentration, his curly hair falling over his forehead and his tongue stuck out ever so slightly as he works.

What a creep.

At home after school, I help clear up from dinner and then tell my parents that I'm off to my room to do homework. Mum's face instantly crinkles with worry, like I have just announced I'm going to pop upstairs for a bit of one-on-one combat with a WWE champion or I want to dash out and scale Mount Everest before bed.

'Are you sure you've got the energy?'

Everyone has told her it's OK and she doesn't need to worry so much, but I guess one of the countless crappy side effects of having had a defective heart is that people, especially ones who love you, worry about you all the time. Mum knows she can't *wrap me in cotton wool*, like she used to say when I was a kid, but she finds it hard to let me just be myself. It's normal, according to Dr Cam, because she's suffered an enormous trauma with my illness. *Your parents have been through a lot.*

Upstairs, I shut the door quietly so mum can't hear – she prefers it to be open a crack, *just in case* – and go through my school bag. There, at the bottom, scrunched under the weight of my science textbook and my planner, is Joe's copy of the poem, annotated in his curvy handwriting. If you look at it through half-closed eyes, it almost looks like little flowers on the page. I smooth out the paper and catch a whiff of the scent of classroom and the murky depths of my bag and somewhere, very, very faintly, Joe's deodorant. Then I place it carefully on the desk, weighing down the edges with books to flatten it out.

Mrs Kirk told Joe to give me his paper to *copy the salient points*, and of course he did because he's a total teacher's pet. I find my own copy of the poem before setting to work, carefully writing, word-for-word, every letter and arrow and underline. I am coming to the end of the poem when I notice the last two lines:

So long as men can breathe or eyes can see
So long lives this; and this gives life to thee.

There, nestled close to the final word, hugging it almost, is a tiny smiley. It grins up at me, and I feel a weird surge in my chest, like my new heart is doing star jumps. What does it mean? Is this just a random doodle, or is it a message from Joe? I try to think back to when we were in class together. Did Joe write the smiley then, when we were looking at the poem? Or was it at the end, after he'd been told to lend me his notes? And what does a smiley mean anyway? *Never mind loser, you can copy my notes.* Is that what he's trying to say? Is he laughing at me?

I stand up and start to pace the room, unable to keep myself still. For some reason, this smiley is really bugging me and I'm feeling like my brain will explode with thinking about it when Jake bursts in, not bothering to knock as usual.

'Have you seen my Pokémon Encyclopedia?'

My first thought is for the piece of paper, like it contains some embarrassing, totally revealing information about me, not just a smiley at the end of a word. I instantly move between Jake and desk.

'You're supposed to knock!'

My brother is totally incapable of *respecting other people's privacy.*

'Why? What're you doing in here?' Jake looks at me like he can see right into my brain. He can be too clever for a ten year old. 'Are you doing something dodgy?'

'Just go away, Jake. I'm trying to do my homework.'

Jake ignores me and cranes round to see what's on the desk.

'Have you got it then?'

'What?'

'My encyclopedia. Duh.'

'No. What would I want with that? I'm *thirteen*. Not some little kid.'

Jake shrugs. 'Could have fooled me.'

It's a lame shot, so I let it slide. I've got more important things to think about, anyway. I steal a glance at the desk again, but it looks like my brother's not going anywhere. He flops onto my beanbag. 'Can I hang out in here for a bit?'

The thing is, my brother is OK, for a year 6. There was a time, when my old heart wasn't working properly, that I didn't feel like that at all. He was just this annoying little kid, constantly buzzing around me like a fly or a wasp or something. I was really ill and couldn't do anything, and there he was running around, doing all the stuff I wished I could do, but couldn't. But now, I know he's not actually that bad as far as kid brothers go. Ellie Fallon at school has a brother who burned down their whole extension and Social Services were called out to the family and Ellie had to live with foster parents for a bit (although everyone had to make out like they didn't know and *not draw attention to Ellie's home situation*), so I think I've escaped quite lightly, in comparison. Also, to be fair, Jake did save my life. So I reckon he can hang out on my beanbag every now and then. As long as he doesn't talk too much.

Jake starts scrolling through his phone and I go back to my desk to finish copying Joe's notes. We sit there in silence for a while, just me and him. I almost forget he's there, until he pipes up behind me, his voice sounding more uncertain than usual.

'Callum?'

'Hmmmm?' I am supposed to be working on my homework, but instead I am tracing the smiley into my planner; rows upon rows of round, happy faces are now staring up at me from my Homework Agreement.

'What do you do if you, like, really fancy someone?'

'What?'

My head jerks up and I am suddenly giving Jake my whole attention. Is he playing games with me? But my brother is staring at his phone, a little bit too hard, like he doesn't want to catch my eye.

'I was just wondering. A friend of mine wants to know.'

'Well, maybe he can ask his own brother then.'

Jake shifts uneasily. 'He hasn't got one.'

I turn round in my chair to face him.

'Is this kid in your year?'

'Yes.'

'And is the girl he fancies in your year?'

'Yes.'

'And has he said anything to her?'

'No. No way.' Jake looks horrified at the thought.

'Good. Well, he shouldn't. 'Cos he's way too young to be messing around with stuff like that.'

'But—'

'Shove off, will you? I've got homework to do.'

Suddenly, I'm really angry and I stand up so quickly that Jake looks shocked. He scrambles to his feet and scarpers out of the room, leaving the door swinging behind him. I give it a firm kick shut and stand for a minute, looking into the eyes of Darth Vader, blu-tacked to the back of my door. I gaze into those dark eyes, the ones that betrayed Luke Skywalker, the ones that are actually hidden by a metal helmet to cover Anakin's disgusting injuries, and I breathe deeply and slowly, as Dr Cam has told me to do when I get stressed. Eventually, I feel my new heart start to slow with my breaths.

In.

Out.

In.

Out.

Calmed, I turn back to my desk. The first thing I see is the smiley, looking up at me from its nest among the curling flowers of Joe's handwriting. And truth comes washing over me like water, cool and soothing and yet also in danger of drowning me completely.

Houston, we have a problem.

I like him.

OMG.

I *really* like him.

Downstairs, I can hear Jake's muffled grumblings, and then my mum's voice floats up through the banisters, across the landing, and into the quiet of my room.

'Callum? Are you OK?'

No, mum. I'm not OK. My little brother is going to end up getting a girlfriend before me and I don't even want a girlfriend because actually girls aren't really my thing and I've just discovered I'm in love with the most popular boy in school and I don't know what to do because I don't even know if I like boys and I think he might like me but I don't know because what does a smiley mean really when you think about it.

'Yes, mum. I'm fine.'

Vanishing Streets

Anna Lodwick

Chapter One

Heat pressed down on Damek's back, sweat sliding its way under cloak and shirt. With a thought, he willed the sensation away. The air in his lungs also cooled, though the sun was as bright as ever, glinting off the bronze fittings on the harness of a nearby horse. As he slipped through the crowd, the chatter of thoughts washed over him: ingredients for evening meals, blocked chimneys and a quarrel about the payment of rent.

The street was a maelstrom of tiny, charmed movements, overlaid with the larger, more purposeful ones of the people. Flowers fluttered on ladies' hats and in window boxes. Flags and banners curled suggestively above his head, beckoning people into shops. A little way off, a street crafter was fashioning butterflies from molten glass. One stretched its wings and leapt into the air. The spell was poor and the flight clumsy but a few people had stopped to haggle.

Damek turned to scan the crowds again. He'd been following his quarry off and on for a week and had almost convinced himself that he'd been mistaken. That the boy was just clumsy or stupid. Then he'd seen him walk in front of a carriage: walk right under the hooves of the horse as though he'd neither seen nor heard its approach. True, the lad had recovered well, disguising it as a stumble to the onlookers who rushed to gawk. There had been no attempt to save himself though: no righting of his balance or nimble jump to his feet. Gravity had acted on him as it would a bag of grain. If only Damek had been close enough to listen… or at least been able to track down those who had.

Damek scowled and refocused on the colourful chaos. With a thought, he flicked away the headache threatening to build behind his eyes, nearly missing the slow, deliberate movement to his left. A slight figure was carefully making its way down a side street: too carefully. Damek paused, then moved with the outflow of people down the narrower passage. The figure came into view again, trying to be at one with the crowd and their fluid, careless motions. But there was something a little stilted, a little tentative, about the gait. Damek smiled.

Cen pivoted on a heel, narrowly avoiding a woman who bore down on him out of nowhere. He righted himself and glanced around the side street. The movement had probably looked graceful and organic enough. But he had to get inside. His nerves were shot to pieces after a mere half hour outside. People seemed to be moving even faster that day and his senses were fogged by the heat. His head throbbed and the dull, sourceless reek of the city felt as though it were coating his sinuses. He scowled and edged into a gap, feeling prickles on the back of his neck.

He risked a look over his shoulder. His scowl intensified when he realised the watcher was only a golden owl on a lady's hat. It stared at him out of ruby bead eyes, the sun making them flash as though it blinked quizzically at him. To everyone else around, it probably was blinking: blinking properly and with just a hint of lofty contempt. Cen's fingers itched to snatch the little thing and crush it beneath his foot.

'Watch it!' The voice in the hushed street made Cen jolt so hard that he nearly crashed into the woman with the owl. Hardly daring to breathe, he glanced back around to find a large man in the blood-streaked apron of a butcher glowering at him. Cen ducked his head and sped away, eyes on the cobbles, checking for anything that might trip him and once again make him the centre of attention.

What was wrong with him today? How had he been so slow-witted as to make someone shout at him? He fought the old, childish urge to claw at his ears. He could not afford another blunder like that. For one thing his ankle still throbbed from the carriage incident, making it even harder to move as he should. As he needed to.

The shop fronts petered out and so did the people. Cen couldn't relax though. More than once he had to dart to the side to avoid someone moving with a speed he could never hope to match. The final time he did this he nearly pitched down a gaping hole in the cobbles where the ground had subsided. The world seemed intent on exposing him that day and still safety was a good few streets off.

Cen turned into the court with the dead tree at its centre, checking left and right. He walked forwards and paused a moment under the branches. He eased his stance and tilted his head back to catch the imaginary shade on his face. The sun had bleached the bark to a sickly yellow. He squinted, then hooded his eyes. Out of habit, he moved his head from side to side, straining to catch the illusion. But there was only the shimmer of heat and a moment later he felt like slapping himself. He lowered his head and hurried on. Two streets to go.

He paused in front of the house, staring hard at the boarded door and at each shutterless window. After a few seconds, he glanced around him and dove down the narrow gap between the house and its neighbour. A brief scramble over the barricade of debris led him to the yard and the back door.

Cen ducked inside. Feeble light shone through the splintered hole in the floor above him. Setting his jaw, he began to leapfrog his way up the collapsing stairs. He launched himself across the final gap, fingers scrabbling over the old wood to find purchase on the roof beam. He paused for a moment, letting his knees sag. The building around him was dead quiet and cooler than the yard. His eyes itched and watered, whether from the dust or all the looking, he wasn't sure. And it made no odds.

Levering himself up, he edged away from the yawning gap. The room beyond was a tiny space beneath the roof. There were no windows, just an opening at one end where some planks were missing. Cen went over to it and peered down. A chicken scratching in the street below was the only thing moving. That he could see. If anyone had noticed his slip-ups today, they had either lost him … or were approaching either too fast or too stealthily for him to see. It wouldn't take much stealth or speed.

He eased back from the gap and sat down hard on the worn boards. Covering his face, he breathed in the reassuring dark and stillness for a moment. His dry tongue passed over drier lips and without removing his hands, he shuffled over to the bucket in one corner.

He groped in the inch or so of water for the ragged bit of tin he used as a dipper and scooped some into his mouth. He needed to make a trip to the well. But hauling a sloshing pale up those stairs was always difficult. He was lucky if a quarter of the water remained by the time he got it up here. When he'd first found this hide-out, he'd entertained grand plans of stealing some rope and devising a way to pull the bucket up from the ground. He'd gone so far as to eye up likely pieces of rope when he was out in the street before realising how stupid a plan it was. Such a system would make people think a very weak magician lived in the building and that was an open invitation to murderers, thieves and sadists.

At last, he pulled the rough cloth bag from his pocket. Inon hadn't had much to spare and the bread had been reduced almost to crumbs on the journey. He picked out one of the larger fragments and ate it very slowly. That done, he crawled over to the pile of straw and cloth he'd pilfered piecemeal over months. It wasn't as impressive as the one he'd been forced to leave behind the last time but it was getting there. He flopped down, only for his head to rebound off an unpadded patch of floor. He wriggled around until he had things distributed slightly better, then shut his aching eyes. Providing nobody had physically seen him clambering up here, he was safe until he emerged again.

The building was dilapidated. The magical shell that kept it intact flickered spasmodically; it hadn't been renewed in a decade at least. Damek calculated that the structure had a few months at most before its floors began to cave in and its walls buckle. He listened hard but felt no sign of life from inside. But then he'd expected that. All the same, the movement he'd noted ten minutes ago (without the corresponding flash of thought that ought to have accompanied it) had still stirred up feelings of revulsion and wrongness in him.

He waited a few more seconds, letting his senses rove out. If there were more than one in there, then he might have to be more cautious. He couldn't hear any other presence in the building though, save the scuttling of rats and the lighter skittering of insects. Pulling his cloak away from his hands and forearms, he strode towards the doorway.

The stairs were pitifully maintained. There were huge sections that felt spongy underfoot, a clear sign that the magic was deteriorating almost as fast as the original wood. Damek tried to ignore it and focus on what was up ahead. How keen were the boy's senses? Surely as dull as mud. But still, not useless. Damek felt the prickle of apprehension that always came over him when he remembered that for the briefest of times, he was vulnerable. His cat-like quiet would fool any other person but …

There was a noise above. A creak, followed by a footstep that thumped loud in his ears. The footstep sounded again, then again, each a blow against the inside of his skull. It took him crucial seconds to switch the enhancing spell from his ears to his eyes. He peered upwards.

White hot pain lanced through the front of his head, crashing from side to side and shattering into spears. He lost his footing and toppled backwards down the stairs. His senses were in such uproar that it was only when he was five or more steps down that he was able to right himself with a fierce jolt. He took a long, ragged breath. Tears forced their way out of his hooded lids as the rational part of his brain ordered them open. Very, very cautiously, he refocused on the top of the stairs again.

A lithe figure crouched there, something that sparked and flickered clutched in one hand. Without thinking, Damek lashed out with a brutal spell. The force should have slammed the boy into the wall. Instead, it just passed over him like a strong wind and hit the timber behind with full magnitude. Shards of wood exploded outwards and the air crackled as the destructive intent of Damek's spell battled with the preservative ones laid on the wall.

The boy rolled away, shielding himself from the rain of wood. Damek was up the remaining steps in two bounds, whipping the shards into a whirlwind that pursued his target across the floor. The spell might not be able to hurt him but the physical objects it carried certainly could.

Cen felt the slight breeze on his cheek as the wood narrowly missed him. He threw himself flat and began trying to inch forward on his stomach. He needed to circle back. His only hope of getting out was the stairs: right now, the magician and his lethal shards were in the way.

He swore as something stabbed into his shoulder. His hand went limp and the bit of mirror he'd used to blind the man dropped. He rolled, wrenching his wounded arm but narrowly escaping another projectile. This one flashed as it swept over head. The man had already seized on Cen's own weapon and was hunting him with it. With his good hand, Cen yanked the knife from his belt.

He had backed himself into the corner with the bucket. Could he throw it? But what good would that be? Don't fight, just flee. He inched along the edge, barely breathing, listening for the sound of a fresh attack. Sooner or later the man would lose patience and start to tear the room apart. Perhaps it would be less painful to launch himself out of the hole in the roof? Something shimmered in front of his face. Cen flinched back but the thing kept coming. He reached up to try to protect his eyes. Instead, his mouth was forced open.

It took him a few seconds of desperation to realise that his throat and nose were full of choking water. He couldn't breathe. He couldn't even exhale. He tried to swallow but the water refused to move. Dark spots danced at the edge of his vision. He clawed at the gelatinous, unyielding substance that blocked his mouth. Water, yes, but magically twisted. Pain was racking his chest and skull, making it hard to focus on anything but how it felt to die. Cen tried to claw his way into a sitting position. He was slammed back down by a foot on his back. Any flicker of hope that the impact would shake the water loose was snuffed out along with his consciousness.

She settled back into the cushions. Light from the skylight sparkled off the incorporeal water lilies in the pool at her feet: a silly affectation of the last mistress the patron had stashed here.

'You're fairly sure about this one, then?' she asked and Damek scowled. He hated expending energy on speech. Unfortunately for him, she wasn't about to allow even superficial access to her thoughts.

'Certain.'

'Yes, well....'

'You'll test for yourself.'

'Naturally.'

One of the swirling lavender lines that decorated the floor eddied around her feet, then coiled away.

'Will the lor—'

'I have been given full control of this matter.' Not for the first time, she regretted how much of the finer detail this man had been allowed to glean. The patron would not look kindly on his involvement being dragged into conversation.

'Very good,' Damek glanced away. She reached down beside her and tossed a pouch onto the floor between them. Or would have, had it been allowed to land. For all his dangerous curiosity in the operation, there was no hiding where Damek's true motivation lay.

'I shall let you know when I am ready to proceed to the next stage.'

He nodded, 'Will I find you here?'

She glanced around at the space: they could throw all the beautifying charms they wanted at it, it was still just a storehouse.

'No. Besides, I have something else to collect.'

Cen knew at once there was no hope of opening his eyes, not yet. Instead, he tried to listen. His ears told him nothing. But that didn't mean there wasn't anything to hear. He twitched his fingers and found that the rest of him hurt slightly less than his head. He raised a hand and felt over himself: no missing limbs at least. He still had all his possessions too, as meagre as they were. Apart from the mirror and the knife.

That made him sit up and finally open his eyes. His head smarted, then cleared. He was in a dim, cool room. Stone. Unadorned. A shaft of light fell through a window high above. There were no holes though. No cracks in the floor that only he could see. This place wasn't held together by magic. But it didn't need holding together. It had been so long since he'd seen completeness like this that it made his head swim. He blinked. The room remained the same. It was about five foot square and there was nothing in it but him. And the puffs of dust that he kicked up when he gingerly pushed himself to his feet.

His injured arm throbbed so hard he nearly fell back down. Cen hissed a few swear words and reached up to investigate with his good hand. Someone had rapped it tightly in cloth. The bandage wasn't tacky yet: the bleeding had stopped. Not that that mattered much. He didn't know why he was here. Maybe just for sport. Maybe the man who'd attacked him wanted to have a round two where all his friends could see.

There was a metallic click and Cen stepped back. The door had been unlocked. An actual lock too, not a spell. He searched the gloom, looking for anything he could use against whoever was coming in. Short of screaming and kicking dust into their face, he had nothing.

He took a breath. Whoever was out there was making him wait. Or perhaps they'd come in too fast for him to see. There was no disturbance in the dust though. No sign that a person was moving too fast for sight in here. Cen listened hard but he couldn't hear anything outside. Of course they were playing with him. What had he expected?

Stepping lightly, he crossed over to the door. He squared up to it, prepared to yank it open and startle whoever was out there first. To his chagrin, he realised there was no handle or bolt on the panel that he could use to open it. He was still stuck. There was another click and it swung open, nearly hitting him. He braced, ready for an onslaught of some kind. Nothing. Just a cool breeze that fanned his face.

The corridor outside was even darker than the cell; there was light coming from the left though. It was diffuse and greyish but definitely there. Nothing stirred. There was no trace of the door opener. Cen inched out of the cell and checked over his shoulder: no signs of life at the darker end of the corridor either. That didn't mean much though. He began to move slowly towards the light. Surely they'd strike soon? This couldn't be at all amusing to watch. His hands curled into fists. Not that punching his way out had ever been a viable option.

The sudden movement of air on his face made him shy back. That hadn't been the directionless draft of the corridor but something much swifter.

Like something passing with purposeful force right in front of him. Like the swing of a sword. He crouched, every sense straining for warnings of another attack. Nothing. An instant later, his pride had him up again. Very slowly, he inched by the place. The sensation wasn't repeated.

Cen reached the source of the light. The corridor opened out into an atrium of bare stone. There was a pool at the centre, filling the room with greyish reflections from a skylight above. It was all he could do not to back away from the water. Only when the memory of the transformed liquid and urge to gag had faded did he realise there really was someone there this time.

The Lambeth Walk

Vanwy MacDonald Arif

I'm going nowhere and coming from nothing. Rain pushes under my clothes and I'm not sure I'll get any sleep tonight. I'm already cold and wet. Walking ahead, as if he owns the street, is a Paki. He's wearing a long white shirt and a thin cotton hat. Wee Willy Paki. A white woman's with him. She looks upset. I wonder what the bastard has done to her. I call to him and tell him what I think. It's my right. I can say what I like on my streets.

'Fucking Paki.'

He stops and challenges.

'What did you say?'

His voice is posh. It winds me up some more. Free English schooling has given him that voice. He's small and doesn't look like a fighter. I could take him on. I'm no scrap starter, not since I've calmed down a bit. But if he starts something...I move closer to him as an answer to his question. And when passers-by approach, they take my side. Of course they do. We stick together us Londoners.

For one moment, one warming moment, I'm not the enemy. I belong.

I'm with Ahmed on a London street. I don't know the name. It's grim and grey. Night has fallen quickly. We don't talk as we walk through drizzle. We've argued. Cold and the drone of traffic sharpens our disappointment with each other.

It's the late 1980s. We haven't heard of the Taliban and don't know where Iraq or Syria are. Afghanistan is vaguely Romantic. Rugged mountain warriors have defeated the trigger-happy might of the Russian Bear. Childhood memories of Abba's Fernando and stories of the Spanish Civil War cast a warm glow on the word Mujahideen. It sounds like poetry

Ahmed's dressed like a trader from Old-Delhi. Someone at the Mosque told him that to expunge Western clothes represents simplicity. British values have not been born yet. In our multicultural society difference is everything. So called community leaders endlessly demand the right to express their own values. Nobody seems to have noticed that these leaders are in the main old men and that their values have not even been discussed with the voiceless ones they claim to represent.

A wiry, ill-dressed man in late middle-age, shouts.

'Fucking Paki.'

Usually Ahmed knows that to survive is better than to protest. But we've argued. He's cross.

'What did you say?'

The street man moves in menacingly, delighted to take offense. I see two people walking along the road and run to them.

'Please can you help?'

They weigh up the circling man. He looks dangerous. They say,

'Fuck off dirty Paki. Leave the white guy alone.'

The louring man grins at his supporters. We take our chance and run.

The Famous ~~Five~~ **One** Investigate the Fall of Man and Original Sin

Vanwy Macdonald Arif

Aged eight I asked why having babies is painful. An important question for someone living in a female body. Mum continued knitting, all pinks and lilacs. Another jumper for me.

'Eve ate of the tree of knowledge; got humanity chucked out of the Garden of Eden. It's Eve's punishment.' Her voice told me 'counting on' was more important right now than questions. As the unacknowledged member of *The Famous Five*, I knew that adults, speaking in dialect, always lied to *The Famous Five*.

'Don't go there chil'ren. The ztation iz 'aunted!'

'Sitthee stay out of the contaminated site!'

It wasn't betrayal to think that Mum had lied. Didn't Uncle Quentin keep, even from George, his own daughter, that he was a Government Scientist working on state secrets? I didn't believe that the Garden was Eve's fault.

Julian would've asked Dick and George to investigate secret locations for clues. But going out for clues wasn't an option. The small library next to the betting shop was banned; I'd have to pass Teddy's house, an actual Government confirmed Paedo. Mum said that Teddy would rip me apart. I couldn't recall Baddies threatening to rip *The Famous Five* apart. It was a warning I heeded. Anyway, we couldn't afford rent, never mind a torch, bag, spare rope, ham sandwiches and ginger-beer.

However, a Fiver was always plucky. Even Anne in her frilly summer dress, had the courage to investigate a garden. I climbed Ma Parker's fence, entering her overgrown garden. Dark, dank, damp; nettled, brambled and thorned. It smelt of cat pee, mould and squelchy soil. Spiders squatted invisibly; ants loitered, ready to carry you back to their nest; worms oozed towards you and wouldn't die, no matter how many times you chopped them.

If it had been sunny, flowery, in Eden, so what? Flowers weren't fun. You couldn't even pick them. Pulling tulip heads when I was in the children's home taught me that.

Julian would ask where God was when the serpent slithered in. I thought of men on the estate who were not inside prison or a mental-hospital. There was Ian Smith's Dad! He had a shed. God must've been in the shed, overalled, dirty-fingered, like off *Gardener's World*.

And Adam? The children the Five met were limp, lisping, posh and mean. I imagined Adam; skinny, wearing a bow-tie and shorts, yellow haired with crayon-blue eyes; scared to ask God questions, scared to talk to an interesting snake. A bossy boots, pushing Eve around, as boys did. 'You're my rib Eve. You have to do what I say!'

Weighing the evidence, Julian-like, I knew Eve did us a favour. Getting flung out of that boring garden, where she went nude and couldn't climb trees, was a good move. If having babies hurt because Eve wasn't a wimp like Adam, life was unfair; history was false. I remembered the lilac- pink jumper, growing daily. I wasn't going to wear that thing. Ever.

Godiva Ahmed

Vanwy MacDonald Arif

'This area must be clear of vagrants by Tuesday.' Leo continued. 'Filming starts at 6 am.'

'Won't they be interested in the cathedral and the guildhall?'

He looked at her for the first time since their dawn mission to calculate how many rough sleepers lived in the precinct. He nodded, eyes brown like a muddy puddle.

'They want to film the market opening.' His voice became elegiac. 'Fruit and veg unloaded heroically in the pale dawn; salt of the earth bantering over hot tea; the city wakes to the chimes of the fabulous Godiva clock.' Leo marched onwards. 'How many tramps are there? How much rubbish and what type?'

Godiva stepped over rotting cabbage leaves, mouldy yam and crushed beer cans. She jotted down types of food debris and estimated amounts of waste. Under the rubbish, part of the rubbish, the rough sleepers lay.

The market came to. Metal shutters moaned as they were pulled up. Once-white vans juddered as their rusty doors disgorged plastic wares and stall holders greeted each other with early morning whispers. The homeless, sallow as the bilious sky, cursed the day. Bone-weary, they sat up in their ancient sleeping bags, lit a cigarette and watched the daily performance.

Back at the City Council offices Godiva worked on her plan. She detailed how the council could ensure a detritus free market, ready for the BBC.

'By midnight the streets will be clear of sleepers. We'll bring the rubbish wagons and street cleaners in. There aren't any residential dwellings so no worries about the noise '

'The vagrants?'

'I'm renting school halls; they need the income. Itinerants will be bussed out Sunday.'

Leo pondered.

'Tuesday.'

'Sunday. The sleepers will need time to get used to the idea. We want them to board the buses, not run off and re-appear in the precinct a few hours later. By Tuesday word will have spread amongst the community...'

Leo laughed.

'I'll ask the gurdwara if they could provide a langar. Maybe churches, mosques and the mandir could make donations?'

He sniggered.

'This is Coventry Godiva. You of all people should know that.'

She blushed.

'So?'

'So no one speaks to anyone unless they look the same, speak the same and believe the same.'

Godiva ripped at the corner of her presentation.

'There's a hate crime every week. And nobody gives a damn about the homeless. Budget?'

She squinted at her figures. When she told him the costs Leo spluttered as if he'd swallowed feathers.

'We need them removed not treated to a spa weekend!'

Godiva looked down at the scratches on the desk top.

'Don't stay all evening. It's a council internship not bonded labour.' Leo pulled his ski-jacket from the back of his chair and hurried out of the small beige office.

By the fire door was a cardboard box, big enough to store a double freezer; the trendy type with an ice dispenser. Inside the box was a baby, golden skinned with black curls; swaddled in a red budget store blanket. Did being dumped in a box as a newborn, Godiva wondered, mean that she too had been homeless?

The thought made Godiva turn left instead of going home along Irongate. The eerie emptiness of the precinct better matched her mood. Cardboard barrows demarcated each derelict soul in their doorway of choice. Stygian sky shrouded the sleepers in eclipse. Resting on a graffitied wooden bench was a box, the sort fridges are delivered in. Inside a baby, golden skinned with black curls, was wrapped in red. Godiva started as the mechanised clock clanged the hour. A cadaverous, pallid woman, hair heaped inside a woollen hat, appeared at Godiva's side.

'You'm jumpy,' the woman remarked.

'It's the clock. It surprised me.'

The woman peered up at the magnificent fairground-style clock high on the Broadgate wall. Wooden Godiva, naked but for her red shiny hair, trotted on a painted horse along an automated track whilst Peeping Tom, laquer-eyed and lecherous, snooped and was blinded.

'I expect it keeps you awake at night,' said Godiva, noticing the red sleeping bag trussed to her back. The woman looked doubtful.

'Can't say I've 'eard it in the night.' Her voice softened and a blueish hand darted out. 'Spare a pound for a cuppa?'

Godiva removed her fur-lined mitts and dug into her pocket, pulling out some coins.

'Ta me duck.' The woman clattered her cardboard cheerfully. She asked in a thin voice, 'Don't suppose you needs them gloves? Only I do live in a box.'

I used to live in a box too, Godiva wanted to say. Only it would be a lie. She hadn't lived in a box. She'd been found in a box. Which was different. Godiva handed her mitts over.

'What's yer name lovie?'

'Godiva.'

Instead of mocking, the response Godiva was most used to, the woman smiled.

'Good name. Means you'm born to fight for some'at right. You'll win too.' She looked at Godiva with a concerned expression. 'Chuckin' out time soon. You'd best get home. Most drunks just wobble to the taxi rank, but there's always one who's trouble.'

Godiva nodded, wondering whether the woman would be safe in her doorway.

"Don't worry 'bout me,' the women pointed to fellow door dwellers. 'We'em all friends 'ere. It's turned out to be a warm night after all.' And the woman was right. The wind had disappeared.

Dad was still up when she let herself in. The small terraced house on Wendover Street was notable only for the fact that the Germans hadn't considered it worth a bomb. Godiva walked through the small dining room and into the back living room, hoping to make it to the stairs without Dad coming out of the kitchen, for that's where he'd be; cooking.

'I was worried,' he said, tea-towel in hand.

'I'm twenty two Dad.'

'And still my baby.'

'I texted that I needed to work late to change my report.'

'You sacrificed for a great degree so you could make a difference. Will your new report help anyone?'

Godiva played with her coat zip.

'You want cocoa?' he asked, returning to the kitchen anyway.

The box was underneath her grubby plastic table the next morning in the canteen. Godiva could go for months not acknowledging that she had begun life as a thing, unclaimed, handed in to the police station like a purse found in the gutter. But now the box was digging uncomfortably into her knee. It was large, big enough to contain a microwave oven, the fan assisted type. In it was a baby with golden skin and black curls.

'What's up?' Amrit from PR put down his breakfast tray. Godiva explained how Tom, council Media Manager, had refused to shelter the homeless even for one night; insisting that the police move them on. After all, threat was free.

'Poor bastards.' Amrit's loam- coloured eyes seemed to flash angrily. And when she joked that riding naked through the streets just like her name sake would show everyone how cruel the council were, Amrit told her that she should. And when she left him to go to her office she noticed that the canteen, bathed in a late showing of the winter sun, looked warm and homely.

By the end of the day the sun had retired, exhausted. Rain pricked Godiva's face as she searched absentmindedly for her mittens on the council offices' concrete steps. The wind picked up cigarette butts and litter, shaking them maliciously. The sky was girder grey. From the shelter of the newsagent next door stepped Mustafa, Godiva's adoptive father.

'Dad!'

'Don't "Dad" me. I heard about your wanderings last night. Benedict saw you and kept an eye on you. He phoned me this morning.'

'Oh.'

'Don't "Oh" me girl. I'll walk you home.'

'It's only five!' The clock gave five dongs as if to concur.

'And the night will soon be as dark as Shaitaan's backside. I want to know. Why were you speaking to precinct tramps like they were blood?'

'Maybe they are. Social services never did trace my parents.'

'You're my mystery girl.' He spoke gently, pointing to the *Dutchie Pot* across the road. Over hot coffee, she told him. About the T.V. crew, the rough sleepers, the conversation with the woman carrying the cardboard box.

'A slice of your coconut cake,' he said to Mercy, the matronly owner of the tiny café.

'Roger,' she shouted in her Trinadadian bur, 'Slice of coconut. Now.'

Roger, a thin youth in an apron, rushed from a back room carrying a generous slice of cake.

'Hey,' he greeted Mustafa.

Mustafa looked at the boy with what seemed to be approval.

'Home for the holidays?'

'Dad. Obviously,' said Godiva.

'You should have studied medicine girl. Then you'd be helping people instead of sweeping them off the streets like they was junk.'

And then Godiva was telling Mercy and Roger about how she'd been ordered to remove the rough sleepers from the precinct.

'Things don't change,' said Mercy. 'When I first come 'ere it was okay to put up a sign in the window sayin' "no blacks wanted!" and now they sweep 'omeless folk into the bin.'

And when Godiva joked that she could ride naked just like Lady Godiva to show what Coventry really was, Mercy told her that she could.

'Muum!' Roger said.

'I will say what I will say. Thank 'eaven Godiva fightin' this. The cake on the 'ouse girl. I build you up to stand against that bloody council.'

'The grim reapers?' A wrinkled woman sat in a wheelchair behind the only other table.

'Eh?'

'Cut cut cut.' She mimed cutting with her gnarled fingers.

'What you having?' asked Mustafa.

'Jerk please.'

'Him meant coffee. Mustafa ain't no banker wandered into my lickle cafe by mistake,' admonished Mercy.

Mustafa reddened.

'If the lady wants jerk the lady gets jerk. She and I have sat here for years and never talked. It's time we get to know each other.'

The woman inclined her head gracefully as if Mustafa had sent over a bottle of Champagne. She looked at Godiva.

'My daughter Godiva.'

'Wonderful name. God's gift.' She adjusted a red car blanket covering her knees.

And Godiva explained to the old woman how the rough sleepers were to be forcibly removed for the sake of a T.V. show and how she wanted to stop it. The old woman looked hard at Godiva.

'You ride through these streets my darling if you truly believe in something.' She looked around at her audience. 'I lived through the Coventry Blitz.'

'You may 'ave mentioned that several times before, you know,' said Mercy.

'And,' insisted the pensioner, 'we all stood together. Rich or poor. Man or woman. Some say that Churchill knew all along that Coventry was to be wiped off the map. And still he let the Luftwaffe come. So you can't trust those that claim to lead you Godiva. Stand up to the bastards!' and she waved her knife like a Bastille Revolutionary before attending to the large plate of jerk that Roger placed in front of her.

Instead of wishing Leo 'good morning' in the office the next day, Godiva said, 'I'm standing up to the bastards.'

'Who?'

'The council.'

'You are the council.'

'Not for much longer.'

Godiva told Leo that she had been found in a box, the kind an old fashioned-table lamp might be delivered in. And she told him that as the social worker who had found her had saddled her with the name Godiva, she must take it as a sign. And Leo smiled which made his eyes crinkle and told her that he would be her friend, whatever happened.

Tom, entering the canteen unseen despite his pugilist's physique, interrupted.

'What is you're doing?'

'I'm going to ride naked through the market place to show everyone that Coventry is a city where the homeless are treated as if they are rubbish.'

'You are a silly little girl. You don't care about anyone but yourself. And even if you did, you don't have the guts to act.' And even though Tom's deep voice and solid presence had always frightened Godiva, when he lowered his voice and put his face directly in front of her face, Tom seemed less tall, less strong and less powerful.

When Robert the security guard arrived, Godiva found herself packing her belongings into a bag without shaking and sharing her resolution with the burly Scot.

'Good luck with everything,' he said as Godiva stepped out into the wintery brightness.

When the clock announced that four a.m. on Tuesday had finally arrived, Mustafa parked on the service road next to the market. In front of the grey shuttered doors stood Tom with Leo, Amrit and a woman in a Canada Goose coat who was clearly from the BBC. Leo gave Godiva, still in the car, a discreet thumbs up whilst Amrit winked at her. Then Tom gestured and Robert, with two men and a woman dressed in florescent security uniforms, approached the car.

'Cold morning,' said Mustafa.

Robert narrowed his ocean blue eyes.

'In Aberdeen, we call this spring.'

'We call it summer in Hungary,' said a man who had the girth of three.

'In Russia we call this a heat wave.' The woman with bottle-red hair added. They grinned and hands were shaken. The elegant BBC presenter walked over to the car and Godiva clambered out.

'Matilda. BBC. We spoke on the phone yesterday. Are you still planning to re-enact the...'

Matilda's words were lost as a rusty coach rumbled to a halt and fifty homeless people disembarked. Next two red mini-buses parked; here were older men in suits and women in saris, boys in turbans and prayer-caps, dark eyed girls in long ruffled dresses and shawls; younger men in black business coats and women in extravagant hats adorned with feathers, flowers and lace. When finally a Ring and Ride van arrived and unloaded pensioners in wheelchairs, stallholders stepped forward and there was Turkish coffee, builder's tea, bagels and halal bratwurst all round.

Whenever anyone who was there that morning chatted about the planning of the event, they said it ran like clockwork. Each attributed it to the marvels of the BBC. All agreed that the license fee was not wasted that day. For her part, Matilda tried in vain to discover the name of the person who had organised such a public spirited extravaganza. It would have made a wonderful follow up BBC documentary.

The clock struck the hour. And as if automated, homeless men and women shuffled to form two lines, their backs to each other. They held red blankets up creating a wall. The human corridor was extended by the congregations of churches, mandirs, mosques, synogogues and gurdwaras. Market stall holders gathered at both ends of the lines, facing outwards, holding aloft bubble wrap, shutting off the corridor of people which stretched from the market hall, along the precinct to the Godiva clock. When the security guards took up positions on four corners, two taxi drivers pushed an electric wheelchair inside the corridor.

Then, Godiva Ahmed, found in a box, stepped with her adoptive mother Maryam into the human walkway. Maryam helped Godiva undress and step onto the wheelchair. Maryam guided the unsteady chair, with Godiva standing upright on the red blanketed seat; through the human alley.

'Social Justice for all!' shouted Roger, Mercy, assorted medics and shop owners who had gathered. Cameras captured Godiva Ahmed's body, proving its nakedness but preserving her dignity whilst Matilda interviewed Mustafa.

'Godiva Ahmed may have been found in a box but her mind has never accepted limits. She wants to live in a city where justice is real, not a fable told by a clock,' said Mustafa.

Matilda turned to Tom, who seemed to have become as stiff as the figures in the clock. He rubbed his eyes as he spoke.

'My employee, Godiva Ahmed, is celebrating our plan to house all homeless people. The diverse crowd in front of us is making legend fact. We are a city of diversity and a home for...all.'

The clock struck 6, 7, 8, 9, 10, 11, 12 all in a row. It seemed to Godiva, as she stood upon the wheelchair and trundled past the backs of men and women she had never met, to be pealing for joy.

Nobody, not even Tom, dared sneak a glance at the naked Godiva.

If they had done so, they would have seen what Godiva and Maryam saw. A muscular white horse trotted slowly ahead, upon which perched a young woman, naked but for her long red hair. Maryam made the wheelchair move faster until it caught up with the horse's head.

'Mum!' said Godiva.

'It's alright for you. You're standing. Me, I'm walking. If that horse drops something smelly. Ugh!'

The rider smiled and introduced herself.

'Lady Godgyfu.'

'Not Lady Godiva?' asked Maryam.

'Not until it gets translated into Latin,' she grinned. They moved on at a speed comfortable for horse, chair and walker.

'How big is that box of yours now?' asked Lady Godgyfu.

Godiva considered.

'It's about the size of a shoe box. You know, the type that trainers come in. The baby fits quite snugly.'

'There's a lot to be said for flat pack,' Godgyfu said as the blue and yellow flag on top of Ikea came into view. ‘They don’t take up much room, you can carry them easily and they can be turned into actual boxes if you need one.’

‘That’s an excellent point,’ said Maryam.

Slightly ahead of the white horse Godiva saw the baby, golden skinned with black curly hair, climb out of the shoe box on the ground. With a red bootied foot, the baby stamped the sides of the box down. When the box was flattened, the baby picked it up and put it under her arm as she walked off into the crowd.

Lost

Missy Reddy

Chapter One

Saturday 9 July 2005

6.23am

LORENA: A small primitive cry. Lights flickering in the dark. Air, she needs more air. Can't get enough air. Something fluttering in her chest. Now thumping, thumping. Try to breathe. It's so dark. Got to get out of the dark. *Help me.* No sound coming out. That cry again. Is it me? There's some other voice. Then another. Can't hear them. *Somebody help me.* There's still no sound coming out, she hears a beep, beep, beep, and there's a flash of light. What was that? Where am I? I can smell blood. My blood? Where's my body? I can't feel my body. I'm numb.

No, not numb. There it is. There is pain. It starts from her stomach and surges through her body in a great wave. She clenches her teeth. *Help me.* She can almost hear the sound of her own voice. Push through: *Huh… Huh...*

The crying: someone else needs help too. It is more urgent even than the pain she feels. There are others around her but she cannot reach them. In the darkness, her darkness, she must try to open her eyes. It feels like there might be light out there. It feels like there might be help, if only she could get there. She pushes open her eyes, but a fierce light invades and she can't take it. She's back in the dark, with the pain. Slowly this time, she tries squinting her right eye, then both, further opening one eye and then the other. She's made it. She stares straight ahead and bit by bit the room comes into focus.

White walls, strip lighting, blue curtains; a hospital ward. What's wrong with her? Something happened at the office, then nothing, now she's here.

The curtains to her left are drawn. A woman in a dark blue uniform stands to her right: a nurse who looks concerned. Lorena's breathing has steadied but her heart is still thumping in her chest, her whole body screams with pain.

The nurse has something in her arms; a small crying bundle with a crumpled red face. She's looking at Lorena, expecting something, holding out the bundle. Lorena stares back.

The nurse glances at the baby and then back at Lorena. She wants to pass Lorena the baby. Lorena is meant to do something, to soothe? She tries to lift her arms but the tubes from her hands weigh her down. There must be someone else who can help. Where's her husband? Where's Cam? And then the baby is in Lorena's arms and the crying has stopped.

Thursday 7 July 2005

9.49am
45 hours earlier

CAM: Cam's been sitting in his car, waiting for almost an hour now. It's unlike Harriet to be late. In his hand are the notes he scribbled down earlier. What else does she need to know about these guys? Maybe they'll close the deal today, then it will just be a case of making sure the order goes through. He'll be able to retain most of the commission that way. He looks at his watch, only 10 minutes until the meeting. Where is she? He gives her a call.

He hears the dull hum of traffic as she answers.

'Harriet, where are you? The meeting's in five minutes.' Cam checks the clock on his dashboard, four minutes.

'Not coming, Cam.' Her tone is flat. 'Haven't you heard the news?'

'Why, what's going on?'

'Switch the radio on, Cam.'

A number of bombs have exploded on London's underground this morning, he switches over: *London tube bombings*, another station: *suicide bombers*, it's the same news on every channel.

'Shit, Harriet, gotta go.' He ends the call, speed-dials Lorena, and turns down the radio.

The call fails to connect. Fucking hell, what's happened to her? He tries again. Nothing. Shit, what's he gonna do? He starts up the engine. No, gotta get through to her. He tries his phone again. Where did they say the bombings were? Still no connection, he dials again and turns up the radio: *Liverpool Street. Aldgate.* Is that near her office?

Okay, it's ringing. Pick up. Come on, pick up.

A few more rings and then Lorena's voice: 'Cam, I've been trying to get through to you. Do you know what's going on down here?'

'Yes, yes, I just heard, I've been trying to call. Are you okay?'

'Yeah, are you?'

'Yeah, yeah, of course!' He kills the engine, it's so good to hear Lorena's voice. 'Are you sure you're okay?'

'It all happened on the other side of the city.'

'Oh, so, where are you now?' Cam asks.

'Still at the office.'

'At the office?'

'We were all gonna head home but the streets are mayhem, so we're just gonna hang here for a while, until things have calmed down a bit, carry on as normal I guess.'

'What? Carry on as normal? What are you talking about? Get the hell out of there!' He starts up his engine.

'Cam—'

'—I'll leave now and come and pick you up—'

'—Cam, Cam, listen it's best to stay clear of central London right now, until things have calmed down, I know it's not ideal but I'll take a cab back to my car later.'

'What?'

'Think about it, Cam.'

'What? Okay, okay, I'll just start heading home then. I'll be back as soon as I can.'

'Cam, love, the motorways are bound to be jammed right now, you're really best to stay where you are until the evening. The worst is over. I'll be alright, I promise.' And that's final.

He kills the engine. 'Okay, I can do that. If you're sure?'

'Yes, just continue to work your magic with that Northern lot, okay?'

'Look, Lorena, I'm not getting any more work done today, but I'll do what you said, I'll head back to the hotel after this meeting, just until things have calmed down. Text me when you get in, okay? And give Mia a hug for me.' His little girl will be sleeping by the time he gets home.

'I will do, love, bye.'

5.35pm

A call comes in from an unknown number.

'Is that Cam?' It's a man's voice on the line.

'Yes, who is it please?'

'It's Ivan, from TAO.' Lorena's boss.

'Lorena?' Cam asks, fumbling with and almost dropping the phone.

'Okay, Cam, I know this isn't what you wanna hear right now, but Lorena has had a shock, gone into labour early, was struggling to deliver and is about to go in for an emergency C-section.' Ivan's voice is as calm and slow as someone trained to talk down a jumper.

'But she was fine, earlier, when we talked? What do you mean, she's had a shock?'

'We're looking into it Cam, that's all I can tell you right now, but you need to get over here as soon as possible. We're at the Middlesex.'

'Looking into it? Okay, I'm in Manchester at the moment, but I'm on my way. Can you stay with her?'

'Yes, of course.'

By six, Cam is in the thick of rush hour traffic, all trying to get to the motorway. The radio is full of regurgitations and speculations about the events in London earlier that day. He hits the power switch, preferring to sit in silence bar the sound of his own hand tapping away at the steering wheel. Can't fucking reach her, fucking hell. The steering wheel takes a thump. And what about Mia? He reaches for his phone.

'Tom.' Cam's never been so relieved to speak to Lorena's dad.

'Cam? Is everything okay?'

'It's Lorena, she's gone into labour early, she's in hospital, and I'm on my way from Manchester. Look, it's Mia, she must still be at school, can you get her?'

'Of course. I'll give the school a call now to let them know I'm on my way. I'll bring her back to ours, okay?'

'Great, thanks so much, Tom.' He'd never let *his girls* down.

'No worries. Call me when you can, with an update.'

'Will do.' Cam ends the call. It'll take Tom at least an hour to get to Mia but it'll take Cam much longer to make it down the motorway to Lorena. He should have ignored her advice earlier and just come straight back, but she could be so insistent at times, it prevented him from making his own decisions.

Around six-thirty, Cam checks his phone, no messages. He's nearing the motorway where he can put his foot down.

11.03pm

It's late by the time Cam makes it to the hospital. Each scenario's played over in his head at least a hundred times already.

He's in the entrance hall, looking for a sign for the maternity ward. He spots a wall of blue felt notice-boards: *Celebrating 260 years of care; Middlesex Hospital set to close in December 2005*; endless photos of the hospital 'over the decades' but no map of the fucking wards.

Now he's scrabbling through crowded corridors, scouring walls and ceilings for signs. The damn place has gone to shit: peeling paintwork, taped off light fittings. And then, at last, a sign for the maternity wing.

Walking through the double-doors to the ward, Cam recognises Ivan sitting in the reception area next to a young woman with long dark hair. Ivan stands up when he sees Cam and walks over to him. The young woman follows.

'Are you okay?' Ivan asks, firmly gripping Cam's shoulder.

'Yes,' Cam says. 'And Lorena?' The words almost fail to come out.

'Your baby girl was born around seven and transferred to the intensive care unit. Lorena was in the operating theatre a bit longer but she's now in recovery.'

That's all he needed to hear.

Ivan guides Cam over to the reception desk to a young Indian woman in a blue and white striped uniform. 'This is Geeta, the midwife who's been keeping us updated.' Geeta smiles at Cam. 'This is Lorena's husband, Cam, we're going to hand over to him now.'

'Okay, thanks, love,' Geeta says in a warm tone. 'Hello, Cam, we're just about ready for you to come and see them.'

'Great,' Cam says. 'Thanks, Ivan, you and...' he gestures at the dark-haired woman.

'...sorry, this is Andrea, one of Lorena's work colleagues,' Ivan says, 'she found Lorena and raised the alarm.'

'Pleased to meet you, er, thank you… look, you should really go home now, I'll take it from here. Thank you for everything,' Cam says. He watches Ivan and Andrea walk back through the double doors and down the long corridor. For a moment he envies them, as it feels like their journey has ended and his has just begun.

'This way, Cam, love,' Geeta beckons him. She escorts him through a small series of corridors to a side ward. She opens the door and Cam enters the room.

Lorena is lying in bed, wearing a hospital gown. Her face, usually radiant with an olive glow, is blanched and her hair is slicked back with sweat. Her eyes are glazed. Cam pauses for a moment, mentally navigating a pathway to her through the array of tubes, wires and machinery. She stares blankly in his direction. Where is the woman he married? He longs for her to smile, to reassure him that everything is okay. He mustn't think that way, he needs to be the strong one now. He makes his way over to the bed, reaches in to touch her hand and kisses her on the forehead. She blinks and gives him a weak distant smile before drifting off to sleep.

Next to the bed is a small creature in an incubator similarly covered in tubes and wires. His baby girl. She has a little tuft of blonde hair on the top of her head. Now there's a surprise since Lorena and Cam are both dark. Mia, too, had a thick head of dark hair when she was born. The baby is much tinier than Mia had been. Cam looks at the chart clipped to the end of the incubator, five pounds and one ounce, well, she wasn't due for another five or six weeks. Looking at her tiny fingers and toes, Cam has a strong urge to reach in and touch them, but is put off by the thought of disturbing the medical aides attached to her. The rise and fall of her stomach gives him hope that she's going to be strong, like her mum. He looks at Lorena, sleeping, and wills her to get better quickly. They can make a new start. He brushes away an uncomfortable memory. Why can't he be more like Tom? More dependable.

On his way out of the hospital, Cam checks his phone. There are a number of old messages from Ivan giving updates as and when events in the hospital occurred, a couple of messages from Harriet, and a message from Tom. Cam sends a brief message back to Tom.

Friday 8 July 2005

4.03am

CAM: It's been about an hour since Cam arrived back from the hospital. He's exhausted but he can't sleep. The house feels so strange and quiet without Lorena and Mia. He'll visit them both tomorrow. Mia will be at school all day so he'll call in to Tom's in the evening on his way back from the hospital.

He switches on his laptop and flicks through the headlines: *London's day of terror; Al-Qa'eda brings terror to the heart of London; Terror comes to London; 700 injured in England's worst ever terrorist outrage; We Britons will never be defeated.* He remembers the World Trade Center attacks as a time when people in the West had ceased to feel safe - that was the first time the notion of killing oneself to kill us had come to these parts.

And now in London, that was just too close for comfort. Cam looks at a map of where the bombings took place. Lorena was right, it *was* on the other side of the city to where she was working, but even so, it could have been her.

Cam checks over his phone messages. First Ivan's:

19.06: Baby girl in intensive care. Lorena still in operating theatre. Will update soon.

20.15: Lorena out of theatre and now in recovery.

21.34: Baby still in ICU, Lorena still in recovery, but both okay.

How could he have missed out on all of this? Not been there to support her?

He deletes the messages from Harriet without even reading them; he hasn't got time for her right now.

Tom's message had come through just after nine:

21.03: Mia collected, fed, watered, tucked up in bed. Update me. Tom.

7.40pm

Cam pulls into Tom's drive. Lorena had been pretty out-of-it again today, so he hadn't stayed too long at the hospital, best let her rest. A quick glance in the rear-view mirror; his chin, usually clean-shaven, has amassed a 48-hour shadow, his cheeks are drawn in, bags under his eyes, he looks like he's been through hell and back. But he must put on a show for Mia. He attempts a smile, it's weak but will have to do, yes Mia, everything is okay, things will be back to normal soon. God, he hopes so.

Lorena's dad opens the door of the house, his eyes bearing the conflict between blame and concern. He escorts Cam through the hall and to the living room. Tom's wife, Blessing, is sitting on the sofa watching TV, next to Mia. Blessing turns her head as Cam enters the room, giving him a kind and sympathetic look. This notifies Mia of his presence but she continues to stare at the TV, whilst scrunching up her little face. As Cam approaches the sofa, he can see the TV programme reflected in Mia's dark brown eyes. Thick, dark shoulder length hair, just like her mum's, her nose is starting to lose its squishiness, bringing her further away from the baby she once was.

Suddenly from the silence, Mia speaks up: 'Where were you? I was at school until seven o'clock and then Grandpa came, but I didn't know anything, I didn't know where anyone was, what was happening, where *you* were.'

Cam is so tired; he's not really up to this. Blessing is as calm and cool as she always is. Cam approaches Mia, his arms outstretched.

'Mia, Mia, love.'

She beats him away with her hands.

'Oh, Mia, stop it.' He holds up his arms to defend himself. 'I was trying to get to Mummy, you know that.'

Tom arrives in the doorway.

'But what about me? I was just left there.'

Cam can see that she's tired too. 'I know, and I'm sorry, love, I was far away, that's why I asked Grandpa to collect you.'

'You're always far away, that's why these things happen.'

Ouch. 'Mia, it's not like that. I'm going to be much closer to you all now, anyway.'

'It's too late,' Mia says, standing up and pushing past Cam. She runs by Tom and up the stairs.

Cam follows her and finds her lying on the spare bed, sobbing. She can barely get her words out between the sobs. 'I.... want... Mummy.' Cam puts his arms around her which she resists momentarily before giving in to his embrace. 'I... want... Mummy.'

'I know you do, love,' Cam says and a warm tear runs down his cheek.

Your Warrior: A Working Mum's Story

Missy Reddy

We are not members of the Old Boys' Network; we cannot sort our problems out by fraternising in the right circles. We are working mums and we swim hard against a strong tide, managing our complicated lives in our own creative, exhausting but effective ways. Here, in a combination of prose, short sketches, and poetry, I share my own story.

You know when you're sat in the gynaecologist's office with your new boyfriend and the man who's just cut you open, removed a cyst the size of a grapefruit from an ovary the size of a walnut, and sewn you back up again tells you that you shouldn't wait to try for a family; that can be make or break for a relationship really.

Well, I guess I hadn't read the signs properly. I remember having to pull over on the hard shoulder of the motorway because I was in so much pain in my stomach that I felt I might die if I had to sit any longer in traffic with my leg raised, feet hovering over the gas, over the clutch, stopping, starting, stopping, starting. That feeling, that meant something. Later, when every time I sat down on the loo and felt that the whole of my insides were pressing down on my bladder. That meant something too. There was something growing inside me that wasn't meant to be there. I was sick and needed to be healed. This growth had implications for life too, for new life.

We bumped into him again, the gynaecologist, whilst we were buying maternity bras. He was pleased for us; said we'd done the right thing. There was a whirlwind wedding, simple by Indian standards, but just right by us. And an English wedding too; finger sandwiches, scones and jam, and a glass of champagne. I really was the centre of attention for a while there, it was fun. But the real story, the one I want to tell you about now, is what happened afterwards; the story of me as a working mum.

Having children is akin to inviting a wrecking ball into your home; into your life. Your relationship, as you knew it, will at least be temporarily destroyed as you are no longer freely able to share the fundamentals of eating, sleeping and sexual relations together. Your friendships will also go to pot as you find yourself no longer moving in the same circles, no longer being able to remember those important dates that let people know you still care, and no longer being able to keep in touch with anyone who lives more than a mile down the street. Anything resembling your former adult life will have to be stashed away to make room for the endless toys and equipment required to raise a 21st-century child. There is a new boss in town and you will do anything to fulfil their needs, desires and wishes. And then, before you know it, the issue of returning to work arises.

I will tell you, now, that I did not want to go back to work. I would have been happy to be a stay-at-home mum. Despite all the changes to my life, worries, sleepless nights, not to mention all the washing, I was enjoying motherhood. My daughter was an incredibly sweet and beautiful baby. She was a wearable baby, preferring to be carried, a breastmilk-only baby, a real mummy's girl. We spent our days at mother and baby groups, coffee shops, music classes, parks and baby swimming. It was a real change from the working lifestyle I had become accustomed to over the previous 12 years; the one-hour commute, the nine-to-five, the treadmill. But, I had worked my way up to a senior position with a good salary that was hard to walk away from. My partner and I decided I would go back part-time just before our daughter's first birthday.

As a child I was conscientious; I picked up litter, became a vegetarian after seeing animals taken away for slaughter, created a playground club where I could share my toys with others. My family had little in the way of means but I treasured what I had. As a teenager, I wrote poems about animal rights and the environment and wore my heart on my sleeve. I had my own mind and preferred not to go along with the crowd. I always had a job or means of making pocket money. At university, I wrote poems about love and war, volunteered for a local mental health charity and joined a theatre group for disabled and able-bodied actors. I cared about the world, about people, about animals. This led me to a career focused on improving the wellbeing of others.

Even in my early days as a worker within caring settings, I naturally challenged any injustices I saw. This was not always taken well. Then I joined the voluntary sector, a children's charity, and felt I had finally found a workplace that would appreciate my personality and skills. I was working with some of the most disadvantaged groups of young people within the UK. Part of my role was to advocate for them and challenge practices that negatively impacted on them. As with all other workplaces, there were issues around organisational change and managing interpersonal dynamics but the wider context of doing something worthwhile overshadowed these issues somewhat.

A workplace has its way of letting you know you no longer fit in. The full manuscript of this piece details the journey I took after realising I was now an outsider.

*

This is the poem that gives name to the piece:

Your Warrior

When I held you in my arms, my first feeling was fear
Blue
Then you opened your eyes and reassured me
A wave of euphoria
Mine
I created you

Keep you alive, safe, warm, nourished
Watch you breathe, stretch, grow

Who could have known how much I'd needed you
Who could have known how much you'd need from me
Close
Who could have known how much I'd suffer for you
And that I'd do it all over again, one hundred times over

I'd survive the day on coffee and kindness when no sleep materialised
I'd swallow the bitter pill that was my depleted body
I'd no longer know where I end and you begin
You are precious

And I am Mum

Your Warrior

Fur Coat

Katharine Rowe

'I've put her in the library for now. I'm not sending her home, I think she'd see exclusion as a reward. Miss Aldred . . . ? Hello? Can you hear me?' The calming authority of the headmistress.

'But Anna likes Laura,' Lee whispered.

'She cut a chunk of her hair off! This is serious.'

'I'm so sorry.'

'I think it'll be alright. Laura's doing some healthy rationalising, she's still laughing about it right now. But Anna didn't even try and justify herself.'

'I've been trying the reward . . ,' her thin voice was pinched by a screw-tight throat.

'Sorry? The reward stars? Any luck?'

'She likes them but forgets about them,' Lee said, faint as the ghost of chalk on a blackboard. 'You know. She's flighty.'

'Yes, flighty can be a feature. I know the stars are babyish but I think we need to try everything at this point, don't we. Who knows what combination of tricks might crack it. And we will crack it, my dear, but we're on dangerous ground. If there had been more intent . . . Anyway, my decision, no exclusion. Though we all know she'd rather be with you.'

'I don't know why,' a faded murmur over a turned-down radio.

'Pardon?'

Louder, 'I don't know why. I don't encourage . . . she just fastens on.'

'Well it's a very natural thing, isn't it? A mother and daughter? I'm not sure why . . . Well, I don't want to send her home anyway.'

'No,' she managed.

'Indeed. I'm just, I think we're reaching a point here where I'm not clear on the way forward. . . Miss Aldred?'

'Call me Lee.' She whispered, tears in her eyes.

'I'm sorry? I'm having a lot of trouble hearing you. Bad line, I think.'

'Nothing . . . Bay?' she asked.

'Oh, yes, okay this morning. He's been engaging well with his playground guardian. I mean Yammi. He was playing with Yammi. The Vortex Game. Or he was certainly round the edges of it at least. But he will be coming to the Assertiveness Mentoring on Thursday won't he, Miss Aldred?'

'Yes, Mrs Lancashire.'

Sitting at the kitchen table, Lee saw a sparrow land in with the rabbits. Lovely to see; the natural world in communion with itself, indifferent to its human surroundings. But because it was happening behind the wire fence it looked artificial, posed. She looked away and straightened a pile of bills.

Ten days ago she'd taken her lunch out into the fresh air to try and get rid of a headache. She'd sat on the low wall, put her face to the hexagons of the wire fence and watched the rabbits. They were sitting with their haunches pressed together, heads in opposing directions. The white one had its ears down and its eyes closed, its wedged head facing doggedly into the future. It was a philosophic rabbit; stoic or maybe nihilistic. Bay had named it Road, which she liked, but sometimes it made her think of roadkill. The other one looked exactly like Peter Rabbit, the peppered grey of a common, wild coney. It was cheerful; ears up and eyes open. Optimistic. Anna had called it Bunny. Sometimes they leapt round the garden like mad Olympians. Retired Olympians put out to pasture. Then gone mad.

The phone rang on the table. It was her mother. Her father was stuck in town, Lee would have to go and get him later. And her brother had shouted at his feckless tenant again and he'd left owing three month's rent. Lee would need to advertise for him again. Lee kept the receiver to her ear but pushed the phone away in increments until it was balancing right on the edge of the table. As her mother went on she let it slowly keel over the side, held only by the flex. Her father was worried about an anti-virus message and wanted her to check all the internet providers again. Up and down went the phone, sawing against the table edge. She dutifully described what Anna had done at school. Her mother despaired. Anna was getting worse, Lee was doing nothing to help. Anna needed guidance, she was only eleven, they must force her to change or lose her for good. And Bay's unsociable behaviour was just as bad, and Lee must stop calling him Boy, it was bad for him, bad for his self-esteem. 'But he likes it,' Lee whispered. She asked to borrow some money and was offered fifteen pounds. She thanked her mother.

On Saturday, watching the rabbits feed, she'd taken her lettuce in both hands and nibbled the edge experimentally. Taking her plate she'd gone into the garden and sat in the enclosure. Lying the plate in the grass, she'd slowly shifted over and got right next to them. They'd been so placid they'd let her stroke them without flattening themselves down. She'd gently pressed her hand in until it was covered in soft fur and she'd stared at the point where her flesh disappeared under pelt.

She folded clothes on the kitchen table. She liked it when the static in Boy's pyjama trousers kept them open as if they had legs inside them. It reminded her of the Dr Seuss story about a pair of scary green pants with nobody inside them. The green pants would turn up in dark, lonely fields or be speeding past dangerously on bikes without arms to hold the handlebars or feet to touch the pedals. They were drawn on very dark pages. They were frightening to a child, the whole story was. Up until the end when you found out that the pale green pants were scared too and the narrator had to put his arm round them to stop them crying. Lee's kitchen was pale green and the black of the mahogany surfaces was like the black of the Seuss drawings.

The phone rang from the floor.

'Lee, the National Trust have said Thursday so I need the drawings by the end of the afternoon. I'm importing tonight, editing tomorrow, so it's end of the afternoon without fail. I know you said you'd nearly finished but that was Monday.'

She tried to think about her office on the second floor but her mind couldn't get past the stairs. She laid her head down on the table, unplugged the cable from the back of the phone and put it between her teeth. She hummed Vivaldi's Four Seasons as waiting music. Her trembling eventually wore off but without it she dropped into a slack sleep.

When she came to, she rose shakily. She pushed her empty cup on to the countertop but it was too crowded; everything kinked out of place like a jerky snake and oily water slopped out of the wok. The grease spread among the dirty dishes, under the cork coasters, into the wrapper of the pittas, along the seam of the bread bin. She was afraid of the oily water. Afraid of its brown and rainbow shine. Afraid of having to clean it out of the cellophane, where it would stay in any case. Of deciding whether the coasters should be thrown away. Of working out if kitchen roll or dishcloth was the greenest option. Afraid because she'd already been afraid about this once already, earlier when she left the water in the pan in the first place.

She left the back door open for the flies to come in.

Lying on the grass, the breeze was cooling and brought scents with it. Bunny was right next to her. She could see the mild pink of his inner ear. The strange 'v' of his nose opening and closing, that diamond shaped piece of flesh moving up and down just like a mouth, more expressive though, softer, more vulnerable. He seemed immune to the wire fence, wild if he chose to be, content, filled with hair and breath and the understanding of scents. He slowly hopped over to Road where she sat snugly in a bower behind the two holly tree trunks. Lee took off her suit jacket and crawled in beside them, getting grass stains on her shirt.

Having walked Bay home from school, Anna came out into the garden looking for her mother. She found her crowded into the rabbit hutch, not quite all in. Bay came out to see. They hunkered down and talked softly to her for a while. Eventually they trailed slowly alongside as she bunny hopped awkwardly up the path to the house, her human body ridiculous in the animal pose she'd assumed. At eleven o'clock, Anna went into the living room to check on her. She was lying stretched out on her side in the close, hot room, her flanks heaving with her moist, heavy breaths. In the morning, they took her out into the garden again where she seemed much more comfortable and left some lunch on a plate, with another plate turned upside down over it to keep out the flies. Anna took Bay to school again.

At first she wouldn't let them cuddle her without flattening herself right to the ground but the next day she allowed them to stroke her and even hopped over when they first emerged from the house. They brought out the one-man tent and a sleeping bag, since she overheated if she came inside at night.

Two days later they found scratch marks against the boles of the tree and the water bottle pulled down from the fence, though she looked content enough. The day after, they found a hole dug under the fence and their mother and Road gone. Bunny was eating lettuce by the hutch. Anna held her brother's hand and they gazed at the hole. After some thought, Anna made a poster that said, 'Have you seen this lady? We have her slippers and want to give them back, so please let us know if you find her.' Bay drew some pictures on it. Over the weekend, Anna continued to cover for her mother. The first time she'd answered the phone she'd used an excessively polite voice, thinking it would make her sound older, but remembered that her grandmother's phone voice was like that and instead just deepened her tone a bit and posed as her mother's younger sister. She was polite to Granny, rude to her mum's work, confusing with cold callers.

By Sunday night Anna was leaving the phone to ring. She found herself contemplating the way Bay's hair hung so regularly, so neatly and thinking about the kitchen scissors lying in the utensil draw.

On Monday morning there was a knock on the door and their mother stood there, sheepish, muddy but unrepentant. She took them in her arms and sighed a deep, home-coming sigh.

They all lay in a huddle in the bed. Lee with her arms and knees tucked up under her, back rounded towards the ceiling. Anna lay next to her, one hand tucked under Lee's stomach. Bay copied his mum, still being of an age where the position was comfortable.

The children woke first. 'Her knees are going to go,' observed Anna.

'She can flop over on her side again like she did in the sitting room,' said Bay. He continued to regard her. 'She'll never get a husband though,' he worried.

Anna laughed until it woke her mother.

Lee jumped up and put on an angora jumper. She shepherded the children forward and the three of them bobbed loosely down the stairs together. Bay bunched his hands up to his chest and ate his breakfast straight from the plate with his mouth. Anna rolled dry cereal to him and he nibbled it up off the table.

Lee took up the phone. 'Kirsty! Yes, I know I left you in the lurch. Yes, that's fair enough. But if you still want me, send it over and I'll get it done in the next three hours.'

She dialled again. Her mum was aghast, Anna had hidden it well but she knew something was wrong, Lee couldn't have lost her voice for a week, and they'd been in desperate need of help choosing their autumn holiday and getting her brother's Chesterfield back from the upholsterer. Laryngitis, Lee said. She'd be over tomorrow but not again until a week after that, so trim the requests, get it down to the one most important.

Dialled a third time. 'Mrs Lancashire, Anna's going to apologise tomorrow. We've talked it over and she's agreed she can't expect Laura to cope as if it didn't happen.'

'Well that's wonderful. I did think we'd never be able to visit it again and was worried it might fester.'

'But Bay is not going to the assertiveness classes. He's fine.'

'Are you sure? Mrs Aldred, they're designed to help, not to pigeonhole or label.'

'He's fine. He's got me.'

'Well . . . well and that sounds good. I'll leave it to your judgment then, Lee.'

The three of them cuddled in a tangle on the couch.

'Mum,' said Bay, twisting Lee's head round towards him, 'what happened to Road?'

'I don't know,' she replied, pinioned by his hands and looking him frankly in the eye, 'We split up. I'm sure he's fine.' Bay snuggled down again. She was lying. Anna rested her head on her mother's arm and closed her eyes peacefully.

Curvy Roads

Miloni Shah

I finally have a secret. Something about myself. Something that only I know. Okay, my parents know, and even the doctors know. But nobody at school does. I want to tell my friends but I also want to keep it to myself, see if they're able to find out my secret on their own. Will it matter to them? Will they see me in a different way, think that I'm not good enough to be a part of the group anymore? Will I lose them?

Probably not.

Right before walking through the black gates of Angel Land High School, on a cloudy morning, I make a pact with myself: If my friends find out about my diagnosis and decide to ignore me, I'll start reading all the books that I wanted to for so long. First on my list is *Big Girl* by Danielle Steel. I always wanted to read books by her. But my mum thought I was too young to understand them properly. Yesterday, when I was in Crosswords, I saw the cover page, the lower half of a girl's face zoomed in, and she was licking a spoon dipped in sugar. The title, *Big Girl – One woman's journey to discover who she really is,* was in bold. I picked it up and read the blurb; a story about Victoria, a girl who is harassed by her parents because she's ugly and fat. Her parents prefer her little sister, their perfect definition of a daughter: tall, thin, dark eyes and sharp features. This book was different from the other books I'd read before: *Harry Potter and the Philosopher's Stone, The Scarlet Pimpernel*, and *Around the World in Eighty Days*. I bought *Big Girl* without a second thought.

I haven't been able to get past the scene where Victoria comes across the photograph of the Queen in her later years, when she realises that she's named after a not so pretty Queen, because every time I pick up the book my parents start talking about my condition. Mum and Dad definitely don't like it when I avoid our recent visit to the doctor. They want me to talk to them, tell them how I'm feeling: Am I okay? Do I want to talk about my recent diagnosis? Am I worried about anything in particular? So every time I flip open the book, they start talking to me.

I'm one of the first to arrive in class 6-E. The walls are pale yellow. There are two green soft boards on both walls and a blackboard on the wall opposite the window. There are three rows in this room with fourteen benches arranged one after the other at equal distance. I head to the closest bench in the middle row before the rest of the thirty nine students come in. My desk is placed in such a way that I can see the corridor leading to class. An opportunity to escape the teacher's boring presence if necessary.

My back is straight, like a wall, so uncomfortable that it feels like it's not a part of my body. I wiggle my shoulders a little, not that it makes me feel any better. I take out *Big Girl* and as I'm about to turn the front page, Pooja and Samantha walk in from the adjacent class. Before I have a chance to smile at them and say 'Morning!' their fists smack against my back, they say 'Ops', and immediately cross their fingers. Their eyes widen, their hands creep towards what they assume is my back. I have a vague sense that their hands are touching the hard surface. I forgot about this stupid game that we have been playing, Ops and Bats, since grade five. Every time a person sits down they have to announce 'Bats' and when they stand up 'Ops'. But if someone fails to do so then the other person gets to punch them really hard. We agreed to only punch our backs: the pain becomes a lot more bearable then.

Samantha looks at me and pokes her index finger a couple of times on my back and asks,

'What's this hard stuff?'

Pooja looks around all nervous like a lost puppy. But we can hear voices getting louder. My classmates are arriving.

'Meet me after class in the pre-school playground and don't tell anyone,' I tell Pooja and Samantha. They nod and go back to their class, right next to mine.

I try to settle back in my place but my eyes are on the verge of turning watery.

A group of girls who have cut out two inches of their pinafore skirts so that it reaches mid-thigh are outside in the corridor. They see each other and hug, the whole thing looks so darn fake that I cringe. Their Instagram story says that they met each other yesterday. Their voices are mixed with the Vice Principal's taking over the PA system, at 7 am sharp.

'Good morning and welcome to the first day of school…'

Her voice is drowned out by students chattering about their summer: What did you do during the holidays?; Did you watch the new movie that was released? It was gross; I met my favourite actor; I went to Australia, it was so cool; Did you see the finals for the Cricket World Cup? I saw it in the stadium and it was awesome.

Five years in this school and everything's the same. The same discussion about the summer vacations on the first day. The same people trying to show off about the cool places they visited and the expensive hotels they stayed in.

Unless a teacher is present in class nobody gives a damn about keeping their mouth shut. They will continue their conversations in whispers if the teacher is there. The mumbling will continue all through class.

I look up at the door waiting for the class teacher to enter. I hope it's Meena Miss. Everybody loves her and listens to her. She's the nicest teacher in secondary school, her classes are not the boring ones where the teacher talks nonstop for thirty five minutes. She tries to do different things in class: in primary school she explained to us the concept of rotation and revolution by assigning the role of the sun, the moon and the earth to us. She doesn't give very low marks to anyone, even those students who are not able to write good answers get decent enough marks like a fifteen on twenty, which encourages them to work harder the next time. The most fun part is that once a week, in the last fifteen minutes of class, she makes us play games.

But it's not Meena Miss at the door. It's Silly Mili. She's doing a terrible job at running, dragging her feet at a quick pace down the corridor. The sleeve of her pinafore is slipping off her shoulders. One of the chains in her bag is wide open and we can see all the unnecessary and insane number of textbooks she's carrying. She stops right at the door, peeks in. The tension that was built up and quite visible on her face is gone in seconds. There's no one to scold her today.

Mili sees me sitting at the desk, right opposite the teacher's table and scowls at me. She sees me looking at her reaction. Everyone who has been in Mili's class knows that the first desk of the middle row is for her. If I'd known that she was in my class I would have definitely left that place out for her.

I'd like to say she is a teacher's pet. But, unfortunately despite her various attempts in the last few years, Mili has failed. She is always late to class, her pinafore is always two sizes bigger which makes the already ridiculous red, black and white uniform even more ridiculous, and if a teacher asks her to borrow a chalk from the teacher in the next class she will take six minutes to complete the two-minute task.

I don't want to create any trouble for myself, especially since I'm still not sure whether Pooja and Samantha and possibly the others in my group are going to talk to me. I move one desk over, and Mili tries a lame attempt to smile, making herself comfortable in her spot, and turns to me.

'Hey! What's up?'

'Nothing?'

'How were your holidays, Zara? I saw on Facebook that you and your family had a vacation in the States?'

'Yeah. It was good.'

'Which places did you go to? We went there last year and it was amazing. We went to New York and Boston mainly. I wanted to go to California but my dad said it was on the other coast. He said we'll take a trip there next time.'

'Okay?'

I want to answer her question in detail, but I want Mili to cut out that annoying nasal voice of hers. If I'd known that Mili was in my class, I'd never have dreamt of choosing this particular desk. Ugh.

The conversations are getting louder and louder. Parth and Rohan are playing mini cricket at one end of the room, with a crumpled paper for a ball and a writing pad for a bat; Ria, Mehak, Dan, and Shrey are playing red ants: slap-piling one hand after the other to see whose hand turns the darkest shade of red. So it takes a while before we notice that Deepa Miss, who must've been passing by, is standing by the door. She doesn't have to say anything. One by one, everyone glances towards her and the voices disappear.

Deepa Miss is short, her hair combed back in a pony tail with a few bangs covering her forehead. She is dressed in a pale pink salwar kameez with a matching dupatta draped over one shoulder. She has freckles all over her face and she doesn't bother to cover it up with make-up either. That's the only thing I like about her. As soon as the class is quie

t she leaves. Everyone is so scared of her that we remain quiet for some time.

The only sound in the classroom is that of the Vice Principal going on with her welcome back speech. 'Lastly, please take part in as many events as you can that occur during the academic year: Sports day, Annual Day, Traditional Day. But the same rule applies: do not under any circumstance skip class to practise performances or to organise these events. If you do so, your parents will be called in and it could result in possible rustication from this school, which you are privileged to be a part of. I would like to leave you with some words by Nayyirah Waheed to start off your new academic year, "let a new life happen to you". Have a rainy day.'

I think that's the only thing the forty students in my class hear, as all of us turn around to look out the window. The rain, the first of the season, is light but has enough force, that the students on the last bench have to slide the glass windows shut in order to avoid water from splattering on their books. It rains every year. Almost every day during the monsoon season. But the rain manages to make everyone quiet. For me, this season is anything but a welcome. It makes everything mucky and drowsy and an already dirty city more dirty. But there are the romantic people, who love to get drenched, enjoy a cup of chai or coffee and listen to the sounds of the rain crashing against the ground.

But we stop thinking about the rain as soon as we hear the scraping of the chair against the marble floor. The class teacher is here.

She is wearing a shiny silk sari, a big red bindi, placed exactly in between her eyebrows, thick winged eye-liner and kajal and a dark red lipstick. A bunch of sweet smelling mogra flowers is tied to the middle of her plait.

'Good morning class! My name is Bindu. Sorry for the delay.'

That is enough for us to know what the entire year is going to be like. The teacher's South Indian accented English makes the class laugh as if we're listening to the stupid, comedy show, The Takeshi's Castle commentary by Javed Jaffrey on Pogo. I don't know how many seconds or minutes we laugh for, but it is uncontrollable. The three simple sentences keep playing in our heads. Bindu Miss walks out of the class. I see tears forming at the corner of her eyes. But just as the class is becoming more sober from the laughing exercise, Dhrumil- the class clown takes his place at the centre of the room. He mimics Bindu Miss's introduction and sends us all back to a rolling-on-the-floor laughing situation.

Everyone's talking amongst themselves. The class is systematically divided. The first row and half of the second row consists of girls and the rest of the second row and the third consists of boys.

Moksha, who has been in the same class as me since the first grade, smiles and waves her hand but I think she realises that I've always tried to avoid her, so her hand goes down mid-wave. I give her a weak smile, returning my attention to the book.

I hope I can read in peace now. I try sagging my shoulders, whatever I can manage, book in my lap and try to use the desk as a shield because according to school rules I'm not allowed to bring non-academic books to school. Well, the school authorities have got to blame themselves. The teachers explain us the concepts like robots, as if they have mugged up the main points from the textbook. This is the reason why most of us end up reading other books like fiction or autobiographies. I've barely reached the part where Victoria's sister, Grace is born, when the class goes silent again. Bindu Miss is standing behind her table. She has an entire piece of white chalk held weirdly between her four fingers. Her eyes are puffy. But she walks up to the blackboard and starts writing a quote, a school tradition where anyone can write a positive or an inspirational quote on the board.

"It's time to learn how to love and forget how to hate." (via hellish-b0y, Tumblr)

I look at Bindu Miss again. Not in the way she dresses or behaves but more as an actual person, a person different from her profession. She just quoted something off Tumblr and that in itself finds in me a way to connect with her. I feel that Bindu Miss and I have a common interest now, she is someone I can be friendly to, someone who might understand me. I don't know about the other students. Most of them are addicted to Facebook, Instagram and Snapchat. But Tumblr has its own kind of people: the hilarious yet sarcastic comments on every day routine events; nobody has to confirm to a particular norm and everyone is free from judgement. The line itself is relevant to the incident that occurred a couple of minutes back. Nobody apologises; we only stare at Bindu Miss. Eyes occasionally moving from the floor to where she's standing but never really meeting her eyes. We've aced the game of avoiding eye contact with any adult when we've done something wrong.

I close my book and put it back where it belongs. Bindu Miss doesn't mention anything about us making fun of her, in fact she ignores the whole event like a pro.

'It's the first day of school. You all are full of energy and have stories to tell. Let's do something interesting. Write down something funny or awkward or unexpected that you did during your summer break. The note can be anonymous if you want it to be. After you are done pass it down your row.'

Nobody laughs this time. We open our books, tear off a page and do what we're told.

There are whispers, 'You should write about that time when…' 'Dude, I can't think of anything interesting.' But eventually everyone starts writing down their stories.

I think hard. If there was a trophy or something for being the most awkward person it will, without doubt, be gracefully handed over to me. I am a hundred percent sure that no one can contest me in this matter. I have way too many stories to contribute: the awkwardness in approaching a waiter at the restaurant to simply giving my order or asking for the bill, the times when I meet someone unexpected at the mall or the movies or the shopping mall. One would expect me to learn from my past mistakes but it just seems to get worse. I bring my hands around my stomach and try to avoid my lack of social skills with a mix of laughter, smiles and embarrassment.

I debate with myself whether I should write about that time when I fell smack on my bum in the middle of a busy café and everyone just turned to look at me, or that time I was going for a handshake with my mathematics tutor but she went in for a hug and basically my hand was on her stomach while she hugged me for all of fifteen seconds. Instead, I wrote:

Last time I was entering my dad's office, I didn't notice the glass door and I walked right into it. This was fine until I realised that everyone around me had seen what had just happened. Mr. Verma and Mrs. Sharma were staring at me, pursing their lips and trying to maintain a serious expression in order to avoid laughing right in front of me.

One by one, we pass down our notes. When everyone is done, Bindu Miss, who has been watching us, says: 'I'm going to shuffle these and give each one of you a note to read out loud. But don't read it until it is your turn.'

She shuffles the notes and hands them to us.

I hold in my hand a piece of scrappy paper. The black smudges on the paper make it look as if it has been dragged across a really dirty desk. My fingers turn to the edges of the paper to unfold it but I see Bindu Miss, her eyes wandering around the class, and I decide against it. It can be a surprise for me as well.

'Let's start from the last bench, introduce yourself and then read the note handed over to you.'

'My name is Parth. *Um*, I was nicely leaning against a stationery car when all of a sudden the car started moving. Luckily nothing much happened other than the mini shock my brain and heart received.'

'My name is Yash. My friends and I were having a sleepover. They were prank calling my crush. Fortunately for me, her mother picked up the call.

The look on their faces was worth taking a picture.'

Up till now everyone has been quiet. We're not sure whether Bindu Miss is going to explode and scold us or whether she had left the class earlier to complain to the Principal. But as soon as the first note is read out, the stony silence lifts, and all of us laugh a little bit. We continue this for the rest of the period. All forty of us. Everyone is surprised because for the other classes most of us don't get a chance to speak.

Soon it is my turn to read out the note. I realise everyone is looking at me. With trembling hands I open the chit.

'*Um*. My name is Zara. I met my crush during one of the summer camp activities I took in school and I was so excited I leaned in to kiss her on the cheek but she kept leaning away. *Um*. It took me five full seconds to realise what I was doing and how everyone around was staring and laughing. It was um super awkward and embarrassing.'

I look around. Sitting two desks away is Saurabh, looking anywhere but at me.

The bell rings. Break time. There's a rush of energy and excitement. I don't have to wait too long for everyone to leave. I see Moksha lingering by the door. She comes back in to ask,

'Hey Zara! You wanna come to the cafeteria with me?'

'Maybe next time. I promised to hang out with Samantha and Pooja today.'

I'm surprised nobody in class has noticed that my back is not my back. I grab the sandwich mum packed for me in the morning and make my way down to the playground. My pace is slower than usual, especially when I walk down the stairs from my class.

The space at the back of the school is huge. There are tiny swings, slides and a see-saw for the pre-primary students. The mini train which brings the kindergarten students from the front gate to the entrance of the building is parked on one side. But right now the ground is empty except for Pooja and Samantha, who are half whispering half shouting something one after the other. From afar, it looks like they are not stopping for breath. They see me approach and I hear, 'Guess we'll find out soon.'

I look at them. Samantha and Pooja follow me. They look like they are waiting to be told something gossipy, I guess I'll have to reveal my secret and see how they react.

'So about the thing earlier, I hope you haven't told anyone.'

'Oh no I swear we haven't told anyone. But what's wrong? What is that hard thing here?' Samantha asks pointing at my back again with her index finger.

'It's a brace to correct my posture.'

'What is wrong with your posture? Everything was fine the last time we saw you,' Pooja continues the questioning.

'So it is actually called um.. Adolescent Idiopathic Scoliosis.'

'What?' they both say.

'A back problem. Basically, I have to wear this brace so my spine doesn't curve in a different direction.'

Pooja halts her swinging for a few seconds and says,

'So we can't play ops and bats anymore? Because it was actually fun to hit on something hard like that.'

'Well we can as long as it doesn't hurt your hand.'

Samantha excitedly moves towards me and asks: 'It was fun. Can I do it again?'

'Go ahead.'

Bam, she smacks my back and giggles. Even Pooja leaves the swing and follows Samantha, 'This feels so different Zara. Will you be wearing this every day?'

'Yes, I have to wear it every day. But I wanted it to be a secret of my own you know. I don't want to tell the others in our group right now.'

'Oh don't worry about them. We told them we're going for a secret meeting of our own. We were just joking but now we do have a secret of our own,' Samantha giggles, 'This is going to be so much fun!'

Dorothy Darling

Charlotte Symons

Chapter One

A Pug Named Maud

The bus rattled away in a cloud of dust, leaving Dorothy standing in the lane, afternoon sun beating down on her felt hat. It was May, but already it felt hot enough for summer. If only she'd been able to get the earlier bus that went through the village. But the bus conductor's instructions had been quite clear. A couple of miles down the lane, on the left. 'You can't miss it,' he'd added, cheerfully. Dorothy, suspicious of the countryside and its wiles, rather thought she could. Still, there was sure to be someone to ask. Adjusting the grip of her overnight case in her hand like a soldier taking a firmer hold of his rifle, she set off.

She had to admit, it was pleasant to be away from London. The air was fresh and clean, and she could hear birds singing, and not just sparrows, either. Was that a thrush? she wondered, hearing the repeated phrase and remembering Browning from her schooldays. But there were lots more she didn't know. If she got the job, she'd learn all about the birds and the countryside and everything. But, oh dear, she would miss London! It was grimy and dreary sometimes, of course, but it was home. Even the dinginess was lovable, in its way. There were moments, like the other day, eating her supper of beans on toast made over the gas ring, while the sky slowly turned pink and the starlings wheeled and twisted over the rooftops, when she knew that London, for better or worse, was part of her, in a way that this rural paradise could never be.

But that sort of thinking is not going to get you hired, Dorothy Darling, she admonished herself. Stiff upper lip and all that. London would still exist. There were such things as trains. And maybe she could save enough to have a little flat in town someday. Anyway, dreams could wait. She had to get the job first. And for that, she had to find the place.

It was hot on the road. The sun was relentless. Its light seemed to have a clarity that London sun just didn't. Despite her hat, she found herself having to squint. She must have gone two miles by now, surely. Still there was no sign of the house, nor anyone to ask. Ah, here was something, at least, she thought, rounding the bend. 'Something' proved to be a complication. The lane forked into two. Neither way was signposted.

Dorothy regarded the potential options. The bus conductor had said 'on the left', which was, perhaps, an argument for taking the left-hand fork. Then again, a case could be made for the right-hand fork being the continuation of the road she was on, given the fact the other road seemed to join at an angle. After all, he'd said nothing about turning off. The left way, however, was temptingly shady. Maybe she should try that one first. It would be a relief to be out of the sun for a bit. No, she wouldn't succumb. The right-hand way must be the one.

After half-an-hour, Dorothy began to wonder if the left fork would have been the one to choose. If only there was someone to ask! She was beginning to feel very thirsty and slightly desperate. Ah, there was an opening into a field. Dorothy stopped and gazed hopefully over the gate. Surely there must be a farm worker somewhere.

A herd of cows was moving down the slope towards the far end, lowing as it went. Amongst the mooing, she could hear the sharp yaps of a dog. And where there was a dog, there was a person, Dorothy told herself, grimly. The gate, on inspection, proved to be tied shut and recalcitrant. Nothing daunted, Dorothy tossed her suitcase over and began to climb after it. Having retrieved the case, she set off at a trot over the grass, trying as best she could both to keep away from the lumbering beasts and not to tread in anything unpleasant.

She arrived at the bottom of the slope, having incurred one dirty shoe and one turned ankle for her pains, to find that there was indeed an available human – a man, perhaps in his fifties, fitting the role of farm-worker.

'Hello, there!' Dorothy called, trying to keep a note of panic from her voice. The cows were worryingly close, and one was stretching out its nose to her like it thought her hat, or indeed her person, was something to eat.

The man turned around. 'Arternoon, miss,' he called. 'Can I help you?'

Dorothy edged gingerly around the cow and made her way over to him. 'I'm looking for a house called Whiteladies,' she said, when she was near enough. 'I'm afraid I must have missed my way.'

'Whiteladies, you say? No, I wouldn't say as you've missed it. Not if you've come from the main road, anyday. It's 'bout a mile down the way,' the man said. 'Left-hand side.' He pointed, further on in the direction she'd been travelling.

'But I've been walking for ages, and the bus conductor only said a couple of miles!' Dorothy exclaimed.

'Well, there's miles, miss, and then there's miles. I reckon his miles were a bit on the large side. I'd call it more like five, from the road.'

Still, at least she hadn't gone wrong. Dorothy thanked the man and began the slow trudge back up the field. The cows, at least, seemed to have no inclination to follow. She wouldn't have put it past them to chase her up the field, like so many dogs, but she supposed they had other things on their mind.

It seemed the dairyman's miles were also on the large side. She almost missed the house in the end. From the road there was no sign of it, only a moss-green path winding away between trees. But the path *was* on the left. Dorothy had already dismissed it and walked past, but she retraced her steps and peered down the winding track. After her long walk, the way looked cool and inviting. On either side of the lane a froth of greenish-white flowers grew, airy as lace. In fact, Dorothy seemed to remember the plant was called Queen Anne's lace. Certainly, if she had been out for a stroll, the path looked ideal. But was it the right way? Unsure, she half turned away. Then she saw it – lying almost hidden by the tall grass at the side of the path. A roughly-cut piece of wood, painted with the word 'Whiteladies'.

After searching for so long, the house had achieved a near-mythical status in Dorothy's mind, so that the fact of having found it came almost as an anti-climax. Still, she reminded herself, finding the place was only the beginning. Now she had to get the job.

The path wound its way along, barred by shadows from the late-afternoon sun. After a few minutes, she began to catch glimpses of a building between the trees. An old, tiled roof; stone chimneys. And then the path wriggled its way round a sharp bend and there was the house, lying before her in the golden sun of a May evening.

Whiteladies was large and rambling, as if it had grown slowly in this place, adding to itself over the centuries. For even Dorothy's unpractised eye could tell that it was very old. The centre section had a row of narrow, arched windows, such as you might see on the side of a church. Another wing had an upper part that was half-timbered, jutting out over a stone-built lower section. The oldest part, as far as she could tell, was the bit that looked like a squat, square-built tower. The windows there were tiny, reminding her of the arrow-slits at the Tower of London. The house looked over a garden, half-hidden from where she stood by tall yew topiary and hedges. Near the gate, a lilac was in full flower. Late as she was, Dorothy was unable to resist the temptation just to stand and drink in the scene. A sense of peace seemed to dwell in the air. As she watched, a pair of white doves came winging over the trees to settle on the roof.

She should go in. She lifted the latch of the gate and pushed it open.

On turning from fastening the gate, Dorothy found that a small animal was barrelling down the path towards her, making a noise akin to a miniature steam engine. Thinking it prudent to offer the line of least resistance, Dorothy remained where she stood. The emitter of the noise proved to be a fawn pug-dog carrying a stout Meerschaum pipe in its mouth. The dog came up to her and sniffed her feet carefully.

'Hello there,' Dorothy said. The dog wagged its tail in a cautious fashion.

'Maud! *Maud!*' The voice came from the house.

'Is that you?' Dorothy asked the dog.

The dog snorted.

Maybe the voice was calling a maid. After all, who named their dog Maud?

But nervous though she was, she couldn't stand by the gate forever. 'Come on then, Puggy. Lead the way,' Dorothy said. She took a step forward and the dog ran off in front of her down the path.

The front door stood open, showing a flag-stoned hall, furnished only by a dark oak chest topped with an unlit lamp. The pug went through the door and disappeared, still carrying the pipe, leaving Dorothy alone and feeling slightly daunted. She looked at the door. It was huge, studded with nails, the sort usually seen on a church. There was also a large iron knocker. Dorothy rapped it sharply.

Just as she was wondering whether to knock again, she heard footsteps, both human and canine.

'Hello?'

The woman who appeared, accompanied by the pug, was wearing corduroy trousers and a loose white shirt. Her hair was short, and she had a weather-beaten appearance, like someone who spends as much time outside as they can. Like the dog, she was carrying a pipe, though in her case she held it in her hand rather than clutched in her teeth. She regarded Dorothy with a bright, bird-like eye.

'Now, who might you be?' she said, cheerfully.

'I'm D-Dorothy Darling,' Dorothy stammered, and waited for a light of recognition to dawn in the woman's eyes. When it failed to do so, she added: 'I've come about the job – you wrote, giving me the address.'

'Dorothy! Of course! The new secretary! You must forgive me – I've been writing all afternoon. Tends to scramble the brain. But wasn't I expecting you earlier?'

'Yes, I do apologise, there was a problem with the points on the line, so I missed the right bus—'

'No, don't apologise, nothing I like less. So tedious! Come on in.' The woman, who must, Dorothy thought, be Miss March, held the door wide. Gratefully, Dorothy slipped past her into the hall.

Miss March led the way down a corridor. Dorothy followed, with the pug bringing up the rear, still carrying the pipe. Halfway down, Miss March opened a door and stepped inside.

'Have a seat. I'll see about some tea,' she said.

'Thank you.' Tea came as welcome news indeed.

Left alone, Dorothy was able to do what she really wanted, which was to look around her. It was, she thought, the most interesting room she had ever been in. Pattern and colour were everywhere, from the paintings that crowded the walls to the Turkish carpets on the floor. Even the walls themselves were painted. Around the fireplace, stylised figures danced and the spaces between the picture-frames were filled with geometric patterns. Dorothy didn't know where to look first. On the mantlepiece, a primitive-looking sculpture of a man, either very old or very new, sat side-by-side with the skull of a bird and an ivory statue of the Virgin Mary.

The chimney was huge, Dorothy noticed – another sign of an old house. On either side, well-packed bookshelves cried out to be examined. Just as Dorothy was trying to resist the temptation, for books, particularly other people's, always held an overwhelming fascination for her, Miss March returned, her hands disappointingly empty of tea.

'Mrs Oxley will be along in a moment,' she said. 'Did you find the place alright?'

'In the end,' Dorothy said. 'The bus-conductor's miles were a bit on the large side.'

'Country miles,' Miss March acknowledged. 'We are a bit out of the way here. I bought the house seven years ago, thanks to *Murder on the Lawn.* It suits me, but it wouldn't be everyone's cup of tea.'

At that point, the door opened, and a woman came in carrying a tea-tray, followed closely by the pug, who appeared to be keeping a keen eye on proceedings. 'Speaking of which… Thank you, Mrs Oxley, that's grand.'

'Will there be anything else, madam?'

Miss March cocked an inquiring eyebrow in Dorothy's direction. Looking at the tray, which was virtually heaving with sandwiches and cakes as well as tea, Dorothy couldn't imagine any desire that hadn't been amply provided for. She shook her head. 'It all looks wonderful, thank you.'

'Well, tuck in,' Miss March said, as Mrs Oxley left the room. 'If you're anything like me after I've been travelling, you'll be ravenous.'

'It does seem a long time since lunch,' Dorothy admitted. 'And it was only a bacon roll.'

She helped herself to a selection of sandwiches, while Miss March poured the tea. The pug was watching expectantly. 'I haven't forgotten, Maud. Wait a moment.'

'That's an unusual name for a dog.' Dorothy was unable to resist commenting.

'Maud? I suppose it is. When she was a puppy, she didn't like going outside, so I was always trying to tempt her into the garden. Tennyson, you know.'

'Of course.' Dorothy laughed, recalling the refrain 'Come into the garden, Maud.'

'No stopping her now, of course. Chases the doves when she thinks I'm not looking, bother her. Here you are.' This last remark was addressed to the dog, as Miss March put a small plate of bread-and-butter sandwiches down on the floor. They watched as Maud delicately ate her way through them, before washing it down with a cup of milky tea. Having finished her repast, Maud settled down on Dorothy's feet with a sigh.

'Well, I think Maud's hired you already,' Miss March said. 'Now, tell me about yourself. You said in your letter you've been working as a secretary?'

'That's right,' Dorothy said. 'I work at a small publishing company. I type, take dictation, write letters, keep accounts and make notes in shorthand.' She crossed her fingers under cover of her tea-plate as she said the last.

'I don't doubt your qualifications, Dorothy. You came with a very good reference from Mr Johansson. What I do wonder about is whether you'd be happy in the country, after being used to London. It would be a big change.'

'I know,' Dorothy said. 'That was what made me apply. I want something different.' She hesitated, wondering how best to articulate her thoughts. 'During the war, we were all just waiting for it to be over, for everything to get back to normal. Then, when it ended, things didn't get any better. Our wages went down when the men came back to work, and it doesn't seem like that's ever going to change.' And then there were the people who weren't there anymore. The ghosts.

'The war has a lot to answer for,' Miss March said. 'My brother lost his only son. Eighteen. Lasted ten days at the front.'

'I lost my brother,' Dorothy said. It was still hard to say the words. 'It was in the summer of '18. When we got the telegram, Mother went to pieces. She never really recovered. She died of the influenza that winter, along with my sister Elsie.'

'I'm sorry,' Miss March said. 'I sometimes think the deaths of that last summer and autumn were the cruellest ones of all. And then that beastly 'flu. How rotten for you. Have you got anyone left – your father?'

'Daddy died before the war started. It's just me, now. So you see, I haven't got any reason to stay in London.'

'I understand. Well, if you want a change, you've come to the right place. It may sound silly, but there's something about Whiteladies that gets you after a while. It was a nunnery, you know, way back when. Perhaps all those centuries of prayer create an atmosphere, but I'm certain I can feel it. Something spiritual, for want of a better word. Not that I'm really a believer.'

'I think I felt it when I arrived,' Dorothy said. 'A sense of peace.'

'I'm glad you think so. It's a special place, and I hope, if you accept the job, that you'll be happy here. More tea?'

When they had supplied themselves with fresh tea and a slice of cake each, Miss March said: 'Is there anything you'd like to ask me? Not that I've really told you what the role would entail. I should perhaps warn you, I haven't had a secretary before,' she went on. 'Never really saw the need. But the publishers have been on at me to answer the people who write to me. I tried to persuade them that's their job, but to no avail. So that would be one of your tasks, writing to thank them for their kind letter. Very dull, I'm afraid. The other part, probably also rather dull, is typing up my drafts. I write in a very labour-intensive way, writing long-hand on paper, then typing it up, chopping and changing, before typing it all out again. I've tried writing directly with the typewriter, but it just doesn't work.' She looked over at Dorothy. 'Have I put you off yet?'

'Not yet,' Dorothy smiled.

'What I was thinking in terms of hours was nine till four, four days a week, an hour off for lunch, then nine till noon on Wednesdays. Weekends off. Regards pay...' She named a sum that was more than Dorothy got paid at her current job, even though that was longer hours. 'Bed and board included, of course.'

Dorothy could hardly believe it. Most of her wage at present went on the rent. If she wasn't paying out for food or lodging, she'd be able to save some money, for the first time in her life.

'Are you sure? The pay seems very generous…'

'These books of mine may not win prizes, but the public like them, and more importantly, they pay for them. I'm not short of a few pennies, though that hasn't always been the case, and I don't believe in being mean. I'm prepared to pay well in return for good service.'

'I understand. I'll see you're not disappointed, Miss March.'

'I'm sure I won't be,' Miss March said, with a sudden smile that lit up her face and made her bird-like eyes sparkle.

Later, standing at the window of the guest bedroom, watching the light fade from the garden, Dorothy wondered if she'd made the right decision. She would miss London and the independence of her bedsit. But she had to admit, the last few years had been hard. It wasn't just the constant scrimping, the feeling extravagant if she did so much as buy an iced bun in a tea-shop. There was the loneliness. Robert hadn't been the only one she'd lost to the fields of France. She never mentioned Harry. 'My young man' she supposed she could call him; always young, now, while she grew older, alone. Perhaps Miss March was right. After so much death, maybe she did need a time of healing, and maybe, just maybe, this strange and beautiful house was the place to find it.

Chapter Two

The Lyttons of Lytton Hall

Dorothy woke to find the room filled with the pearly light of morning. She lay looking up at the white ceiling, letting the feeling of peace wash over her. Any doubts she might have had last night had disappeared. It was as though the house, having held her safe through the hours of darkness, had now taken her as its own. She was welcome here, she was sure.

A strange noise came from the other side of her door. It sounded like someone blowing through the crack, though going by the height from which the sound seemed to emanate, they'd have to be lying down while they did it.

The sound went on. *Huff. Huff. Hwroof.*

Dorothy smiled to herself and got out of bed. When she opened the door, Maud burst in, wagging her tail nineteen-to-the-dozen. The little dog proceeded to seize hold of the bottom of Dorothy's nightdress with her teeth and wind it around her legs, wagging her tail in triumph all the while. 'Hey,' Dorothy laughed. 'Where's your pipe?'

Maud made no reply, save to carry on snorting, winding and wagging. Looking about for deliverance, Dorothy's eyes lighted upon her dressing table. She hobbled over to it, casting her eye over the various objects that lay there. 'Here you are,' she told Maud, handing the dog her hairbrush. She needed a new one anyway. Distracted, Maud dropped the hem of the nightdress and seized hold of the wooden handle with a delighted gurgle. Head held high, she paraded the hairbrush round the room, wagging her tail so hard her whole body shook with excitement. Dorothy stood in the middle of the room and laughed till her sides ached.

They found Miss March already at the breakfast table, munching toast and marmalade and reading the morning paper. A cup of villainous-looking coffee sat at her elbow. 'Morning. Help yourself.' She indicated the table. 'Or Mrs Oxley will bring you anything else.'

Dorothy's usual breakfast was tea and bread-and-marg, with sometimes a kipper or an egg as finances allowed. Her experience of coffee was limited to what passed under the name at the Lyon's corner house. Now, tentatively, she took a cup and poured some of the dark liquid. The taste was rich, bitter and strong. She could get used to this, she thought, letting the flavour roll round her mouth. It certainly beat the watery Lyon's offering into a cocked hat. The rest of her breakfast was also a great improvement on her usual fare. Toast, spread with golden butter and Mrs Oxley's chunk-filled marmalade, was almost unrecognisable from her customary cardboard slabs smeared with cheap apple jam.

'You'll find there are some young people in the village,' Miss March was saying. 'The Lyttons, up at the Hall, for a start. They must be around your age. There's Cynthia, and her brother Ned. He's just inherited the title, of course – the old Viscount died last winter. Nasty bout of pneumonia. Well, he would go out hunting with his bad chest, and him nearly seventy. His wife's a lot younger – he married money. American, you know.'

Dorothy made interested-sounding noises. Privately, she rather doubted that a young Viscount and his sister would be interested in being friends with a humble secretary who, until yesterday, had been living in a bedsit, managing on a few shillings a week.

But Miss March hadn't finished. 'I'll ask them to dinner on Friday. Oil the wheels of social intercourse. We'll launch you on Little Strachey society!'

***Dorothy Darling* is a murder-mystery novel set in the early 1920s.** *While largely light in tone, it also depicts its characters struggling to deal with the emotional aftermath of the Great War.*

Animals of Unprecedented Need

J. A. Velasco

Broken English

Enzo said to me I am up to something bad, that I mean bad to him. I enigma, he say.

He don't understand me, I think maybe because of my English. Or maybe because we different, very. He has all I want, he can buy clothes every now and then, he can go to lunch in places with shiny floor and big crystal doors. He can have a taxi to go to town, even when is just 45 minutes walking. I think Enzo sees easy many things, he think life is easy. That because things and life have been easy to him since he was born: he never worked before (he just studying all his years) so I think how can he know about things and the life if he always been in bubble of school? Is he going to read book when he is in trouble or has to put a smile to his boss? Sometimes I think he will be not have a boss anyway. He lucky.

Enzo text me first, that is truth. I was putting my clothes in the closet of my room when I hear the phone doing *beep beep*, message came from him. I don't like the room because the floor is carpet and when I have no slippers my foot feel sticky, but is so much better than the coffin room I have in home. Here at least I am free to use my two legs to walk from the bed to the desk. The bed is so big, my feet are not touching the wall as it use to be back in Hong Kong or Japan, where my foot will be touching the wall and I do not move much because the person upstairs me complain that his bed move as well.

Enzo has a nice English, he have live here for many years now so he even has the sounds of the English people a bit, he still has to become better. I told him I was lived in Hong Kong all my life because I still think people of England don't like Chinese around, and Hong Kong people are not Chinese from China, they are Hong Kong people. Different system.

Enzo write text to me in very difficult English the first night we talked. He use the words like *arrival, conversation, cultural-shock, longing, mindful, thoughtful, careful, accommodation, bedding* (which is not bed), *chores, adaptor, plug*, and the one that I like so much how it sound is *conjugation*, that words is so very beautiful. He has so many different words when he talk about things of his wc: he say t*oilet, toilette-seat, sink, shower, shower-gel, shower head, shower, a shower, the shower, bath, a bath, bath-tube, bath-cream, bath-bomb, towel, hand towel, gym towel, a towel, the towel,* and also says *towel rack.* Why he complicate things so much? He has many things to think about and that is only about his wc, I don't want to ask about his room because he might write book about it. He says things have own name and form part of 'a whole', that not all of it is a wc but I tell him that's not matter much as long as you know how to use it. But he say language is more than just knowing the name of things.

I think I can see opportunity here and Enzo can help me learn things, I was about to tell him to teach me but he say it first, he say if I give him chance he can teach me new words and what they mean so I can speak better in time. I say yes, he can teach me.

I ask him why he text me so late at night, why he awake.

He says if I know the word *lonely,* and I tell him I do. I say I am lonely right now because is just me in my room, alone sound like lonely. Maybe he means in deep sense, always be alone even when people with you? He always thinking way too much about one single thing. I think this is sad for late night, to be lonely talking bad things with stranger so I want to change the talk, I want to listen good things instead of sad. I ask what's his favorite word and he says *affection.* Sound like affect, of something bad. I tell him I want to know what affection mean and he say he too, he also wants to know what affection mean.

How can he use a word he don't know what it means?

And I thinking *my* English was bad.

I saw Enzo when he was walking in campus the next day, I can see him but I far and he can't see me. He look more tall than what I think he was, he actually look much better in real life than in my phone screen but I can only think of eating a banana with the chopsticks, they not meant to be. I don't know why I know this so fast about him and me. I text him later because the past night he said we can meet for coffee, I telled him that I want to learn to drink the tea like the Queen and he says he knows how she drinks it. "It's pretty straightforward, Angus. You just literally fill the teapot with boiling water and empty it, then just drop two teabags and fill it up again, let it brew for three minutes, pour it in a mug, add a bit of milk and sugar to your own taste with a teaspoon" he said, but I don't understand what he means by 'brew' and 'pour' so I just text back 'O.K. u teach me'. If he can do it for me then why bother to know these words. And again he complicated things: *teapot, teabag, teaspoon.* I can use teapot to put something that is not tea, maybe just water. I can use teaspoon to eat something that is not tea, I think of honey. So a teaspoon is just a spoon, a teapot is just a pot. And I can use bag for nearly any thing, so a teabag is not correctly said, it's just tea.

The past night, before I put clothes in the closet, I was met with my neighbours. I live with thirteen other people, they say this is cheap place to live for university, that why we live in a big tower and there are 14 of us. I hear the white boy, Christopher, say something about class and the system, but I don't understand what he mean, classes start tomorrow and the system can be anything. My room is in floor 11, the kitchen divides the floor in two and we can sit in the long table. I can see all campus from the big window in here, is so big and long I can see the lake and the fountain and the building, I look down and I can see people pushing boxes down in the floor, some old people are helping them. I think how is that people in the Europe bring the family today. I look to the left where all the cars are and some people are giving hugs and say goodbye to the kids, is so much drama. They live not far so I don't understand why mothers be cleaning their eyes after they hug the young person. In China that happens when we children but not in university, some parents don't go to university until graduation, but here thing is very different. I hear someone back me and I turn around, is one of my neighbours, his name is Evan. He says he from a place called Sarry Near London, he ask me if I know it and I just move my head up and down so I not look stupid, it remind me of my English teacher in my first school because she say if one day White people ask us something we are Chinese so we never must answer 'I don't know', she say we always must say 'I'm not sure' so we don't embarrass the all country, but now I am embarrassing every one because I forgot how to say what she said me and I am standing here completely silence moving my head up and down looking at Evan. His face have blue eyes, they are beautiful and he has a beautiful smile. He is tall and look like a model, he has muscles and he speak fast and simple, I can understand what he say most of the time. He say he will go out to a party and ask me to go with him. I say yes. He is very acute.

I did not told Enzo about my neighbour because I don't want to make him feel sad, and the past night in the party Evan drink too much and he was funny and kissed me on my face. I am drinking the tea with Enzo and I just think of Evan, I afraid Evan will walk in here and see me. I tell Enzo we can go to his room because he say he have a TV and we can see a movie, this is one of the things we both share. Enzo room is very big, he even has a wc inside so no need to go out in the hall to wait for others to wash, he can do it right there. His room is so big he can put an extra chair and a small table to put the pizza. I tell Enzo if he want to teach me more words, and he say he wants to teach me not word but a *concept*, he call it 'the tense'.

'It just means that, if you use the correct tense for a verb, people will understand you in a more accurate way' he say and I tell him I don't know what accurate is. He say that it means correct. 'If you conjugate your verbs, if you apply the proper tense, it assures that we know when, whatever you're saying, took place.' He say, then he quickly tells me that to assure is to make things secure, *certain*, he so funny because I know what assure means, I am a very assure person, very confident. 'For instance, if you say *I was happy*, then that could mean you were happy and now you're not.' He say. Then he use the print machine to give me a sheet that say 'Prepositions' and he teaches me that too. I learned so much in so little time, I say to him. He said that time matters in whatever we say or write, because otherwise we can say things 'without really expressing with *certainty* what we mean'. He telling me about the difference in say *in, at, on, to, with.* I tell him that I think he is right in all he say, I always believed that the past is very important because our present is the result of that. Then he laugh so loud when I said that, he say he was not talking about past in a deep sense and that he not sure I get what he is 'trying to do'. He laughs so loud again and I laugh because his laugh is very loud and funny and his face gets red and he is a bit overly weighted so he looks like a tomato, I imagine his hair is grass and is green so he looks like a tomato more and more. We are both laughing at the same time, but I think he never understood I am laughing *at* him, not *with* him.

I enjoy his company. He reminds me of one of my client back when I live in Japan.

I have not tell him I live in Japan, that I swear to my self I was not going to tell anyone. Sometimes late at night I still think to my self who I'm. I still dream with two of three client, I dream of Akari and her Mother, the Mother really like me. The Mother will cook me very delicious Japanese foods thinking Akari and me were *fuufu*, that we were marrying, she believed I very rich. The Mother die thinking I was marrying her daughter, and once she die Akari just pay me the rest of the money she owned me and with those I pay my plane ticket to Hong Kong to see my father and mother.

I liked working for womans in Japan because most of those client had a good reason why to use the order-form. They usually love womans but can not be with them because the family gets very angry, older people want the female childs to marry men, not womans. So I went to Akari's Mother twice in one months and stayed in her house in Ohara. Akari hired me when she know her Mother was having a dying cancer so the job took about 4 month only, then she said she was happy her Mother was not suffering and she can be with Miku together.

I ask the company if I could find client in Hong Kong or Shanghai but they say no unless I finish the jobs in Japan first, I have to wait to finish my job with Eiko, she hired me because his Mother mind was going forgetful and asked for Saku every day. Saku was the Mother dead son, Eiko's brother. This is a typic client, is always the dying Mother or dying Father. Is never about the client unless they want sex or accompany. So I wait until Eiko calls me and I become her brother, I am Miwa's son, and visited her in hospital every day until one day she forgot she has a son and forgot she has a daughter and forgot how to speak and who she was and who she has been. One day she forgot how to breathe and then she die.

It was female that I liked working for, I always get thinks for free and is usually easy job and I liked to think I was helping some one, some how. The only person I do not charge money and did for free was Momo because she work in the OTEIL office and I needed to pass the English tongue test so I could inscribe in English University. She wanted to move to China so we marry and she got her visa and she help me get my OTEIL exam. Job done.

With mans is different, mans just wanted my body, tho few times they have similar case like Akari so I will dress like a girl and put dust colours in my face and go and see the older Mothers.

Mens mostly it was the sex they wanted. I will asked the mans to buy the clothes they wanted me to wear, they must have to be expensive clothes and I get to keep it, they always say yes to that, the usually thing was to go for a elegant dinner to places with shiny floor and the man working in the restaurant will put the white cotton square in my belly so I do not get the food in my clothes. It was when we go to the room in the hotel or the home when I will feel the job was a bit difficult, some people wanted me to do things I don't want to do but I am a professional and I needed the money to study in English university. Hisato will hand me a heavy book, which was very expensive he said, and wanted me to rip the pages as we were having the sex in hard way, I was order to moan ans scream as I rip pages apart.

Hisato wanted me to do gross things with him and I forever said yes, he worked for the local college and was the secretary, I need him to have me very good grades to English university. He say for every meeting he was going to put high mark in the ballot of one topic, then another day another topic, then another topic. Good thing I just need one good GPA.

He was very hard to me, he put all his fat body on top of mine and will not stand up until he finish, he would use his hands, his cock, sometimes his whole fingers and hand and push it to my inside. He will turn my body upside down and now I looking at the ceiling and then he doing things with his mouth in my cock, then he will flip me back and now my face was on the bed again and he pull my hair very very very hard that it hurts so much like a burnt and he asks me to scream more and more and more. Then he come on my body and when he finish he ask me if I want food and I can order anything I want from the telephone.

I am not hungry, but in not many places food is free, so I order food and ask cash for the taxi, then I just walk home to take a shower and sleep, I needed to go to the bank early and make the sum of my money. I pay my illness test every week in the hospital with my own cash, if I didn't do that the company won't give me more client and I sign the paper sheet of contract with some of them, like Akari, because there is no finish to the job at first.

I am getting close to the money target I need, I decide Hisato, the man who fuck me hard, is my last client and soon I will go and see my mama and my baba and I need to get the contract for the floor where they live, I will give that to the bank so they can lend me the rest of the money I need to pay for fees, I thought I could make some client from the order-form people in UK anyway, you can find beasts and animals with money anywhere. Hisato is not the only hard client, most man are hard, they all have things in the head that are not right. They fuck me hard, sometimes they beated me (I asked more money if they wanted to beat me) and if they wanted me to say gross things I did in another tongue, Japanese, Cantonese or Mandarin, I would. Then they had my body and I had my cash, they clean themselfs later in the bath but not cleanse, I know they different, clean and cleanse. Enzo remind me of my client. He is teaching me things and buys me food, he must be wanting my body, I can see it in his eye, he can not be good to me if he does not know me so he must be wishing to have me in bed. He does not know I was order-form, he does not know of me and how much I know and how many people I have been for clients. I scared to tell him this, not because I close to love him, but because he might like it. I want to see how much money he can give me or how much expensive clothes he willing to give before I think of give him my body or not. He wears nice things, he takes taxis and he goes to shiny restaurants many times. He must has to be rich, very.

Mens think my body is the cure for the urges they have but is not, my body makes them want more and more. And is all fake, anyway, that why is 'order-form', they order me to be some thing or some one. I don't understand why they like it, but my job is never to ask why, my job is to be made from order, what they want, what they wish, no questions. That why they pay me much more if I just normal prostitute. If I normal prostitute then they know I am prostitute, but in order form I am who they want me to be, my person is zero, Angus, me, not exist.

I am not there, I am an order-form, the name they say is not mine and the things they ask me to do are not things I will do in normal time, so is not me, it cannot be me, it must not be me. When the men are on top of me, fucking me, using my body like a toy, I think I am not there, I think of England, I think of the big clock tower in the big bridge, I think of the Queen drinking the tea, I think of the soldier man with the tall hat, I think of a beeskit, of a black taxi, of a red bus, of the rain, of the fields. I think of I be free. I think of marrying one English person, I think of never being in the bed under Hisato big fat body again. I think of running, of breathing, of touching.

Is not me.

I am not there.

Is not me.

I am not there

I have my own name.

I am Angus.

I have my own life.

About The Writers

M. René Bradshaw is a Californian-born writer, translator, and editor based in London. She is the UK Editor-at-large for *Asymptote Journal,* and the European content manager for *TuneIn Radio*. Her reviews and stories have appeared in *The Times Literary Supplement, The London Magazine*, *Litro*, and elsewhere. She is currently writing her first novel.

mrenebradshaw@gmail.com

Ed Butterfield was born in 1996 and grew up in Dronfield, a small town in Derbyshire. He writes fiction about the legacy of the past, its echoes in the present and the quietly corrosive things we do to the people we love. He is currently working on his first novel.

edward.butterfield@outlook.com

Born in the US, **Costanza Casati** grew up in Italy where she studied Ancient Greek and Latin: she became fascinated with female characters from Greek Myth and wants to make them accessible to the present. She is currently working on a novel about the life of Clytemnestra, turning the murderous queen into an intriguing heroine.

costanza.casati1@gmail.com

Anna Maria Colivicchi was born in Rome, where she studied Italian Literature at Sapienza University, before joining the MA in Writing at Warwick. In her writing, she seeks the extraordinary in the ordinary, focusing on the details of everyday life. She is currently working on her first novel, *The Doctor's House*, a family drama set in Italy.

annamaria.colivicchi@gmail.com

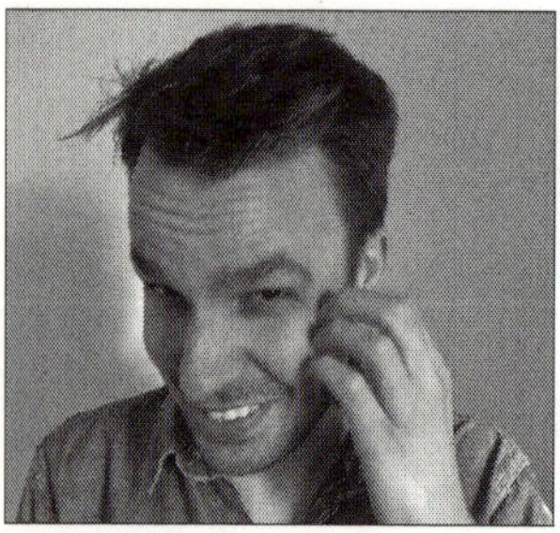

Son of a nurse and an engineer, **David Crowe** has moved every year for a decade. He's writing his way home.

dwcrowe1@gmail.com

After a career in the theatre **Eve Dashwood** completed her Degree in English and enjoyed the experience so much she returned to study on the MA in Writing. She is currently working on a Victorian novel set in the Music Hall and a collection of short stories that re-work classical literature.

evedashwood21@gmail.com

Luke Dean studied Creative Writing at the University of Gloucestershire, where his short fiction has since been taught. After graduating he co-founded Eleven Places Theatre Company, a Cheltenham-based new writing company. He writes about people fumbling in the dark and failing to communicate. He is currently working on his first novel.

lukedean@outlook.com

Will Francis studied Classical and Archaeological Studies at the University of Kent, before joining the Writing MA at the University of Warwick, bringing his love of history and mythology into his writing. His piece *Carter's Folly* draws heavily from Egyptian mythology and the Curse of Tutankhamun.

wpafrancis@aol.com

Annie Garthwaite spent thirty years in business before starting an MA in writing at Warwick in 2017. She is dedicating this time to the novel she has waited many years to write; an account of the life of Cecily Neville, fifteenth century matriarch of the house of York and the longest lived survivor of the Wars of the Roses.

annie@anniegarthwaite.com

Steve Gay writes science fiction novels and thrillers. He also writes short stories and his work has been published in *Litro* magazine. Steve's current project is a historical story set in his home town of Rugby at the time of the Coventry blitz, and based on first hand accounts; *Concrete and Roses* is the first chapter.

stephengay@virginmedia.com

Katie Margaret Hall is the creator and screenwriter of the UK's first Lesbian webseries, the award winning *She's in London.* She released the poetry collection *The Nature of Fragments* in 2016 and was published in the UK Lesfic anthology *L Is For....* Katie is currently developing a TV series and writing her debut novel.

katie.kmhmedia@gmail.com

This is **E. A. Jane**. She is a poet and writer taking inspiration from her travels. Roald Dahl made her love reading and continues to inspire her to write. Though seemingly ordinary at first, she knows a lot about sharks and is persistently quirky in her writing and her life.

emmaalicejane@gmail.com

PS Keynes graduated in English from Trinity College, Cambridge, and trained as an actor at Mountview. She's worked as a journalist, actor and teacher and runs methodinmadness.org.uk. She's the author of a children's picture book and mum to a five year-old son, who keeps her simultaneously on her toes and off her rocker!

penny@penchard.co.uk

Ellen Lavelle was born in 1995. A fan of J.K. Rowling, Scarlett Thomas and Kate Atkinson, she admires their ability to write immersive plot-driven stories. She writes crime and historical fiction and is currently working on a detective novel, featuring a female investigative journalist recovering from a life-threatening injury.

ellenlavelle@btinternet.com

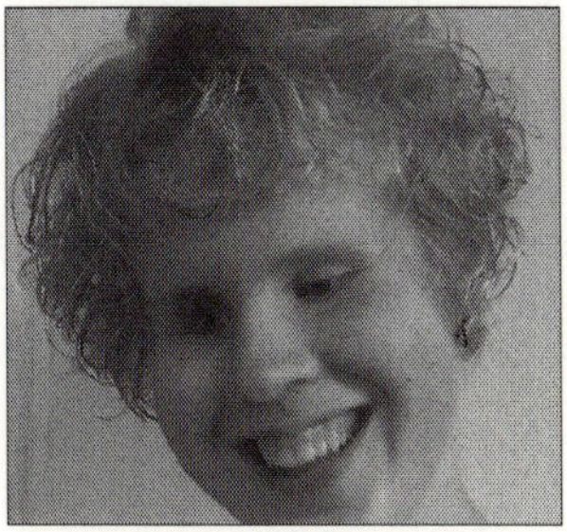

Anna Lodwick is a young writer from Leicester. She prefers working on long-form prose, with fantasy, YA and contemporary being current (sometimes intersecting) areas of interest. As a writer with a disability, she is passionate about matters surrounding equality and seeks out innovative ways to explore them in her work.

annallodwick@gmail.com

Vanwy MacDonald Arif writes about individuals labelled as outsiders. Her background of working in schools in challenging circumstances and experiences of socially disadvantaged communities, as well as her sense of humour, inform her fiction for adults and young people. She enjoys reading magical realism and satire. Her guilty pleasure is crime fiction.

vanwy.arif786@gmail.com

Missy Reddy has been involved in many creative pursuits since childhood: music, dancing, drama and writing. She has studied both psychology and writing at university and has a strong passion for equality and social justice. She writes fiction and creative non-fiction and is currently working on her debut novel: *Lost*.

missyreddy99@gmail.com

Katharine Rowe lives and writes in Northampton. She is currently working on a novel set in a world undergoing an alternative version of the steam revolution. There is another one planned involving Erl Kings and quantum physics. Both her rabbits were eaten by a fox.

tujuh_dua@yahoo.co.uk

Miloni Shah graduated from St. Xavier's College, Mumbai with a degree in English Literature. She is currently pursuing her MA in Writing at University of Warwick. She likes exposing different aspects of society through her work. Her coming of age story, *Curvy Roads*, is about an adolescent diagnosed with a medical condition.

milonishah27@gmail.com

Charlotte Symons writes prose fiction. Her short stories have been published in *The Lampeter Review* and in *The Ghastling* and *Arkana*. Much of her work engages with fantasy or folklore. As well as *Dorothy Darling*, she is working on an historical vampire novel and a retelling of the Arthurian legends.

csymons1@outlook.com

J.A. Velasco graduated in 2015 with honours in Philosophy, Politics and Economics from The University of Essex. He arrived at The University of Warwick in 2015, where he completed an MSc in Economics and is currently pursuing an MA in Writing. Upon graduation, he will start a PhD in Political Narratives and Economic Growth.

javela@outlook.com

Friends of manifest

The following people have shown their support for new writing by helping to fund the creation of manifest: New Writing from Warwick. They deserve our unreserved thanks and we are delighted to recognise them here.

Heather Allford
Sarah Amatt
Ahmed Arif
Susan Aslan
Liz Barclay
Dee Barker
Caroline Bennett
Jonathan Bennett
Peter Bennett
Susan Bennett
Lisa Betteridge
Dot Bond
Nina Brooke
Paola Buccolini
David Butterfield
Gillian Butterfield
Matt Butterfield
Paolo Casati
Giulia Casati Casiraghi
Filippo Casiraghi
Furio Colivicchi
Chris Day
Amy Dean
Diane Dean
Laurel Dean
Peter Diamond
Rosemary Diamond
Jean Escott
Rosie Fawcett
Adrian Francis
Rachel Francis
Gonzalo Ceron Garcia
John Garthwaite
Stephen Gay
Philippa Gee
Kelly Goldstuck
Jo Graham
Elise Graham Benfield
David Hall
Sandra Hall
Marguerite Harrison
Kat Holmes
Jayne Hooper
Suzanne Howe
Sarah Hyde
Michael Ivory
Mike Johnstone
Laura Jommi
Frances Koenig
Caron Lavelle

Ian Lavelle
Joanna Laynesmith
Neil Lewis
Alison Lodwick
David Lodwick
Mark Loly
Eamon MacDonald
Hanz MacDonald
Sandra Maravita
David McGovern
Jane McLeod
Marilyn Miller
Silvia Panceri
Rosie Parsons
Steve Parsons
Eleanor Peters
Valerie Peters
Pamela Petro
Patrick Pietroni
Amanda Pirovano
Flo Quilici
Tazkia Rahman
Ludovic Renou
Clive Rogers
Maggie Rogers
Richard Sandle-Keynes
David Saunders
Trudy Sharpe
Anne Skinner
Carol Small
John Stew
Silvia Strano
Janette Taylor
Alistair Thompson
David Vann
Graziella Volpi
Jude Waddell
Barry Walsh
Kathy Watson
Judy White
Martin White
Caroline Wilson
Ann Wishart
Andy Wong
Christina Wood
Heather Yesson

Acknowledgements

Creating *manifest: New writing from Warwick* has been a joy. It has also been hard work, calling upon the talents, capabilities and support of many people. We would like to offer our heartfelt thanks to the following for their contribution.

Respect and recognition to the manifest committee; Costanza Casati, Anna Maria Colivicchi, Luke Dean, Annie Garthwaite, Katie Hall, Ellen Lavelle, Miloni Shah and Vanwy Macdonald Arif. They met weekly, worked unstintingly and came up with more inventive ideas than anyone could reasonably expect. Their energy and enthusiasm – just as much as their skill – made sure the job got done. Special thanks also go to David Crowe and Penny Sandle-Keynes for their expert data management and market research, which has contributed so much to the effective marketing of this book. A special mention, too, to David for liaising with the University to secure seed funding and to Finnian Brewer for early stage marketing support.

We recognise a great debt of gratitude to everyone who supported our fund raising efforts. Our literary salons drew a high-spending crowd thanks to accomplished readings from members of the MA Writing department, including Gonzalo Ceron Garcia, Tim Leach, Jack McGowan, David Morley, Sarah Moss and David Vann as well as students. A special call out goes to members of the Warwick Comedy Society, who made our Literature and Laughs event such a success.

Most particularly we thank the many and varied Friends of manifest, whose generous contributions of hard cash helped us to create an outstanding book and to launch it to the world with something of a fanfare. It would be hard to express how much we appreciate the vote of confidence you have given us. We hope very much that this book brings you all the pleasure you so richly deserve.

Waterstones Piccadilly and Warwick Books deserve special thanks for providing such exceptional venues for our national and regional book launches.

Finally, when it comes to the book itself, we particularly thank Gonzalo Ceron Garcia for writing an insightful foreword, Alexa Whitten at The Book Refinery for support with production, and Gaia Lamperti for her stunning cover artwork.

Previous anthologies of work by students of the University of Warwick's MA in Writing are:
Moonshine (2017)
Palimpsest (2016)
Fractals (2015)
Tinderbox (2014)
Inklings (2013)
Papercuts (2012)
The Draft (2011)
Onwards (2010)

Depending on remaining stock, copies of previous anthologies as well as manifest: New writing from Warwick are available from:
The Warwick Writing Programme
Millburn House
Millburn Hill Road
University of Warwick Science Park
Coventry CV4 7HS 210